Books by Fran L. Porter

*When the Ship Has No Stabilizers: our daughter's tempestuous voyage through borderline personality disorder (2014)*

*The Wrong Brother (2019)*

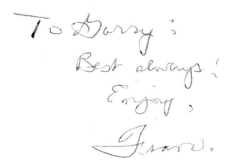

To Darcy;
Best always!
Enjoy;
Fran.

# The Wrong Brother

## by Fran L. Porter

## A Novel

CROSSFIELD
PUBLISHING

Porter, Fran L. (1947- )

ISBN-13: 978-1-7751496-5-1 (Crossfield Publishing)

ISBN eBook 978-1-7751496-6-8

Cover artwork by Lawrence Stilwell

Interior layout by Harald Kunze

Manuscript prepared by Ernestine Crossfield

www.crossfieldpublishing.ca  1-226-301-4001

publisher@crossfieldpublishing.ca

Printed in Canada by www.rapido-books.com

2269 Road 120, R7, St. Marys, Ontario, N4X 1C9, Canada

Library and Archives Canada Cataloguing in Publication

Title: The wrong brother / Fran L. Porter.

Names: Porter, Fran L., author.

Identifiers: Canadiana (print) 2018906806X | Canadiana (ebook) 20189069430 | ISBN 9781775149651

(softcover) | ISBN 9781775149668 (ebook)

Classification: LCC PS8631.O734 W76 2019 | DDC C813/.6—dc23

CROSSFIELD
PUBLISHING

# The Wrong Brother

Fran L. Porter

# Dedication

To all who long for true romance and happy endings. To all who insist on being optimistic, despite the sometimes-horrific ups and downs life insists on throwing at us. Your longings, and your insistence, are also mine.

سلام

# Prologue

## Of Jump Starts and Mind Retreats

*'Jump start' seems a trite phrase to use for such a shocking beginning. But there it is. I start down Reminiscence Road precisely because Des jumps me. It's a 'jump-start' to the middle of the story, followed by a drifting downward through layers of my consciousness to land at the first time we met, where I can, at last, put perspective on it. Always I shall remember it that way.*

*My babies sit in the back seat of the Echo, holding hands. I know their faces reflect the terror in mine. I know also that, young as they are, they've come to realize—just as I have—that their dad is not merely a little sulky sometimes. He is not simply an alluring man who occasionally has his moods. He is truly and horrifyingly (one recoils at the mere thought) capable of murder.*

*Which begs the question: why had I married Desmond so impulsively? Despite my smug immaturity, I wasn't oblivious to the warnings from others. In retrospect my behaviour seems heedless and self-destructive. But at the time, Desmond appealed because he was subtly dangerous. He represented abandoning predictable tameness and venturing into perilous uncharted waters. He was my version of quitting a nine-to-five job and making a split-second decision to sail around the world.*

*Can he be pleaded with to spare my babies? They're his babies as well, after all. But no, he doesn't see them that way. Desmond is a misogynist; he hates all women, and he has never forgiven me for having girls. Police cars appear, bringing to a head his hatred of me and his daughters. If it would help, I'd pray. But God and I have never really been on speaking terms.*

*I close my eyes and plead with whatever deity might chance to be listening. Please—don't let him touch the girls! Please—keep him away from my babies! With the gun's barrel jammed against my temple, it's a wonder my mind functions at all, and yet self-preservation in crisis is a well-known phenomenon. It can bring on a mental state of utter calm, and that's what it is doing now. Floating in stasis, I begin my journey down Reminiscence Road, knowing he can't torture me if he can't reach my mind. Possibly I'm being a coward. Possibly I'm just seeing it flash before me, the way one is supposed to do in the moment before death...*

\* \* \*

*With a bump, I land at age nineteen. I'm flippant and all-knowing, spouting sarcasm like an unruly geyser as I sit with Mother sipping coffee and informing her I've applied for that special Board of Governors Hepplewhite Scholarship at the university. I don't see myself then as the kind of lofty academic people love to hate, but that's exactly what I am. My GPA is my only self-worth barometer. Mother I regard as my intellectual midget.*

*Her strangely negative shrug makes me smirk. Education is fine, she says, and she's proud I do well academically. But I shouldn't be so insensitive to life's truly important things—love, most of all. Why can't I be more loving—and more lovable? Yeah, right! That turns me silly with laughter. This from the woman who didn't even take my father's hand when he was on his deathbed!*

*Let her preach, though. I am immune.*

*Or am I?*

*Even as I mentally mock her, a modicum of her influence prevails. She's a professed believer in romance as well as the joys of passion. Being with Father was sensual and exhilarating for every minute of their life together until he got sick, she claims. Sure! That's why she couldn't even be bothered holding his hand as he was passing away. But I make no comment. Instead, I file romance and the joys of passion under 'not for me'. 'Sensual and exhilarating' is a beautiful fantasy that has no home in humdrum reality. Not in my reality. Romance and the joys of passion, I reflect, are two of the most lied-about human experiences on this planet.*

*I hardly date. Unless you count my classmate Teddy Kelly— whom I'd rather not count—my past encounters with those of the male persuasion have been eminently forgettable. They're all hands and hormones, having no interest in my thought processes or in anything not of the flesh. They talk at me, not to me, and a lot of what they babble is prosaically dull. Then I meet Desmond. And I'm forced to concede that Desmond, and the aura he emanates, is the furthest thing from dull. Discovering a man who excites me in any way whatever is so novel I forget to be sensible for the first time in my life.*

*That he's 'courting me' (her expression) should overjoy Mother. It doesn't. Perversely, she won't like him. I see it in her behaviour: stiffly-polite, ever-so-slightly chilly. Defiance floods me. Who is she to criticize my taste in men? I go so far as to make the reckless declaration that I'm expecting a proposal from him any time now—to which my answer will be a resounding 'yes'. The effect is satisfactory. She opens her eyes wide and gives a kind of hiccupping slurp, like a drowning fish.*

*So when Desmond does propose marriage, I'm suddenly between the proverbial rock and hard place. I can refuse and lose face with Mother because I backed down from my original stand. Or I can accept, winning her reluctant respect for sticking to my guns but plunging myself into a giddy and excitingly unconventional future.*

*Given my nature at nineteen, only one answer is possible. Of course I accept.*

ﷲ

# Chapter1

Since I'd entered adolescence, Mother's formality had become more grating than ever. Previously, we lived together by maintaining a sort of guarded truce, with Father providing a buffer zone. He had a lubricating way about him that neutralized friction. When he died and Mother went to an 'adults only' condo, I was left to manage on my own. Nothing could have suited me better.

With high school behind me, I moved into an apartment building just off the university campus, populated mainly by students. Isolde, my roommate, had a better relationship with books than people and socialized only when absolutely necessary. Something called her back to Switzerland soon after the term started, and she never returned. Accepting parental help I wished I could have refused, I stoically picked up her half of the rent and didn't take it personally.

Once a month, Mother and I met for coffee in her elegantly-furnished French-Provincial sitting room. Widowhood had given her a certain tragic beauty, which I admitted to myself even then. She talked of movies she'd been to see with her other widow friends, or of clothes she'd managed to find that didn't show her non-existent midriff. And she talked of how much she missed Father, whose reaching hand she hadn't even seen, never mind held. Why could I not forgive her that?

The day I first saw Desmond fighting with Damien was the same day I told her I was applying for the Hepplewhite Scholarship. We sat demurely across from each other, like two Victorian ladies at tea. She had just finished reprimanding me, using all three of my names, the way she always did when I was in trouble. "Marigold Iona Anderson, for a smart girl you've got an amoeba's attention span! Can't you try and stay with the tour? Or are we really such worlds apart?"

I grimaced at her use of my full name, not only because it meant a raking-over-the-coals but because I hated it: first name an unpleasantly pungent flower, second name a brand of kitchen appliance. I assumed I must have been a difficult birth.

"Sorry." I gave her a feeble grin. My cell phone was vibrating in my pocket; I turned it off. Mother refused to have a cell phone of any description, decrying them as impediments to real social interaction, so I didn't enlighten her about what had distracted me. "You were mentioning your friend's nephew?"

"Yes. Theodore Kelly. Teddy, he goes by. He's apparently a lovely fellow. Apparently also, he's in one of your university classes. Do you know him?"

I shrugged. "Vaguely. I haven't noticed him that much."

"You're amazing!" She shook her head. "At your age, I..."

"I know. You had a salivating string of beaus slobbering all over you. You were meticulous about your makeup, your hair and your nails. The boys sent you roses and jostled for your coveted favours. Well I'm not you, Mother. I like my life. Maybe it seems cloistered and uninteresting to you, but seventeenth-century France was actually a period of fascinating happenings."

"*Was* is the key word there, Mari. It's all very well to study the past but living in it is unhealthy. You *like* boys, don't you? I mean, you're not...? I would understand, you know, if you told me you were..."

"I'm not gay, Mother. I'd tell you if I were, and strangely

enough, I do know you'd understand." I smirked. "Maybe I'm just an odd duck, like Shakespeare. Some claim Shakespeare was freakish: a literary genius born into a respectable but relatively ordinary family. So I'm in good company." I batted my lashes. "At the moment, all I 'lust after', in the words of Ben Johnson, is the Lester Hepplewhite Memorial Scholarship. And I think I have an excellent chance of getting it—even though some of the pesky boys you`re so wanting me to take an interest in, are my competition!"

She looked pained as she reached for a piece of shortbread. "Okay, tell me more. I've heard of this scholarship, but I have no idea what it is."

"It's not the stuff of romantic adventure, so try not to let your eyes glaze over. Every year, Barrett University's Board of Governors selects one particularly promising student as its recipient. The award provides enough financial support for the five years necessary to obtain at least a Master's degree in a chosen field of study. I have selected seventeenth-century French philosophers."

She made a face. I pretended not to see it and plunged on.

"The money is administered by the Board of Governors but comes out of the estate of one Lester old-fogey Hepplewhite who felt the need, before he died, to have something named after him that promoted him to society as a nurturer of higher learning."

Mother winced. "If you're being considered as a candidate, you're being very disrespectful."

"Oh, I'll be respectful when the need arises." I gave a tight-lipped smile. "Or maybe I won't. Maybe sass would be a trait they'd admire more. We'll see. I have submitted a formal application, including a promise to stay and give this town the benefit of what I've learned for five years after I graduate. That's part of the agreement. The Board of Governors has contacted me for an interview. That means they've looked at my transcripts and they approve of me on paper. It remains to convince them to approve of me in person. My interview is in three days."

Her answering smile was equally tight. "If higher education is truly your Mecca, you better play their game. They're probably business professionals who enjoy being buttered up a bit."

"What those moguls *enjoy* is putting some poor sap under a microscope and watching him squirm." I was talking that way on purpose because I knew Mother didn't like it. When her lips pursed, I felt a grim satisfaction. "They get their kinky jollies out of counting sweat droplets on tortured foreheads."

"Well, they won't count any droplets on yours." Her voice was tart. "Marigold Iona Anderson *doesn't* sweat. She has ice-water in her veins."

"Thank you, Mother. I'll take that as a compliment."

I left shortly afterwards, descending the stairs from her fourth-floor condo rather than using the elevator—just because I had to defy her warning that stairwells can be isolated and risky places. A rising storm outside lent *King Lear*-type sound effects to my departure: whining wind, the manic growl of distant thunder, and a pounding rain that my high-school English teacher would have described as a *rataplan*. Appropriate, I mused with a snort of laughter. There was always an incipient storm lurking between Mother and me.

And then I emerged into the lobby and found myself smack in the middle of a breaking *human* storm that made me realize how wrong Mother was about that ice-water in my veins. What I saw that night quite literally caused the hair follicles at the back of my neck to stiffen as I watched—and the fear I felt was as palpable as if I were cowering prey at the mercy of some huge looming jungle beast.

# Chapter 2

They could have been gladiators in a Roman arena, the male combatants of that human storm. (And Mother said I wasn't a romantic!) They reeked of primitive blood-lust, a readiness to dive for each other's throats. Because they barred my path to the street exit and to the grey Echo I'd left parked outside, I had to pass by them to make my departure. I found I was afraid to do it. Feet nailed to the floor by the almost tangible violence in the atmosphere, I shrank back into the shadows, a horrified spectator to their unfolding drama.

They had maybe five years on me. One was as blond as the other was dark. Objectively speaking, both were strikingly handsome men, but a feral snarl drew Dark's lips back from pointed incisors. Add the cape and you'd have Dracula, with all the treacherous seduction the urbane count was known for. My nineteen-year-old imagination pictured those teeth sinking into my neck and inducing helpless erotic surrender.

Hypnotised, I had to wrench my eyes away to study Blond. He was the Greek-god type: virile, muscular, manhood in its prime. A shadow of beard on his face emphasized all the more his rampant maleness, and the blue lab coat he wore open at the neck accentuated sea-blue eyes and revealed a fine matting of chest hair the same ripe-wheat colour as the abundant hair on his head. There he stood right here in Mother's lobby: Adonis, whom neither Venus nor Proserpine could keep her hands off.

15

What can I say? When you're nineteen and a smartass and have recently studied mythology, you have thoughts like that. At least, *I* did.

The venom in Dark's voice almost made me reach for my phone and tap in 911. He spat, "You want Donna! Admit it! You want her just because she's mine!"

Blond's voice was as deep and soft as Dark's was strident, yet equally threatening. "Let Donna alone. I'm warning you. Stay away from her."

"Or what? Or you'll kill her? With your knowledge of mood-altering drugs you could do that, couldn't you? I've seen the way you look at her! If you can't have her, no one can! That's what you're thinking, isn't it? It's the same story with every girl I date!"

Blond said, "This discussion is over. Leave this building and get out of Donna's life. Now."

For several moments I thought a physical brawl might ensue. It didn't. Dark ultimately backed down. He muttered, "This isn't over!" and strode angrily through the exit doors and out into the wild night, trailing in his wake that bestial aura. Drawing a shaky breath to slow my racing pulses, I extracted my car keys from my purse and made a move to follow.

"Wait!" Blond's mesmerizing tone halted me in my tracks. It was deadly quiet. "You obviously witnessed that. Who are you?"

Forced to turn and face him, I lost the battle with my heart rate and was mad at myself for feeling afraid. Squaring my shoulders, I went with assertiveness as the best approach. "My mother lives in this building. I was visiting her." My hand tightened on the phone I still held. "If you make a move toward me, I'll press 911. I'm not kidding!"

The intensity of those blue eyes held me, as a rabbit is held in the glaring headlights of a car. For several silent seconds he studied me; then he said simply, "I won't make a move toward you. Go. It's best you forget what you just saw and heard."

"Oh. Is that a threat? I'm not into threats." I could hardly believe my own words. What kind of idiot was I, challenging him when I'd heard Dark declare him not above killing! He himself had just given me permission to escape. And yet here I stood, defying him the way I defied Mother. Was I so anxious to live up to that ice-water statement of hers that I was prepared to risk my life?

His brows lifted in surprise and the blue eyes held a glint of what could have been amusement. How *dare* he laugh at me! But his words were not at all amused; they were stern. "I'm not into threats either. Consider it well-meant advice. Go. I'm right behind you."

"I think I'd rather you went ahead of me. I'm not sure I trust you behind me." I was staggered by the extent of my own gall—my own death wish! For all I knew, I was taunting a Jack-the-Ripper! Why didn't I just shut up and flee, already?

Now his lips twitched as though trying to restrain a smile. I was definitely providing his evening's entertainment. Less sternly he said, "Fair enough. May I know whom I'm preceding?"

"You may not! That's the most transparent pickup line I've ever heard."

He bowed—a courtly gesture that was ludicrously incongruous in this place and time. "So be it. Good evening to you, then. And please—follow my advice." He tipped an imaginary hat and disappeared into the storm as Dark had done, leaving me to catch my breath and rein in my runaway senses before I made my own exit.

It was as I drove home that I realized the impossibility of the task he had set me. Forget what I had just seen and heard? No way!

When I was a child, my father had sat me down one day on an area rug in our living-room and had told me that rug was a magic carpet that would fly me all over the world, as long as I wasn't thinking of elephants while I sat on it. Of course it had never flown me anywhere, and it never would. All such self-sabotage ruses I had since referred to in my own mind as 'The Father Principle'.

Blond's admonition to forget what I'd just seen and heard was 'The Father Principle' times ten.

# Chapter 3

"It was a terrible thing," Mother said to me over the phone three days later. "All of us in the building were woken by the sirens. The poor girl apparently staggered out onto her balcony and jumped to her death. Her name was Donna Wooding. Kept to herself. I didn't know her at all. Now why would a nice-looking young girl in the midst of her prime want to go and take her own life?"

"Is that what the police are saying—that it was a suicide?"

"That's what *everyone* is saying. Poor girl! Probably she was mentally ill."

Or possibly, I couldn't help speculating, she was the victim of a mood-altering drug administered by a jealous lover. Much as I shied from that line of thought, The Father Principle kicked in in earnest. And today of all days, I couldn't afford to let any distractions cloud my thoughts.

"Mother, I have to go. I've got my interview with the Board of Governors this morning."

"Of course," she sniffed. "That's the real reason I called—to say I'll be rooting for you. Break a leg, Mari. Sorry if my news upset you."

"Thanks. It hasn't upset me. Ice-water, remember? I won't let it."

But maybe I *did* let it. Or maybe it was that sass I thought they might admire that explains my conduct at the interview. I'd told Mother I could be respectful when the need arose and I'm still not exactly sure what got into me. I had never in my life seen in one place so many jowly cheeks, sagging boobs and overhanging beer bellies, and I used the standard ploy to diminish nervousness by picturing them all in their underwear. It did wonders. Head on, I met their collective gaze with my standard smirk. The intention was to exude confidence, not rudeness. It failed.

Mr. Lorne Salter, Board chair and wealthy textile manufacturer, was a well-known icon in our town. He'd been honoured several times for various philanthropic enterprises and he was highly esteemed. But in his underwear he cut just as preposterous a figure as did the others. My smirk widened. When he drilled me with gimlet eyes, I drilled him right back.

Salter called the meeting to order and acted as spokesperson. His tone was businesslike but pleasant—though he wasn't fooling *me* in the slightest. I refused to be a bug beneath the microscope of his unwelcome scrutiny, and if it came down to a staring contest, I decided, I was going to outstare him. Much to my annoyance, he seemed to guess my intention and treat it with patient tolerance.

"So." His eyes shifted deliberately from mine to sweep over the assembled body. "Ladies and gentlemen, I give you Ms. Marigold Iona Anderson, whose excellent academic credentials you have before you. They speak for themselves. May I start by asking you, Ms. Anderson, why we should consider you a deserving candidate for this award?"

"You just said it. I have excellent academic credentials. They speak for themselves."

He blinked and his eyes widened slightly, the way Mother's often did at my brazenness. I felt my smirk becoming more pronounced. Then he rallied and struck with a blunt-force brutality that took me completely aback. "Paper isn't everything, my smug young woman. Kindly tell us, in your own words, how you intend to use this scholarship to further the cause of higher learning."

I nodded, thrust out my chin. No, I would *not* let him intimidate me. "Certainly I will. And yes, I'll use my own words. I mean, there's no question of using someone else's, is there? I'm going to specialize in seventeenth-century French literature—Voltaire, in particular. *Micromegas* and *Candide* both fascinate me, as does the political background that inspired their writing. Voltaire, like me, was a rebel. Despite the centuries between us, I identify with him and his need to defy the moral attitudes of the time."

One of the women spoke up then, sounding almost angry. "You're aware, I take it, that Voltaire was no stranger to being thrown into prison? I trust you're not planning on emulating *that* aspect of his life!"

I rose to the challenge, ignoring the titters of soft laughter her remark had caused. "As I'm sure you know, a number of history's more courageous figures have done stints in prison."

"One can only do so much to benefit society from a prison cell."

"There I beg to differ. Take Nelson Mandela, who..."

Salter held up a restraining hand. "Enough! We're not here for a debate, Ms. Anderson. We're here because we, the members of the Board, have been entrusted with the wise dispensation of these funds. We require convincing of your worthiness as a recipient. Your youth may make you susceptible to the thrill of skating on thin ice, but I urge you to be mindful about the risk of breaking through!"

"Nice analogy, sir. But there should be no risk. And I shouldn't be put in the position of having to kowtow just because someone happens to have been born earlier than I was. One doesn't engender respect simply by being quinquagenarian."

He grinned suddenly at my use of the ten-dollar word, and his eyes actually twinkled. "And neither, young woman, does one engender respect simply by spouting pseudo-academic verbiage with the hope it will impress! Youth often despises age, Ms. Anderson. Your directness and refusal to 'kowtow', as you put it, is, if nothing else, immensely refreshing. We white-haired *quinquagenarian* old crocks will want to retire and consider your case. Meanwhile, outline for us, if you please, your proposed program of studies."

I inhaled, let it out slowly as I strove to keep my voice steady. "To balance the literature side of things, I'm taking courses in linguistics, mechanics, and the tracing of language development. Eventually, I intend to propose, as a topic for my Master's thesis, the effect of the seventeenth century on modern times, or possibly the extent to which we are where we are today because of lessons learned from those who have gone before us."

Now he broke into a full-blown chuckle, echoed by some of the others. "I see. That's very interesting. And you don't find it ironic that, as you sit here, you deride our generation and claim it can teach yours absolutely nothing?"

I'd left myself wide open for that one, and he'd driven in for the kill without mercy. I deserved it. I deserved every barely-stifled giggle of it. Helpless, I felt myself drowning in the tidal wave of their amusement and I rose quickly, gathered up my tattered composure, and decided it was over. I may as well be 'hung for a wolf as a lamb', as the saying goes.

"I'm sorry to have wasted your time," I told them stiffly. "It seems I've made a mistake. Obviously I'm not a suitable candidate after all. If I have to pay with my dignity, then the price is far too high. Please excuse me." And I stalked out of the meeting room, closing the door firmly behind me.

Then I went home and cried.

There's no rationalizing stupidity like that. For a smart girl, I had behaved like an ass. Throwing myself under the bus—and throwing that scholarship down the drain—was the very last thing I'd intended; yet I'd heedlessly abandoned caution and done a perfect impression of that iconic bull in the china shop. They must all have doubled over with mirth after I'd made my dramatic exit. No doubt, grand-poohbah Salter was enjoying his triumph even as I sat here in my lonely apartment, bawling...

I had to get out. For one thing, I had to take a walk and ponder Mother's news this morning and whether I should contact the police. Wasn't it my duty as a law-abiding citizen? But then, what did I really know? I couldn't identify the men. Wouldn't I appear even more a fool than I had today in front of the Board?

Shrugging into my coat, I struck off across campus, heading for the student cafeteria where I knew I could get an early supper in relative privacy. I folded myself into a small corner booth and thumbed idly through a copy of the *Barrett Bugle* that someone had left on the table. Barrett is a small enough town to rate a gossipy local rag like the *Bugle*, yet a large enough town to boast not just the university but two hospitals, three fairly ritzy single-dwelling neighbourhoods, several high-rise luxury condos like Mother's, and the *Bugle's* big brother, the *Gazette*. Generally, I skimmed the *Gazette* online every morning and didn't bother much with the *Bugle*. But opportunity had thrust it at me, so I turned its pages and read while I chewed.

The piece about Donna Wooding's suicide was terse and scant on detail. And then I stopped in mid-chew, peered more closely at the article on the page opposite the one on Wooding, and blinked several times at its accompanying photograph. And I thought once more about magic carpets and The Father Principle.

It was Blond.

Only now Blond had a name: Damien Sparks, neurologist. *Doctor* Damien Sparks. *Well, shut the front door...!* There wasn't a doubt in my mind that—even if he *hadn't* killed that unfortunate girl—what I'd glimpsed in Mother's lobby three days ago was something from the seamier side of Sparks' life, some piece of dirty laundry he wouldn't want the world to know about. The article blabbed on about a six-hour operation he'd done at

Blair Memorial to save the life of a little girl who'd been in a motor accident. It was heart-warming stuff—stuff from which a pure-as-the-driven-snow public image is made.

Stuff that no one but a chance witness on a stormy night would ever think to associate with the makings of a cold-blooded murderer...

Okay. Now I really *should* go to the police.

# Chapter 4

If I'd called them right away or walked straight down to the station, it would have been a done deal. But I didn't. I ate the rest of my supper, chewing slowly while I finished reading the *Bugle* cover to cover. By then I'd talked myself out of it.

The fear of appearing a fool, the way I had this morning, had eclipsed thoughts of moral responsibility. Really, I told myself, what had changed now that I'd stumbled upon his identity? I was still no more enlightened about the matter than I'd been before. Yes, a neurologist might know more than most people about mood-altering drugs, but surely Dark's blurted accusation was just a jealous rival letting off steam. People accused each other of terrible things all the time when they were in competition over something or some*one*. Two men fighting over a woman was bound to be just as malicious and—yes, venomous—as two women fighting over a man. And anyhow, if Blond had decided to harm someone with drugs, his logical target would have been Dark, not the woman he was fighting over. Right?

I shook my head, deposited my plate in the 'empties' bin, and trudged back home. I'd have to call Mother and give her some report of the interview. That I didn't relish. Her questions would be probing and my answers would be evasive. What else was new? Temporarily I could put her off by telling her they were still considering my application—which, officially, they were. But ultimately I'd have to own up to being rejected—as I was bound to be—and come up with a good reason why. Rudeness didn't cut it, even though it was the truth. How could I expect Mother to understand when I, myself, didn't?

The light on my kitchen-counter phone was blinking to indicate a message. So she'd called already. And, par for the course, she'd opted for the land-line number, not the cell. I drew a breath, pressed 'play', and braced myself. Then I tensed, frowned, and gave a small squeak of surprise.

Call display showed the name 'Salter' and the voice indeed belonged to the man I'd just talked to this morning. Of course he would have my contact info from the forms I'd completed, but why on earth...? I listened to his silky tone and my surprise grew.

"Ms. Anderson. Lorne Salter here. I'm going to get right to the point. The Board was all in favour of turning you down after your dramatic little speech this morning. I vetoed their decision. More precisely, I requested they postpone deciding until I've had a chance to meet with you, one-on-one. I, too, was nineteen once. If you in any way regret your conduct and are interested in trying to salvage the situation, call me back. If I don't hear from you by tomorrow evening, all is definitely lost. The ball, young woman, is in your court." He broke the connection.

For several moments I continued to stare stupidly at the phone. My breath came in ragged puffs. What was Salter after? Where was the catch? One-on-one...? I snickered. Did the old goat actually think I might be willing to give him a quickie in exchange for his weighty vote in my favour?

I punched buttons. I'd expected it to go to voice mail, but he picked up almost immediately, further rousing my suspicions. I mean, Salter was a busy man and a prominent one; getting hold of him in the snap of one's fingers was surely not a usual occurrence. Neither, I was positive, was the suggestion that followed our formula greetings.

"My dear, you're as prickly as a porcupine." That silky tone of his, as well as the 'my dear', reminded me of crafty friend Fagin in a recent production of *Oliver Twist* I'd seen staged at the campus theatre. No doubt his intentions were just as dishonourable as Fagin's, but I listened all the same. "If I can find a way through your defensive armour, I suspect I might discover a reasonably nice person underneath. Before we give up on you, I'd like to try. So let's meet somewhere for lunch. I'll buy."

A sardonic grin tugged my lips. "That's, uh, kind of you, sir. You didn't strike me as the type who gives people second chances. I appreciate it. How about the cafeteria in the Student Union building right next to Hansen Hall?"

"No. Somewhere off campus will be less crowded and more relaxing. Shall we say noon tomorrow? There's a little place called Robert's Bistro on the corner of Rembrandt and Sterling. They serve a superb lamb stew there and a very hearty chili. It's one of my favourites."

It's also at the other end of town, said my inner voice, not far away from a sleazy hotel. Wow, Mr. Lorne fat-cat Salter, your technique fairly drips with style! I wonder what *Mrs.* Salter would think of this method of selecting worthy Hepplewhite candidates...?

"And if I can't make it, sir?" I heard the mockery in my tone, particularly in the last word. Kiss Lorne Salter's fat behind or kiss the Hepplewhite good-bye: that's the choice he was giving me. The ultimate ultimatum.

"If you can't make it, we'll set another day. Soon. Don't worry."

I laughed outright. "Oh, I wasn't worried, sir. I can adjust my schedule. Tomorrow noon is fine. Robert's Bistro. I'll be there."

"Good. See you then." He hung up.

Well, golly-gee, I had a *date*. Again I giggled aloud as my index finger speed-dialled Mother's number and I mentally composed a good way of telling her. *Guess what? Turns out beer-belly Salter has the hots for me. So I think the Hepplewhite's in the bag—as long as I'm willing to jump in the sack...!* Her voice derailed my puerile contemplation of what I then considered wit. She said, "How did it go? You weren't sassy with them, were you?"

"Mother, your faith in me is underwhelming. Okay, I admit my behaviour wasn't the best. But all is not lost. Lorne Salter wants to meet with me again tomorrow." I didn't edify further.

"Mari, why must you always...? Well, never mind. Tomorrow you'll have to make sure you're as polite and cooperative as you can be. I know it's important to you. Don't blow it."

*Oh, the temptation...!* Quelling the urge to touch that line, I switched topics. "Have things settled down again in your building after that loony-tunes girl offed herself?"

"Don't be crude, Mari. Relatively. The police were around asking all the routine questions, I guess, but I don't think any of my neighbours were able to be any more helpful than I was. Someone said the girl has a cousin out west who has been notified and will look after having the place cleared out and put on the market."

"A suicide, then, for sure? The police see no reason to think otherwise?"

"Not to my knowledge. Why would they? Is there something you've heard that I'm not aware of?"

"No. Not at all. Uh...I should go. I have reading to catch up on. I promise I'll be sweet as shoofly pie to dear Mr. Salter. I'll let you know how it goes."

"Shoofly pie... Hmm... I'm not sure you have it in you to be *that* sweet, Mari. But, for your own sake, do your best. Handle it with all the diplomacy you can."

"Don't worry, Mother. I'll handle it." My shoulders shook with renewed laughter after I'd replaced the phone in its stand.

As it happened I had no chance to complete, as I'd planned it, my discussion with Salter—using either diplomacy or any other form of social finesse. A startling turn of events during our little assignation on the following day wrested the situation completely out of my control.

იც

# Chapter 5

Robert's Bistro was not dimly-lit as I'd expected but bright and cheerful, with a homey quality about it. At the height of the lunch rush its tables, cheerfully draped with red-checkered tablecloths, were fully occupied save for one, where Salter sat alone. I purposely kept him waiting fifteen minutes. It wouldn't do to appear too eager.

He rose politely at my arrival, guided me to my seat, and said nice things about my appearance. I *had* taken trouble with my looks: brushed my naturally toffee-coloured hair until it shone, and donned a lilac dress that hugged my trim figure and featured a skirt short enough to show a tantalizing amount of leg. Salter's appearance was the opposite: he wore a plain tee, blue-jeans, and loafers. I wondered if he was in disguise.

When the female server brought us menus, he pointed out the lamb stew and recommended it highly, thereby guaranteeing I would select the chili. He grinned at me over our steaming bowls as they were put before us and said, "Take a taste before we get to business. You'll be pleasantly surprised. A neighbour put me on to this place. It doesn't look like much from the outside—or the inside, for that matter—but it serves nourishing food that is low in grease and high in fresh ingredients." His grin widened. "We quinquagenarian old geezers need to be concerned about stuff like that."

I laughed, made a motion of waving him away, and lifted my

spoon to my mouth. He was right: it *was* good, and it was non-greasy as well. Ravenous, I fell upon it, suddenly realizing I hadn't had any breakfast this morning. Okay. Whatever his game was, I'd play it for now. I'd play it until I found a way to make him feel as ridiculous as he'd made *me* feel at the interview yesterday. I said, "This is the best chili I've ever tasted. I compliment you on your choice of eatery, sir."

"Thank you." He nodded. "There are times, you know, when it pays to play games." I nearly choked on a piece of beef; was he reading my mind? "There are occasions when it's wise to exercise tact and even a bit of flattery. When the people you're dealing with have the power to determine your future, you give them what they want. Serve it up in doses large enough to ring sincere but not so huge as to make you sound like a sycophant—or 'suck-up', as you young people say. They'll know it for what it is, and they'll have no illusions about the game you're playing, but it'll still get you everywhere. Does that make any sense at all, Mari?"

His sudden familiar use of my first name was as startling as his words. I felt unstrung. With my spoon I fiddled around in my bowl while my mind sought a reply. When I found it, I was disgruntled with the immature surliness I heard in my own voice. "You're telling me that you endorse hypocrisy. No, that makes no sense to me at all."

He shook his head. "What doesn't make sense is the way you acted yesterday. You committed academic suicide. Why? Are you so intent on making older people look foolish that you're willing to cut off your nose to spite your face? Even though afterwards you probably went home and shed a ton of regretful tears?"

Remember how I was going to make him feel ridiculous? I shifted uncomfortably in my chair; *I* was the one who felt ridiculous, and I hated him for it. Attempting to sound casual, I lied. "I had a certain amount of regret of course, but not a lot. With my academic record, I'm bound to get a scholarship somewhere. If it means leaving this town and this university, so be it. I shouldn't be put in a position of having to curry the favour of any 'old geezer', as you so colourfully term yourself."

I smiled again. To my annoyance, he smiled back.

"Righteous indignation is the prerogative of callow—and therefore callous—youth. I remember it well. We're here because I see a lot of the early me in you. My world left so much to be desired, and I was going to change all of it singlehandedly. What I grew up to realize was that, in order to change any of it, I needed the help of—you guessed it—my elders. Sure, you could leave this town and this university and try your luck elsewhere. And no matter where you might decide to apply, the people holding the keys to the doors you want to open will be old geezers like me. That may be a bitter pill to swallow." His smile broadened. "Swallow it."

I poured myself a glass of water from the pitcher in front of me, took several sips while I gathered my wits. Not sure how I was going to respond, I drew a breath. What came out was, "You're telling me I still have a chance at the Hepplewhite if—having said 'yes' to a clandestine off-campus date with you—I now choose to stroke your ego, and possibly more than your ego. Have I got that right, sir?"

His smile became a laugh. "Below-the-belt doesn't suit you at all, my dear. You're not nasty by nature. Let up on the defensiveness for just one moment of your life." He signed to the server to fill our coffee mugs; then he lifted his in a toast. "To your academic brightness, Mari—and to its being tempered very soon by a good dose of common sense. Will you drink to that?"

I felt my mouth turn down at the corners. "I'll drink to Mrs. Salter remaining ignorant of this particular selection process, *sir*."

His eyes twinkled. "You came here with the idea of making me feel like an old fool. Well, I already know I'm an old fool, so any efforts on your part in that regard are purely redundant. I'll drink your toast if you'll drink mine. Agreed?"

I shrugged, and we tapped mugs. The coffee was a dark-roast blend, rich and flavourful. I swilled it around in my mouth, savouring it and letting its warmth tease my tongue. Liking Lorne Salter had not been part of what I'd come here to accomplish. I steeled myself against liking him, as I'd also steeled myself against the knowledge that going up against him in a battle of wits proved *me* the far more poorly-armed adversary. I was playing out of my league.

Even so, I opted to try and get definitive information out of him once and for all. In his phone message he had implied that, provided I went along with this little rendezvous, I still had a hope. Too carelessly, I said, "So...when can I expect to know the verdict? How long am I to be left dangling as to whether I should try my luck elsewhere?"

He never answered. Instead, his attention was abruptly diverted by a deep quiet voice coming from a figure that had approached our table while we were absorbed in conversation. That figure now addressed him with one word only: "Lorne."

And that one word was all it took. I recognized the voice, as I recognized the blue gaze dwelling on both of us. It held me in its hypnotic depths, the way it had held me three days ago in the lobby of Mother's condo building. For the moment, it drove from my mind all thoughts of my chances at the Hepplewhite and brought flooding back my recent quandary about The Father Principle and whether or not I should contact the police.

Blond from the *Bugle* article stood before me, big as life and as profoundly disturbing as ever.

# Chapter 6

Imagining him in his underwear was *not* the appropriate coping strategy! Quickly I fled that train of thought. Salter had risen to clasp his hand and then to introduce me to him. "Damien, Marigold Iona Anderson, our most recent Hepplewhite hopeful. Mari, this is..."

Probably because I was rattled, I sprang immediately to the offensive. "I know who he is: Doctor Damien Sparks, promising neurologist. Good to meet you, Dr. Sparks." I could have said instead, 'We've already met' but something warned me not to. He didn't mention it either; he simply took my hand and applied brief pressure before letting it go. Against my will, I found the touch electrifying.

His brows were raised and the blue gaze had intensified. "A pleasure, Ms. Anderson. Are you a medical student or an amateur sleuth?"

"Neither. I ate supper in the university cafeteria yesterday evening and thumbed through a copy of the *Bugle*. I was looking for something to relieve my boredom. That article about you, by the way, wasn't it."

He smiled—and its whiteness against tanned features was more attractive than I would have wished. "The reporter who interviewed me yawned several times himself."

"He was probably thinking what an egocentric jerk you were even to agree to the interview."

The smile became a mellow laugh—also more pleasant than I would have wished. Salter joined him. Then he stopped laughing and the blue eyes turned speculative. "Marigold. I don't blame you. Were you an unwanted child?"

"Good grief!" Salter's chuckle rang out again. "You two deserve each other! Let me finish my introduction: Mari, this is Damien Sylvester Sparks, the neighbour who first recommended this place to me."

"*Sylvester*. Poor you. You must have got into a lot of fights at school."

"No more than my share." He was still laughing. "Thanks, Lorne. Sylvester was my mother's maiden name. I'm proud of it."

"Bully for you..." I couldn't help smiling back. "Maybe your mother's taste in last names was questionable, but I compliment *your* taste in restaurants. This place is great."

"Thank you. And I compliment Lorne's taste in lunch companions."

My face felt hot and I knew I was blushing. Damn! I needed to duck down a metaphorical rabbit hole and I took the first one that came to mind. "Nice as this confab is, I'm sure you're aware you've just barged your way into a clandestine tête-à-tête —which is awkward for all of us. You'll have to promise not to tell Mrs. Salter."

Sparks did not flinch. After a beat, his gaze shifted to his friend and he said, "I'm sorry, Lorne, for interrupting. When I saw you here, I thought I should tell you that I did take a look at Cindy this morning and I share Lydia's opinion. Lydia..." His gaze shifted back to me. "...*Mrs. Salter*...is with Cindy now and apologizes that she can't meet up with you for lunch today. She's going to phone Carl Branson's office and make the appointment."

Salter nodded. "Wise to do it as soon as possible. I'll finish up here and go right home. Thank you, Damien."

"Not at all." Again he bowed, as he had that night in the lobby; then he raised a hand in salute to someone who had just entered the bistro. "There's Joanna. And a table has just come available. I'll leave you two alone. As I said, a pleasure, Ms. Anderson." And he was gone.

With him he took the last remnants of any attempt on my part to be cute or clever. I felt utterly defeated. Sudden tears pricked behind my eyes and started to flow before I could find a handkerchief. I made a hasty move to rise and was halted by Salter's hand on my arm. With his other hand, he fished the handkerchief I sought from his breast pocket and passed it to me. "No need to run, Mari," he soothed. "Please stay and listen." He paused. "I want very much to convince the Board of Governors that granting you the Lester Hepplewhite Memorial Scholarship would be a good move."

I sniffled. "Theirs is the accurate opinion, it would seem. I don't deserve it. I think you should leave me to my fate and go home to your Cindy. I'm...sorry about my attitude—today *and* yesterday. You're right: I'm super-defensive and half the time I don't even know why." I wiped my eyes. "Thank you very much for lunch— and for having more faith in me than you really should."

He let his hand remain on my arm. "I'd like to settle this before either of us leaves. Give me another minute, please. First, your academic standing is far above any other of this year's applicants. In that regard, you're the clear winner. Second, it's not that you lack compassion or people skills in general; it's that you prefer to keep them hidden underneath that coat of armour you insist on wearing. That has to change. I want you to prove to me—and to the Board, in a second interview—that it can."

"I'll prove anything you want if you'll just go home to Lydia and Cindy! I'm keeping you away from them, and they obviously need you."

He squeezed my arm, removed his hand. "You just have, my dear—proved it to me, I mean. Cindy is a fifteen-year-old miniature apricot poodle who's been circling the drain for the past week. She stares off into space a lot and has intermittent seizures. Carl Branson, our vet, says she has a brain tumour. We wanted a little more time to say good-bye before making the final appointment, but Lydia says we must and Damien confirms it. Yes, I need to go home—as soon as I've pinned you down to a date for that second interview. This appointment you have to keep. It will be this coming Monday morning, ten o'clock. I've already called all the Board members and made arrangements. Can I count on your being there—with politeness and maybe even some deference?"

"You have already called...?"

"You heard me. I didn't get where I am by letting the grass grow under my feet. I'm a self-professed mover-and-shaker. Decide, Mari. Now. Do you want this scholarship or don't you?"

"Gag me with a...! I'm sorry, that was childish. Yes. Yes, I'll be there. Yes, I'll definitely be there!"

"Good." He settled the bill; then we rose together and he ushered me out. On the way, we passed the table of Dr. Damien Sparks, neurologist, whose date was a radiantly lovely girl with raven-black hair and a figure to die for. Salter did not introduce me to the girl or speak to the couple; he just smiled and nodded. Blond smiled and nodded back.

I didn't miss those signals between them—just as I didn't miss it when Lorne Salter gave the barest wink.

# Chapter 7

Instead of driving straight back to my apartment to catch up on that reading I'd mentioned to Mother, I went to Sarah Williams' cozy country cottage on the outskirts of town. Sarah had been my high-school English teacher but she now regarded me as friend and protégée. Like Mother, she was a widow, but the two were very different. I could relax with Sarah. She hated makeup and rarely did anything to her nails. She dressed for herself and nobody else. Amongst other posters on her kitchen wall was the one that read, 'A woman without a man is like a fish without a bicycle'. She was one of my favourite people.

I had no hopes she'd be home, but she had a tenderly-nurtured and peaceful back garden to which I had free access. Cool, spacious, and abundant with trees, flowers and vegetables that its owner fancied, the garden was where I went to contemplate my figurative navel. Sarah believed in the formal practice of meditation; I didn't. But no less than she, I loved sitting in the garden and de-stressing.

She was home, as it turned out. The school board gave its teachers a day off in lieu of two evenings spent doing parent-teacher conferences, and this was the day. Sarah was in her kitchen baking muffins when she spotted me in the garden and came to join me, bringing two mugs and a pot of tea. Without comment, she eased herself into the chaise longue beside me and poured for both of us.

"Herbal?" I asked, suffused with gratitude.

"Rose hip. Drink first; then we'll talk."

For several moments we sipped in silence. I was the one to break it. "Sarah, I need your opinion on this." I related to her the series of events that had just taken place at Robert's Bistro. "Was it a plot between Salter and his interfering, oil-on-troubled-waters bud? Have I been royally had?"

She took another long sip before responding. "If you've been 'had', Mari, I'd say the two gentlemen responsible are a couple of princes. They sound like people I'd like to meet sometime."

"Hah! Salter has a beer-belly, and Blond—that is, Dr. Damien stick-his-nose-in-it Sparks—has a dark and sinister side that most people don't know about."

"Oh? How so?"

I discovered I didn't want to tell her. Telling her would make her an accessory-after-the-fact if *she* didn't go to the police. It wouldn't be fair to transfer my dilemma to her. So I mumbled something evasive. "He just seems...mysterious. I can't put my finger on it."

She squinted into the sun. "Are you attracted to this man, honey?"

"Don't be ridiculous! Yes, he *is* attractive. No, I don't find him gorgeous or anything..." I realized I was lying. Maybe she realized it too. "Besides, he has a girlfriend, a beautiful one. She met him for lunch right after we three had finished our little chat."

"I'm glad for him. People tend to get what they have earned. He sounds like a man who is worthy of a lovely girlfriend."

"You don't even know him and you're taking his side!"

"I wasn't aware there *were* sides." She sipped languidly. "Maybe they're just pals, he and the girl. You could try asking him out. That way you'll know for sure."

"Sarah, I think you've been talking to Mother!"

She shook her head. "I haven't seen your mother in a while—though I'm sure she'd be as pleased as I would to see you dating a nice man, kicking up your heels, giving in to your more basic instincts."

"You shock me thoroughly, Mrs. Williams!"

"Do I?" Her eyes blazed suddenly. "I don't see why. You're not in high school any more, and if you really have the keen intelligence you're credited with, it should have dawned on you before now that I'm a human being first and a teacher second! What do you think I do with my spare time—conjugate verbs and parse sentences? Or make tea and offer advice to former students who happen to wander by? Grow up, Mari, for Pete's sakes! Scholarships and cute comebacks are all very well in their place, but they're not substitutes for the pursuit of happiness."

I scowled, wanting to shock her back. "I see. So you're telling me I need to go on some kind of quest for one of the basic American human rights and abandon all restraint while searching for it? What if I confirm what I suspect: that I'm a cold fish? Both romance and happiness are extremely overrated, in my opinion. I'm in no hurry to experiment further and confirm that opinion."

Her expression softened. "I repeat: grow up, honey. Falling in love is one of life's biggies. *Let* happiness consume you and sweep you off your feet! *Let* yourself be attracted to that special man!"

"What about the poster in your kitchen? I thought what you advocated most was a life without men."

"No. What I advocate most is a life without the *wrong* men. My late husband wasn't one of those. And widowhood is lonely." She smiled suddenly. "In fact, I happen to have a man in my life at the moment, a very wonderful man. Understand me. I'm not telling you to become a man chaser. I'm telling you to loosen up, let people in. I just said it, honey: being in love is one of life's biggies. Don't deny yourself the experience."

I tried to curb my astonishment. "Shouldn't you be telling me to wait until after my studies are over?"

"No." She shook her head. "I don't think I should. Yes, that would be my advice to ninety-five percent of my students—and they would ignore me. You belong in the other five percent: you're *too* serious, *too* practical, and *too* idealistic."

"That's an oxymoron, English teacher. How can I be too practical and too idealistic at the same time?"

"An oxymoron usually makes sense in a perverse way. Didn't I always stress that? A silence *can* be deafening; a feeling *can* be bittersweet; and even 'jumbo shrimps' is oddly understandable. You, Mari, are too practical and offhand about certain things— like happiness and love—and too idealistic about other things, like your expectations of human nature. You need to learn to cut both yourself and others some slack." She drained her mug, rose. "End of today's lecture. I'm going back inside to my baking. You can stay out here as long as you want." She patted my arm. "Give some thought to what I've said. And maybe give some thought to asking out that young man. See you later."

I brooded in the garden for another ten minutes after she'd disappeared; then I made my way thoughtfully home. It was interesting that she felt I should date Blond, despite my telling her he had a dark side. Did I dare ask him out? Wouldn't it be inviting rejection?

Aloud, I laughed at myself. Forget it! Doctor Damien Sparks, neurologist, was way out of my league, just as Lorne Salter was.

Sarah had told me not to chase after men just for the sake of it. But now I suddenly decided to follow up a lead Mother had given me about her friend's nephew, Theodore Kelly, who was in one of my university classes and was reputedly a 'lovely fellow'. I would scout out lovely Teddy Kelly. I would test those waters. Maybe it was time I got some more dating experience under my metaphorical belt.

If I'd had any way of knowing then what dating Teddy Kelly would lead to some years later, I would never have touched the man through ten pairs of triple-sterilized surgical gloves.

☙

# Chapter 8

My second interview with the Board of Governors panned out to be everything the first wasn't. I took pains to behave appropriately. Not only did I keep a civil tongue in my head, I was able to speak with unaffected enthusiasm about my hopes for the future: securing a position at the university and staying within the ivy walls of academia, where I felt sure I could make significant contributions. The woman who'd challenged me about admiring Voltaire the prisoner actually smiled this time and said, "Normally I like to hear the candidate express a desire to benefit us by founding a business venture or researching a cure for cancer. But the real world does need teachers as well—good teachers with a dedication to imparting to others a genuine love of learning. I think you could be one of those, Ms. Anderson." I returned her smile—sincerely.

When I received the news two weeks later that I'd been awarded the Hepplewhite, a childish whoop of joy escaped my lips before I could stifle it. For the next five years, my financial worries had been settled. Project number one on my slate of immediate plans had come to pass. And by then I'd already made a good start on project number two: becoming the apple of Teddy Kelly's myopic eye.

Teddy Kelly was in my comparative religion class. He was a geek of the first order, even to the tape on his thick glasses, and he was shy to the point of awkwardness. Liaisons with the opposite sex were few to none. That made two of us. Any exploration in that realm that we shared would be a classic case of the blind leading the blind. But that had its advantages: no disease-transmission worries and no fear of looking more a fool than my partner. Limited as my own dating experience was, I was sure it exceeded his.

'Fall in love' had been Sarah's prescription, not 'get laid'. My awareness of that made Teddy the obvious choice after I'd scanned the roster of unattached males registered in my courses. Most struck me as self-satisfied goons who thought they were God's gift to femininity. Two or three had initially tried coming on to me but had decided I was frigid after I'd rebuffed them. And possibly they had spread the word because no one else had approached me since. Not that I cared.

Teddy was the kind who would adore me. He'd be overjoyed at any attention I gave him, and he'd shower me with gratitude. I'd be won over by his undying devotion. Sure, it's crazy in retrospect that I actually thought I could base a loving relationship on such reasoning. But at the time, as I've said, I chose not to believe in Mother's romantic sparks of passion—especially since I'd decided that the one who seemed to ignite those passion-sparks in me was strictly off-limits—and possibly even a killer.

Initiating social contact was cliché and took no effort. I dropped a book and Teddy retrieved it for me. Lowering demure lashes, I thanked him. He flushed and nodded back. Piece of cake. When I suggested we have coffee in the cafeteria after class, he gallantly offered to buy. Voilà. I was dating Teddy Kelly.

Mother was thrilled, as I knew she would be. Sarah offered approval with more reserve, no doubt suspecting my motivation might be more selfish than romantic. But I did try, at least at first. I invited Teddy to family gatherings and was seen in his company at town events. Others began to look upon us as a couple, which I did my best not to find annoying.

Did he satisfy me in the devotion-and-gratitude area? Absolutely! He danced attendance on me all the time: helped me on and off with my coat, opened doors for me, told everyone how great I was, kissed me good-night with warmth and tenderness. And as for the stuff that went beyond the kiss? It wasn't happening.

I think people assumed it was; otherwise his ministrations to me could not possibly be so eager. But those people were wrong. He didn't even try to fondle me. No one could say I wasn't patient; before I knew it we'd been going out most of a year. And he'd made zero attempts to get intimate. To be fair, neither had I.

What did happen, in the end, is that we both had rather too much to drink at that year's town New Year's Eve celebration. I'd just turned twenty and felt starting off the year with a bang would be appropriate, whether or not love figured in the equation. I had talked him into consuming, over a time period of an hour-and-a-half, three glasses of champagne. So he was pie-eyed but not totally out-of-it. Me, I'd matched him glass for glass and was in the same state. Neither one of us was that used to alcohol.

After the midnight fireworks, we took a taxi from the town community centre back to my apartment. On the spot we began undressing each other. I said something inane about setting off our own fireworks. He laughed and said he came from a very religious family, and wouldn't they be shocked to see him now. Not the stuff erotic seduction is made of.

"Do you have a rubber?" I asked him.

"A what?"

"Condom, shield, sheath, prophylactic, whatever you want to call it! Do you have one?"

"No. I...didn't think I'd need one." Everything about him, including the physical evidence of his willingness to participate, suddenly grew limp with relief. "Guess we can't do this without one, can we?"

"Nope. Guess we can't."

I slept in the bedroom; he spent the night on the sitting-room couch. In the morning he took a taxi back to his own place. Me, I took a good honest look in the mirror and decided that, where Teddy Kelly was concerned, project number two was dead in the water.

We stopped seeing each other. Even in class, he avoided my eyes. Mother was regretful, Sarah stoic. "You can't *force* fireworks, honey," she sympathized. "They're there or they're not."

"I followed your advice..."

"No, you didn't. My advice was to unbend a little and let people past that piranha-stocked moat guarding the fortress you build around yourself. I think I also suggested you call up Dr. Damien Sparks, your aptly-named neurologist, who *does* set off sparks for you. You haven't done either one of those things."

"Sparks is not an option. I...have nothing in common with him. I haven't even seen him since he stuck his very handsome nose into my conversation with Salter. No, Sarah, I think I'd rather be like you: independent and permanently unattached."

She shook her head. "You haven't been listening to me. I told you, there's a man in my life, a special one. His name is Simon Preston and he teaches science at the high school. He just joined our staff last year." She paused. "We're in love. We're getting married. Happiness, Mari."

Bleakness swamped me. "Desertion," I countered moodily. "In Mother I'd have been all set for it, but not in you. You were my... my stronghold, my symbol of total freedom. I've always admired your contempt for involvement with men."

"I keep telling you this: it's only involvement with the *wrong* men I disapprove of." Her voice was whisper-quiet. Some women, like my sister, tend to choose the wrong men all the time. I'm not one of them, and I don't want *you* to be one of them either."

I sniffled. "I won't come to the wedding."

"No. You won't, because you're not invited. We can do without your sarcasm on our big day."

"Is he moving in here? Will I still get to come and sit in the garden?"

"Yes. And yes." She tweaked my nose. "Grow up, honey. I'm going to keep saying it until you do it. You'll like Simon. We'll have you over for supper once he's settled in here. Now scat! Go back to your studies and chalk up Teddy Kelly to a learning experience! I'm sure the poor fellow is as mortified about the whole thing as you are."

She was right, of course, on both counts. I did dive back into my studies and spent the next while preparing a couple of tutorial sessions on *Candide* and gullibility to share with my fellow students. My professors were required to make regular reports to the Board of Governors that I was indeed pursuing higher learning, and my reputation as a good teacher and an interesting lecturer began to gain some momentum amongst my peers—a development that pleased both me and the Board. Over the following few months, I centred all my satisfaction on building that reputation and, as for the mortified Teddy Kelly, I behaved toward him as though he had ceased to exist.

That was an even bigger mistake than my deciding to go after him in the first place.

# Chapter 9

Our embarrassing incident had apparently affected Teddy Kelly far more than I realized. Also, he turned out to be a jerk in nerd's clothing—not a 'lovely fellow' at all, but one who'd decided the whole thing was my fault and went around telling people I'd behaved like a slut all through our relationship and he'd finally had to ditch me because 'slut' wasn't a quality he wanted in a life partner. Holy guacamole! (I was still pretty juvenile at twenty.) Who knew he could be so nasty?

Most likely what he was really trying to do was salvage his manhood in his own eyes as well as in other people's. Perhaps he thought I might spread something about *him* and decided he'd beat me to the punch. I don't know, and I don't care to psychoanalyse him further. Let's just say Sarah's recommendation that I chalk him up as a learning experience was now more apt than ever.

It took months for the rumours to get back to me, and by the time they did it was nearly spring break. My university crowd had already dismissed them as reflecting more poorly on Teddy than they did on me. My best defense was not retaliation but shutting up and giving Teddy enough rope to hang himself. Sarah—now married to her Simon and happy to invite me over for dinner so I could get to know him—praised my attitude and declared there was hope for me yet. "Barrett is a small town, honey." She winked as she passed the mashed potatoes. "People know you better than that. I'm pleased to see you *are* starting to grow up at last!"

As I'd been prepared not to like Lorne Salter, so I was prepared not to like Simon. Of course I was aware my feelings stemmed from jealousy of his inevitable claim on Sarah's time and attention, previously devoted to me. And as I had liked Lorne Salter regardless, so I liked Simon regardless. He was good-hearted and jovial—and, as it turned out, related to the very Lorne Salter he brought to mind!

"Lorne's my uncle on my mother's side." He grinned. "Maybe if I'd played my cards right and taken more of an interest in his business I'd be a lot wealthier by now. Maybe I'd even be in line to inherit some of his mega-bucks, instead of having to plod my way through life on a lowly teacher's salary." His grin became a chuckle. "I'm being facetious, of course. I decided early on that teaching was for me and textiles wasn't. Even so, Uncle Lorne generously took me on at the factory every summer when I was in high school. He's a great boss. The workers love him. The neighbours do as well, in ritzy old Applewood Grove."

I toyed with my fork at the peas on my plate, picturing Applewood Grove with its tree-lined streets and estate mansions, the oldest and wealthiest of our town's upscale neighbourhoods. Before I realized I'd spoken, I mumbled, "Including, no doubt, Dr. Damien Sparks, prestigious neurologist. Sparks, I believe, is your uncle's neighbour."

"Sparks. Right." He nodded. "I don't know Sparks very well—but I do know he's a former Hepplewhite recipient. You guys have that in common. And he has already made good on the promise the Board of Governors felt he showed back in his student days. He's bound by contract to give the town the benefit of his services for the requisite five years. But he's gifted enough that he may move on after that. Maybe he'll end up as chief neurosurgeon in some well-known big-city hospital. "

"Bully for him." This was news to me—the last bit not such great news. The thought that the good doctor might shortly move out of town troubled me more than I dared admit.

Sarah's eyes became mischievous. "Simon, Mari is like our grade seven boys who show a girl they like her by punching her in the arm or swatting her with a textbook. I'm thinking maybe we should invite this Dr. Sparks to our next dinner—along with your uncle and his wife. I'd like to get to know your relatives better—and get to know the 'prestigious neurologist' as well. Wouldn't you?"

I swallowed a piece of carrot down the wrong pipe and coughed several times before I could speak. "Sarah, stop meddling!"

Deliberately she put on an innocent expression. "Who's meddling? I can invite whomever I want to my next dinner. You have no say at all in the matter."

"I can refuse to come."

The mischief in her eyes grew. "That may not be an option. As with our wedding, I could decide not to put you on the guest list."

"Then what would be the point of inviting him?" I brooded as I carved a piece of roast beef and pushed it around in a puddle of gravy. That one I could answer for myself: given the recent Teddy Kelly fiasco, I was such a lousy judge of male character that my choices required prior vetting by someone more capable. I heaved a sigh and added, "I mean it, Sarah. I'll refuse to come if you invite him. He's not someone I care to meet again. Honestly."

She laughed. "Uh-huh! Thou dost protest too much. But let's leave it for now. You need to get over the Teddy Kelly thing first. Then we'll see!"

Simon suddenly put a new and safer twist on the topic. And what he said next not only relieved my discomfort but riveted my attention. "By the way, Mari, I went golfing with a chum of mine this afternoon. He wants to meet you. And it seems a mystery-man acquaintance of his would very much like to meet you as well. So, Sarah, the plot thickens!"

"Indeed! Who's your golfing chum?"

"Stanley Morris."

"Stanley Morris..." I tested the name on my memory. "He's an associate professor of history at the university."

"Score one for you."

"I think he's written a couple of papers on social conditions in France during the seventeenth century. I've probably run across him in my readings. Simon, the feeling is mutual! I would be very interested in meeting him as soon as possible—your chum that is, not the mystery-man acquaintance."

"Well, I think I can tell you how to go about it. I've never seen an appointment calendar more jam-packed than Stanley's, but Sundays are the exception. They're his 'turn off the clock' days. Here's a hot tip for you: go to his church this Sunday morning and corner him at coffee-time after the service."

I snorted. "Right!"

"I'm not kidding. It was his own suggestion. He goes to Pleasant Heights Church, just a couple of blocks from the university. If you approach him there, you'll actually be able to engage him in a conversation that's not interrupted by his cell phone or his colleagues."

"Simon, that's devious! Anyhow, I'm not a member there. Wouldn't it be a bit ungodly to use the church to further my own ends?"

He waved a dismissive hand. "Comparative religion is one of your courses, isn't it? So go make some comparisons! I don't think God would mind. I doubt Reverend Connor would either. Stan says he's very welcoming to drop-ins. I'll bet he himself would be glad to introduce you to Stanley."

My interest was piqued. "I'm writing a paper at the moment on some of the Jesuit practices of the time. If I can quote from a 'personal communication' perspective, my instructors will definitely be impressed!"

"Listen to the academics junkie!" He punched my arm. "Stan said to tell you the service starts at ten. And the mystery man will be there as well."

"I don't really care about the mystery man. I may go anyway, though. I'll think about it."

When I made my farewells that night, I wasn't at all sure if I seriously intended following through with Simon's suggestion. A number of excuses popped into my head. I'd be completely out of my element. I wouldn't know anybody there. It was a most unorthodox and rather underhanded way of meeting someone. What would really be my chances of getting Associate Professor Morris alone and having a good one-on-one chat with him?

But now the bait had been dangled in front of me. And I wanted that 'personal communication' credit to enhance my assignment. Besides, who was I kidding? I *did* care about the mystery man. Despite my denial, I was dying to find out who he was.

Sunday was two days from then. All that Saturday I let the idea percolate. Several times I changed my mind. But by the next day I had decided I was going.

And by attending service at Pleasant Heights Church that Sunday morning, I set off a life-changing and irrevocable chain of events—not in a good way.

# Chapter 10

I have not had a religious upbringing. But I recognize fully the need to worship a deity that has been part of human culture since the dawn of time. Religion is a firmly-entrenched aspect of society, even if not a part of the average person's daily life as it once was. And most of the mainline churches were no longer stultified in the old bible-thumping traditions; they had moved with the times. Pleasant Heights' congregants had a reputation for being both open-minded and active in the betterment of the community. To attend a service there was not an experience I found uncomfortable.

Studying the assembled throng, I noted the average age to be maybe thirty years older than I—and yet there was no dearth of younger people either. A buxom, creamy-complexioned girl about my age showed me around the nursery and Sunday-school areas. In the Sunday school I counted fifteen children, and there were twelve babies in the nursery. So Reverend Connor's flock contained sufficient up-and-coming members that it would not be dying out any time soon.

People like me—visiting outsiders—might be viewed by some of the more fundamentalist sects as lost sheep looking for a home. An earnest effort to round me up and bring me into the fold would have turned me right off. Pleasant Heights' view was nothing of the sort; it was as pleasant as the church's name. Its atmosphere was more like a social club with religious overtones. There was lots of joking, laughter, and warmth. Reverend Connor (about the age Father would be, were he still alive) was a handsome man with a thick crown of silver hair, piercing blue eyes, and a paternal manner. He was obviously well-loved and considered 'one of the gang'. I felt at ease in no time.

The sermon was upbeat: not one of Lenten gloom and misery or of fasting and giving up things, but one of hope for the coming Easter season, for awaited resurrection, and for a time of celebration on the horizon. I liked the approach. And I liked the reverend.

Finding Stanley Morris took minimal effort: Connor led me straight to him after the service. In line with Simon's prediction, Morris was happy to chat informally, even if it meant touching on subject areas that comprised his work. I entered a few notes into my tablet as I sipped coffee. Then Morris firmly shut down the shop talk, pinched my cheek in a far-too-familiar gesture, and said, "I'm glad you've come, Missy. Simon said you probably would. The rev. is pleased as well. It's his son who wants to meet you."

"Oh. Which one is his son?"

"He was supposed to be here, but apparently he got sent out to cover a convenience-store robbery early this morning. He's a reporter for the *Gazette*. That kind of job doesn't have Monday-to-Friday hours, of course. I'm betting he's on his way here right now."

"Is that likely, since he's missed the service?"

"I think it's highly likely. He tells me he has always been fascinated with Voltaire. That gives the two of you something to talk about right off the top. Frankly, though, it occurs to me he may have other less academic motives!"

"Why would you say that?" I felt my heart beat faster despite my determination to stay cool.

Behind rimless spectacles his eyes danced. "Call it a hunch. You're an attractive girl and Desmond's a red-blooded male. He could have seen you somewhere from a distance and liked what he saw. Who am I not to aid and abet the course of true love?— especially when it's based on a historical figure as interesting as Voltaire!"

I joined him in laughter. "Okay, I admit I'm getting hooked. Does he have any particular reason for his love of Voltaire?"

Morris winked. "Desmond tells me he's a bit of a history buff on the side. He and I got into it a couple of Sundays ago: the power of the written word and all that. He asked me if anyone at the university was an expert on Voltaire. He's thinking of writing some sort of feature piece and submitting it to a magazine. Since my pal Simon had mentioned you to me, I mentioned you to Desmond."

"Why doesn't he just go online and Google whatever he wants to chase up?"

Morris gave a snort and nudged me. "Because, as I say, it's probably you he wants to chase up! Get with it, girl! You're surely not going to miss a chance to meet a handsome and eligible young man, are you?"

Reverend Connor joined us at that point. He apologized for his son's absence and confirmed the professor's speculation. "Desmond will be awfully disappointed, Mari, if you run away too soon. Voltaire may be the bait he's using, but I believe *you* are the one he's trying to catch! He has had other girlfriends in the past, but I've never known him to go to so much trouble to engineer a meeting! Now that I've met you myself, though, I totally understand."

I couldn't help smiling. "Flattery will get you everywhere, gentlemen! Let's hope God doesn't disapprove too much." Their honesty was disarming. "I read the *Gazette* online every morning. I'll have to look out for Desmond's byline."

Connor's chest puffed visibly with pride. "One day soon the

present editor will retire, and Des fully expects to step into that position. He's got talent and ambition: a winning combination."

"You two are both entitled to a commission for the selling job you're doing! I give up: I'll meet him. And I'll keep an eye out for the 'Desmond Connor' byline when I next read the paper."

Stanley shook his head. ""Connor is the rev.'s *first* name. Our sign in front of the church blew down in that big wind several weeks ago and we haven't got around to replacing it yet. Our bad. I'm on the property committee, and we should have taken care of that before now."

"It's 'Sparks'," clarified the rev. "I'm Connor Sparks and my son is Desmond Barrett Sparks. He likes to use his middle name as well; his great-grandfather on my side married a member of our town's founding family." And before I'd even finished digesting this new piece of information, there was a light tap on my shoulder.

"Hi, Mari." Desmond Barrett Sparks' captivating features lit with a smile as I turned to face him. "It's great to meet you at last." His right hand clasped mine in a firm handshake. "I'm grateful to Stanley for telling me about you." Both seduction and danger lurked within onyx-coloured eyes that glittered beneath brooding black brows. I supressed a gasp as I was carried back once more to the night of that scene in Mother's lobby—and reminded of my still-existing dilemma and The Father Principle.

Reverend Connor's son was the other half of the fighting duo, the one I had labelled 'Dark'. He was the man who had induced in me that night a mixture of compelling attraction and raw fear—the urbane Count Dracula.

# Chapter 11

Desmond Barrett Sparks, *Gazette* reporter, had no idea I'd been present at that lobby scene. So I told myself. Only Damien Sparks, neurologist, knew that. Were they brothers? Cousins? Something warned me not to ask, not to give away any indication that I'd ever seen Desmond Sparks before—and not to mention Damien Sparks either.

I think I successfully disguised my initial shock. And my interest was immediately captured by his colourful account of the convenience-store burglary. "They were young teens. They asked the clerk to break a fifty in order to get him to open the till. Once the till was open, they demanded all the money in it and ran, leaving their fifty on the counter. Thing is, it's the store's policy never to have more than thirty dollars in the till at any one time."

We all giggled. He had other stories as well, each one amusing. The man enjoyed playing to an audience; that was clear. And we were an appreciative audience that day. Rev. Connor ended up inviting the three of us back to his place for an off-the-cuff lunch of buns he'd baked himself the day before (an old family recipe), a thrown-together salad of spinach leaves, feta cheese, chopped apples and sliced strawberries, and a yummy orange sorbet for dessert. I loved the quaint bungalow right across the street from the church. We sat in its old-fashioned conversation nook adjacent to the tiny kitchen and balanced our meals on our knees.

Throughout the occasion I became more and more entranced by Desmond's charm. Before I knew it, three hours had elapsed and I was making hasty excuses to return to my studies. He escorted me to the door, and we grinned at each other like a couple of Cheshire cats while I slipped into my coat.

"Okay, I won't beat around the bush." He helped my arm into the sleeve. "It's an old chestnut, but please make me the happiest man in the world by agreeing to go out with me. Make Stanley and Dad happy as well. What do you say?"

"I say this is quite the conspiracy! Even Simon seems to have played an unwitting part. So...I guess I know when I'm licked."

"This coming Friday night at seven, I'll pick you up and take you to *le Chateau*. We'll feast on duck *à l'orange* and *profiteroles* for dessert!"

"That sounds very rich for a starving student's blood."

"Nothing too good for the woman I've been dying to meet! As a writer, by the way, I approve your choice of specialization. Voltaire is my hero! The pen *is* mightier than the sword, even if physically walloping the daylights out of one's opponents might give more immediate satisfaction. We'll indulge our palates on Friday, and then we'll take in a movie. Okay by you?"

I overlooked the bit about getting satisfaction from physically walloping the daylights out of one's opponents. I put it down to a figure of speech. Making my Cheshire-cat grin coy, I replied, "You had me at 'The pen is mightier than the sword.'"

How shall I describe what happened after that? Perhaps it was mere infatuation, but at the time I was sure it was something more. Desmond Sparks whirled me away on a cloud of emotional highs such as my limited experience had never before known. From the moment we began seeing each other, the world broadened into sparkling new dimensions that included dining at many of the town's high spots, mingling with other *Gazette* reporters up on current and global happenings, meeting and socializing with some of our area's most prominent personalities, and attending events I would never have been invited to on my own merit. Des took me to a year-end do at the university, where he dazzled my drooling female classmates. He and I entered and won a Trivial Pursuit contest in aid of children with leukemia. Suddenly, I began to be a better known and more respected person about town. I was floating on air.

That neither Sarah, nor Simon, nor Mother liked Des did not become apparent for several months. It had dawned on me by that time that my new boyfriend was really a small-time journalist, not a brilliant star headed for national or world renown. His assignments were mainly local events, back-pages stuff same as the *Bugle* ran. My elation at accompanying him to them, based on novelty, began to wear off. But my elation at being his girl burned bright as ever.

Sarah resented that he often called me his 'arm candy'. Maybe I should have resented it too, but strangely I didn't. Mother said he had told her crudely that she was too proper and needed a bout of rough sex to loosen her up. I grinned and appreciated the humour. Simon expressed regret that he had ever engineered our meeting. "I'm sorry, Mari," he said. "I'm thinking I got you into something that may not be in your best interests after all."

We were at one of our regular dinners in Sarah's cottage the day Simon said that. Des was off on an assignment, so it was just the three of us. I straightened in my chair, spine stiffening. "Why are you all so against Des? You just don't know him the way I do!"

"He gives us the willies," Sarah admitted. "We've tried to like him but can't seem to manage it. And because both of us are very fond of *you*, Mari, I'm glad we're finally levelling and saying flat-out what we think. Your association with that man concerns us. We can't pin down exactly why, but there's something about him that is..."

"Intriguing," I flared. "You're being totally unfair to him! Mother is, too."

Sarah shook her head. "I'm afraid 'dangerous' was the word I was going to use. Your mother feels the same way."

I stiffened further. "I see. So you've all been slamming my taste in men behind my back. Lovely!"

"Please don't take it that way, honey..."

"How else am I to take it? I'm highly insulted in Des' behalf!"

"Is it serious between you two, or just a dalliance?"

"None of your business!"

Simon sighed. "I shouldn't have brought it up. We won't say any more about it."

Sarah held up a finger. "I'll drop it after this one last comment. I still like the sound of your *Damien* Sparks much better than I like this brother of his. And I'd still like the doctor to come to one of these dinners someday."

I huffed. "For one thing, he's not *my* Damien Sparks. For another, I'm not even sure how the two of them are related. They're so different I find it hard to believe they're brothers. And lastly, Des and Rev. Connor have never mentioned him, so neither have I. I'd prefer to forget him."

"Fine." She pushed the ham and raisin sauce toward me. "Seconds?"

"Please."

I reflected, as I continued to chew, that ignoring the existence of Dr. Damien Sparks had become somewhat of a challenge since Des and I had been dating. Surprisingly, the neurologist had been present at a number of the town events I'd attended with Des. He'd made no move to approach us in the crowd and I wasn't even sure he'd seen us—but it seemed rather a coincidence that he would select exactly the same functions to attend as we did— like the opening of the new John Blair Memorial Library, the Sylvia Barrett Mental-Health-Awareness Benefit Dinner, and the annual Run-for-Cancer half marathon (where Des was present on assignment and Doctor Intrusive showed up as a participant).

Damien Sparks was becoming the elephant that hampered the magic-carpet flight of my relationship with Des—and I began to become as angry about that as I was about Sarah's, Simon's and Mother's negative feelings toward my new boyfriend.

But perhaps what I became angriest about—once I got over the shock—were two discoveries I made about *myself* a few months later, on the night of Lorne Salter's sixtieth birthday party.

# Chapter 12

Salter had reserved a meeting room at the university for the event. Guests numbered close to a hundred and included Salter's colleagues from the Board of Directors, some of his staff from the textile plant, some of his neighbours from Applewood Grove, and a few of his relatives—like Simon. Desmond was there—with me as his 'arm candy'—to cover the proceedings and write up a small piece for the *Gazette*.

I wore a thin chiffon number in dusky rose that left my shoulders bare and accentuated my curves. Des whistled as he helped me into my wrap and crowed, "Yes! Beautiful! You'll captivate him! You'll captivate them all!"

I chuckled my denial. "By 'him', I presume you mean Salter. No way! I don't think Salter is accessible on that channel, at least not where I'm concerned."

Grinning, he nibbled my ear. "Don't be so sure. Anyhow, there will be lots of other men there for you to captivate. I look forward to seeing them drool while I make it very clear to them that you're mine!"

I swatted him playfully, but of course I was flattered by his proprietary words. When we arrived, he immediately relieved me of my wrap and hung it up, saying, "I want you *un*wrapped and luscious, so everybody can stare and envy! You are gorgeous, Mari!" I swatted him again, basking in the ego-boost and ignoring Sarah's oblique glance.

There was live entertainment in the form of a moderately well-known band, a sultry soloist, and a mock-stripper comedian who billed herself 'Ellie the Ecdysiast' and did a stumblebum routine where all her clumsy efforts to remove her clothes went wrong. Following her hilarious act that had us all in stitches, the music resumed and Simon captured me for a dance. Desmond whirled away with Sarah before she could protest but claimed me back not long afterwards. Then, astonishingly, he marched me straight across the room and almost into the arms of Dr. Damien Adonis Sparks!

Blond was, if anything, handsomer than ever in evening wear. I suppose I should have expected his presence there as Salter's neighbour, but what defied expectation was that Des should steer a course so deliberately towards him. Was there about to be another altercation between them? For a moment I held my breath.

"I think it's time you finally met my brother." Des' hand rested squarely in the middle of my back. "We're fraternal twins. He may be more successful than I in terms of wealth and prestige in this town, but in the love area I would challenge him anytime! Damien, meet Mari Anderson—my girl."

Damien Sparks frowned, shook his head slightly during his brother's prior comments, and took my hand, his blue eyes inscrutable. Very softly he said, "A pleasure." He didn't reveal that we already knew each other. And as before—against my will—his touch electrified.

Then he moved aside to include his date in the conversational circle: the same beautiful woman with the raven-black hair he'd been with that day in Robert's Bistro. Equally softly, he introduced her. "Joanna Farley, you already know my brother Desmond. Meet his date, Mari Anderson."

Joanna greeted us both, her musical voice as lovely as the rest of her. I smiled back, admiring her perfection of face and figure and ruefully succumbing to the green-eyed monster. Jealousy of Joanna was definitely a waste of my energy when I'd already acknowledged that the handsome doctor was out of my league, but rational arguments did nothing at all to stave off the beast. I know my grin turned mocking and I know the mockery was self-directed.

Desmond bowed to his brother's date and—to my momentary panic—requested a dance. Joanna nodded and moved off with him onto the floor, leaving me suddenly alone with Dr. Sparks, whether I liked it or not. I didn't.

"Your defenses are going up." His voice was deep and teasing. "There's no need to be defensive. I don't bite."

His self-assurance maddened me, particularly in the face of my own discomfiture. I felt my mocking smile widen as I said, "I have a question that I hope you'll be good enough to answer, considering that it's all water-under-the-bridge now. Did you truly deliver a message from Mrs. Salter that day in Robert's Bistro? Was she actually coming to meet us for lunch?"

His brows drew together in another frown. "Does it matter now?"

"I don't like being counter-questioned! Answer me! Was she really coming?"

"No."

I heaved an exasperated sigh. "Then Salter was going to proposition me. And I was going to nail him to the wall! Why did you rescue him? He didn't deserve it."

"Does something qualify you to make judgments on what people do and don't deserve?"

"You're doing it again! I could have had the upper hand! If he had come on to me..."

"Attractive as you are, I don't think you have any proof he

would have come on to you. Lorne is a faithful man, a family man. I believe his motives were strictly honourable."

"Why did you intervene?"

"Because his dog was dying."

"Was that the only reason? Was your intervention strictly spontaneous? Or was it planned?"

He laughed quietly. "Oh, ye of little faith! I repeat: stop being defensive. None of it matters any more. Let it go." One eyebrow quirked teasingly. "Can we at least dance while we fight—and while you're plotting whatever nefarious new scheme you're plotting to throw me off my game?"

"You're infuriating, Doctor Damien Smug Sparks! Does nothing ruffle that calm of yours?"

He took me into his arms and steered me out onto the floor. "We're still stuck in this counter-questioning rut, aren't we? *You* ruffle my calm, Marigold Iona Anderson. Mia. I prefer 'Mia'. May I call you Mia?"

"Just because they're my initials? Or are you implying that in some way I'm yours?"

He laughed again, pulled me closer against him. He was a good dancer; I can't claim the same. Besides, I was fighting my almost overwhelming response to his holding me like that. Never had I responded with such excitement to being held by a man, and it was making me feel unbalanced. Into my hair he murmured, "Does it fulfil some sort of fantasy on your part, Mia, to think that you're mine?"

"Don't flatter yourself! I meant that I don't like those implications! I don't *belong* to anybody!"

He released his hold, took me again by the hand, and led me toward one of the exit doors that gave onto a small balcony. "Come outside with me for a few minutes. You need to cool down and so do I."

"Oh? So I *am* 'throwing you off your game', as you put it? Give the girl a cigar!" A fresh breeze fanned our faces as we stepped out into the night and leaned over the balcony railing, breathing in the fresh scent of the newly-mown lawns below. His shoulder touched mine, remained against it. I milked my advantage. "In this semi-sheer dress, I realize I'm super-tantalizing. So—did you bring me out here to ravish me under the intoxicating light of the full moon? If I were to rub up against you, stroking you sensually from head to toe, would that discombobulate you at last and shatter that maddening calm of yours?"

Even as the words left my mouth, I could hardly believe the way I was acting. Never before had I been so deliberately seductive with a man. Trying to catch my breath, I felt a momentary dizziness. If he were to try anything, I suspected I'd have neither the strength nor the will to resist. Maybe I *wanted* him to try something.

He broke the contact, encircled my waist with his right arm and guided me to a nearby bench where he lowered himself beside me. Very softly he said, "I think, Mia, that you're what the Victorian novelists used to term a 'vixen'. And I confess susceptibility. How long have you and my brother been dating?"

I shook my head. "Don't try to change the subject."

"Which was?"

"Your overwhelming attraction to me. I'd be no kind of a fighter if I didn't move in for the kill while you're down!"

His eyes glinted with amusement. "For your info, Mia, 'down' is hardly the operative word at this particular moment."

"Uh-huh. Perhaps 'hardly' is the operative word, then?"

The amusement spread. "You're good. You're enjoying yourself, aren't you? Go ahead, make me laugh. It will help."

"Oh, the last thing in the world I want to do is to help you! Shall we go back inside now?"

"You go. I'll stay out here for the moment and enjoy the fresh air."

I eased my fingers beneath the sleeve of his jacket and lightly stroked up and down his forearm. "They're somewhere between aquamarines and sapphires, I think."

"What are?"

"Your eyes. They're beautiful."

"Lines like that are supposed to belong to me. Go. You win. I need to be alone and think mundane thoughts. For the record, Marigold Iona Anderson, you don't fight fair."

I mewed like a kitten. "Isn't *all* fair in love and war? Maybe this is both. See you inside." Still partly stunned at my own conduct and yet revelling in my victory, I left him.

And that's the first astonishing thing I discovered about myself on the night of Lorne Salter's sixtieth birthday party. Handsome Damien Sparks, who was out of my league and who already had a girlfriend anyway, was a man I was thrilled I could arouse so easily. That fact flushed me with a wild excitement equal to his—an excitement that I, being female, could avoid betraying where he, being male, could not.

I'm not the 'vixen' type. Never before had I felt the slightest inclination to behave like that with a man. That I'd enjoyed behaving like that with Damien Sparks was mind-blowing.

The second discovery I made that same evening was more mind-blowing yet.

ـلـ

# Chapter 13

Lydia Salter was proposing a toast when I re-joined the party. She was petite, white-haired, and delicate-featured with a peaches-and-cream complexion and a warm wide smile. Salter had no need to seek hamburger elsewhere; he had steak at home. Maybe the good doctor was actually right about Salter's motives being strictly honourable on the day of our rendezvous. It irked me that the good doctor might be right about anything.

"Here's to my dear husband, Lorne—loved by the family and the town alike! Happy sixtieth, darling!" Lydia's voice rang with sincerity. A passing server offered me a champagne flute from a tray, and I tapped it against that of the person beside me and drank the toast.

Desmond had finished his dance with Joanna Farley and was conversing with a boisterous group recounting off-colour stories. I spotted Farley navigating a course toward one of the restrooms and followed her, telling myself I may as well use the facilities and get to know her better in the process. Again, whom was I kidding? Farley had suddenly become supremely important to me because I wanted to size up the competition. Later, I saw that clearly. At the time, the other rationale served quite well.

"So we meet again." I nudged her. "Seems we're headed the same way."

She smiled. "It's an interesting fact that women always pee in pairs or groups. Where is Damien?"

"We stepped outside to get some air. He's still there." I didn't elaborate further. The rest wasn't her business; it was ours alone—his and mine. I wanted to hold it close, savour it, not share it with anyone.

"It figures. He's a fresh-air fanatic. Loves walks in the woods and hikes in the mountains. Do you and Desmond do things like that?"

"No." I wished we did. "Des is more the around-town type. Being a reporter takes him around town anyway, and he seems to thrive on the event-and-party scene."

While we waited in line for cubicles, she told me she was a psychiatrist who had her practice in the same building as Damien. They both enjoyed several interests in common when their time off coincided. "We don't exactly work together, but our fields can overlap sometimes. Brain tumours can cause strange behaviours. More than once I've thought I was treating someone with a psychiatric disorder and it turned out the patient needed Damien's expertise and not mine."

We continued our conversation over our respective sinks as we washed our hands. My not-so-subtly-probing questions revealed they'd known one another two years and were *both* Hepplewhite winners. My, my, what a distinguished group we were! Did they both prescribe mood-altering drugs in their practices? She gave me a look when I asked that one. Why did I want to know?

I shook my head, pretending it wasn't important. In point of fact, it was desperately important. Steering the dialogue in this direction had been pure impulse on my part, but I suddenly needed to verify if there could possibly be any truth to Desmond's accusations against Damien that stormy night in Mother's lobby. "I was reading a paper," I lied, "about how crucial family honour was in seventeenth-century France and how women carrying illegitimate children were sometimes disposed of by using drugs to make them suicidal. I guess mood-altering drugs have been around as long as have murderous intentions."

She shrugged. "I'm not up on seventeenth-century France, but yes, people have strange reactions to drugs all the time. Of course their use for sinister purposes has occurred."

I risked taking it one step further. "Recently, my mother had a suicide in her condo building. The young girl's name was Donna Wooding. She decided to jump off her balcony. Mother wondered if drugs could have been involved."

"Donna Wooding." She nodded. "I remember the item in the local news. Poor girl! I didn't really know her. Damien had met her—though he didn't talk about her beyond describing her as emotionally fragile. Inducing her to take a dive might not have required anything beyond a very persuasive—and evil— perpetrator." She shivered. "Let's get off this creepy subject and go find our dates before they think we've fallen in!" Summarily she terminated the discussion. I could think of no way to re-open it without seeming overly preoccupied with something that, in a news sense, had already been consigned to past history.

Simon and Sarah were talking to Damien Sparks when we emerged. Sarah was flushed and giggling: proof positive that men like the handsome doctor had that effect on women of every age. "I've invited this charming young man to one of our dinners, Mari," she informed me pointedly. "Desmond says he's on assignment that night and I wanted to meet his brother anyway. You didn't introduce us, so we introduced ourselves. Joanna, you're invited too. It'll be next Sunday evening, seven o'clock. Simon is cooking."

"I'm making Chinese," Simon confirmed. "I love to fool around on the kitchen stove with Cantonese dishes."

"Kinky." I stuck my tongue out at Damien. "You'd better warn these people, Simon, that, even though Chinese has a reputation for not being very filling, they won't be able to eat for a week after one of your dinners!"

Damien quirked the teasing eyebrow. "I'll take my chances. Joanna, are you free? I'll pick you up."

She shook her head. "Wish I was! It sounds delicious. My ladies' hiking group has a trip planned for all day Sunday, and it includes an evening meal. But you go ahead, Damien; don't worry about me." She smiled at Sarah. "I'd love the chance to get to know you and Simon better some other time."

Sarah smiled back. "You have a rain cheque."

They finalized arrangements with Damien while I boiled inwardly and stomped off to give my personal congrats to Lorne Salter. Lorne introduced me to his wife Lydia—a woman as gracious and likeable as her husband. While we chatted, I tried to deny to myself the relief I'd felt when I'd heard Damien tell Joanna he'd pick her up. At least they weren't living together.

And even more frantically—and angrily—I shrank from my second mind-blowing discovery that night: that I desperately wanted my handsome prince *not* to be guilty, not of murder, not of anything.

# Chapter 14

"Love is insidious," Sarah said without preamble. "It creeps up on you when you least expect it, and your heart won't listen to arguments against it. Hard as you try to ignore it, it keeps on nudging until you're forced to pay attention. Is that how you feel?"

She was talking on the phone to Myra McAllister, her sister who always seemed to choose the wrong men. Myra made regular 'gut-spiller' calls. It was the Sunday evening following Salter's party, and we'd just finished Simon's lovely Cantonese dinner. Simon and Dr. Damien Smug Sparks were loading the dishwasher, Sarah was sorting out Myra's love life, and I was immersed to my elbows in dish soap, washing by hand some of the larger pans. When Sarah hung up, I flung both a towel and a challenge at her.

"What makes you so blamed dogmatic, anyway? You're not a licensed authority on love. All you know about is your own experience. That doesn't qualify you to prescribe for others!"

She shrugged. "Myra asks for advice, just as you do. I give it to her. And yes, Mari, I do have some experience at love—*real* love—whether you like it or not." She directed a coquettish glance in the doctor's direction. "Are *you* an expert on love, Dr.

Damien Sparks? With your looks, I'd guess you have to be. Or is that an unfair question?"

Damien blushed but met her gaze. His deep voice was velvet. "I thank you for the compliment, but no, Sarah, love is one subject that is extremely difficult to master. I have by no means mastered it."

"Nice side-step," I said rudely. "I don't blame you, though, for evading the question. Sarah is a meddlesome old busybody."

Damien's spectacular eyes met mine and held them. "I deny evading the question, Mia. I answered it directly." He placed the last plate in the dishwasher and joined me at the sink, rolling up the sleeves of his plaid shirt as he grabbed another dish brush and plunged his arms into the soapy water. "Hepplewhite winners are supposed to be experts in certain areas—but factual expertise is relatively easy when compared to esoteric subjects like love. I would never presume to try to dissect love. It would be like trying to nail Jell-O to a tree."

As I'd done at Salter's party, I stuck out my tongue at him. *What about* lust *then, Dr. Smarty-Pants? You* are *an expert on that, aren't you?* If we'd been alone, that would have been my retort— and, judging by his expression, I think he knew it. Instead, I contented myself with a relatively innocuous comeback. "One of these days I'm going to make some Jell-O, take it outside at freezing temperatures, and test if that can actually be done."

He grinned. "Spoken with that true Hepplewhite lust for further knowledge." Did I imagine it, or did he slightly emphasize the word 'lust'? The man was impossible! When he and Simon started talking sports, I was vastly relieved. Moving over and leaving the rest of the washing-up to him, I grabbed another towel and collared Sarah.

"I hope you don't plan on making a habit of this," I whispered in her ear.

She looked blank. "Of what?"

"Oh, don't play innocent! Of inviting Doctor Damien Conceited Sparks to our dinners!"

She shook her head, whispered back. "He's not conceited, Mari; he's gorgeous—a treat on the eyes and a beautiful human-being besides. Look how he insists on helping out. A lot of men wouldn't do that. And I love that he calls you 'Mia'. I hope you don't let him get away."

I grabbed one of Simon's freshly-washed woks, wiped it vigorously and gave her a daggers look. No use pursuing this conversation. Instead, I said, "When I'm done here, I'm going out for some fresh air and light exercise to jog down my meal. May I borrow one of your bikes?"

"By all means. It won't take us that long to pedal up to the university and back."

"*Us?*"

"Yes. I'll come with, on Simon's bike. Just to make sure you don't get into any trouble. We'll leave these guys to take apart the Blue Jays while they finish putting together the rest of the place. Okay with you?"

"Sure." I slanted another meaningful look in her direction. "But certain topics are taboo. Okay with *you*?"

She shrugged disarmingly. When the two of us made known our plans, the men offered to escort us, Damien suggesting we walk instead. Simon nudged him. "You're right: there are only the two bikes. But let's leave the ladies to their girl talk. There's a hockey game on as we speak. Can you stand to watch the Flames get slaughtered yet again?" Damien laughed and they went back to talking sports as we made our getaway.

"He's everything Desmond isn't," Sarah commented the moment we were mounted and riding. "You're dating the wrong brother, honey."

"I warned you!"

"But you didn't mean it. What's stopping you from asking him out again, maybe to a movie where it's just the two of you sitting close together in the dark?"

"Joanna Farley is what's stopping me. Sarah...what do you know about mood-altering drugs?"

She blinked, and I didn't blame her. No one but I would see the relevance. But she merely replied, "Not a whole lot. Enough to realize why certain of my students sometimes act strangely. Does that question have to do with the handsome doctor?"

"I'm...not sure." Seized by another out-of-the-blue impulse, I turned my front wheel and veered away from the university grounds and toward Pleasant Heights Church. "Sarah, I'd like you to come with me for a quick visit to Rev. Connor. His bungalow is right opposite the church and I know he won't mind if we drop in on him for a few minutes. Let's hope he's home! I need to ask him some questions, once and for all."

She looked quizzical, but she turned her bike to follow mine. By bicycle trail, the rev.'s place was no more than ten minutes away. For a while we pedaled in silence; then she said, "Rev. Connor is both Damien's and Desmond's father, right? So what is worrying you?"

"He never mentions Damien. He has had me over a couple of times, along with Des, but the two of them talk as though Des is his only son. I'd like to find out why."

"Meaning you *are* interested in Damien!"

"Meaning there are issues in my own mind that I need to resolve."

Sarah said, "As long as you don't think we'd be imposing. The guys will be watching the game and won't expect us back right away. Are you sure you aren't being too nosey by asking questions that might be highly personal? Are you sure you aren't wading into murkily-dangerous waters?"

I shook my head. I was sure of neither of those things. But what I *was* suddenly sure of is that I wanted level-headed Sarah to be present while all three of us had a frank conversation about the accusations Desmond had made against Damien on that stormy night I couldn't put out of my mind.

It was an impulse I regretted almost at once.

# Chapter 15

The rev. *was* home and was delighted to see us. That was no surprise. He assured Sarah that any friend of mine was a friend of his, and he ushered us into his quaint little conversation nook just off the kitchen. The delicious aroma of fresh-baked buns teased our nostrils, even though we patted our full stomachs and declined.

"I'll get you some to go, then. I noticed one of the bikes has a basket." He suited action to words and filled a large plastic bag, twisting a tie around its mouth. "Nothing too good for the girl who's the centre of my son's world!"

It was as fitting an opening as any. I smiled at him and said, "Rev. Connor, we're sorry to drop in unannounced like this, but I wanted to talk to you with Sarah present. Something has been bothering me for a while, and I need to run it past you. It's about Des and your other son, Damien—the one you don't talk about."

His face blanched at mention of Damien's name, and small white lines formed parentheses around his tight-lipped mouth. In a scarcely-audible voice he breathed, "No! Tell me it's not happening again."

"What? *What* is not happening again?" I was suddenly not sure I really wanted to know.

He grimaced. "Mari, there's never been a girl Des has dated that Damien didn't end up stealing away. Please...don't be one of those! Desmond so needs a girl who will love him for himself, not because she wants to use him to get to Damien. Please...!"

It was Sarah who interrupted, and her tone was brisk. "If you'll pardon my interjecting an opinion, Reverend, I don't think Damien needs to steal away Des' girls. With his looks, he can have plenty of his own!"

"That's not the point." Connor switched his gaze to Sarah. "The point, for Damien, is that he loves taunting his brother with how much better everything about *him* is." The minister wiped a tired hand across his forehead. "I can't get over my anger at Damien for that."

Something within me shrivelled with remorse at having gone down this road. But I had no choice now but to plunge on. Briefly I recounted their fight in Mother's lobby, Des' voiced suspicion that Damien might try to harm the girl he couldn't have by drugging her, Damien's warning to me to forget what I'd witnessed, and Donna Wooding's subsequent suicide. Despite what Connor had just revealed, it felt good to get it off my chest at last—to share with the only two people I wanted to hear about it my mental wrestling match over whether I should have gone to the police. Connor was paler yet when I finished speaking but he reached out a hand to grasp mine and give it a squeeze. Sarah held my other one. We sat like that for several seconds, set in stone, before Connor blew out his breath in a sigh.

He said, "Mari, I wish you hadn't carried this burden all alone for so long. But I'm glad you've told me." He swallowed. "The boys were day and night all through their childhood. Des came easily, but my Megan died giving birth to Damien. Of course I didn't blame him for that—at least not consciously—but in so many other ways he made life difficult for Desmond while they were growing up. When the boys were twelve, Des built me a beautiful model of a B-52 aircraft for my birthday. I've always had a fascination with military planes, and with trains. Damien destroyed that model plane—smashed it to smithereens. Des was in despair. He cried in my arms, said it had taken him weeks to build it. And I could tell you other similar stories."

Sarah's grip on my hand tightened. She said, "Please don't. And yet I'm glad, Mari, that you and I are learning these things now, before it's too late."

*Before I lose my heart to Damien, you mean? Sarah, I think it might already be too late!*

I returned the pressure of her hand on mine, keeping that thought to myself. "Connor...you don't believe Damien capable of actively *causing* Donna's death, do you? If he is so malicious, could he have drugged that poor girl or in some way induced her to jump off her balcony? Desmond said he knew Damien would somehow bring about her destruction if he couldn't have her for himself!"

Connor released my hand, rose and paced back and forth within the confines of the tiny room. Again he sighed. "This is very distressing. I honestly think the answer to your question is 'no'. But obviously Des doesn't agree with me."

"Should I go to the police?"

He shrugged, helpless. "That's between you and your conscience, Mari. If you do go, it will upset Des enormously. He tells me he loves his brother, despite everything."

Tartness entered Sarah's tone. "I'd hate to be an accessory-after-the-fact by talking you out of going, honey. But I think I'm a pretty fair reader of human nature. Damien is a gentle man, as well as a gentleman. I'm having a lot of trouble reconciling what you're saying, Connor, with what I myself have seen of Damien."

Connor made a dismissive gesture. "Damien stopped talking to me a long time ago. His present character is not something I'm really equipped to comment on. If you do decide to go to the police, call me first. I think I might try to talk you out of it."

I nodded. He reached for the plastic bag containing the buns and passed it to me. I said, "Thanks. This is very kind."

"Those buns have won ribbons at county fairs. Enjoy them. Sarah, it has been lovely to meet you..." Just like that the subject had been dropped and declared closed. We were being given what used to be termed 'the bum's rush'.

Back outside on the street, Sarah shook herself somewhat the way a wet dog does. "That was quite the bizarre conversation, Mari! I like Rev. Connor. But the poor man carries a long-standing sorrow and it seems to be Damien's fault. You're right: I *am* a meddlesome old busybody—and I regret meddling in your love life. From now on I'm keeping my nose out."

"I'm not going to go to the police. That's my final decision. But I *am* going to oust the handsome doctor from my life as of now. That, too, is my final decision!"

Sarah didn't argue. The conversation with Connor had cast a pall over the rest of our ride. And when we got back to Sarah's, I grabbed my purse and made hasty excuses to leave.

Damien's deep voice tantalized. "Why are you running away? Was it something I said?" Those spectacular blue eyes dwelled on me almost caressingly. A sour taste came into my mouth as I wrestled with all my newborn doubts about him.

"It was *everything* you said," I shot back. "You're far too smug for your own good, Doctor Wise-Guy Sparks. And I'm really too busy to waste any more of my precious time on your infantile one-upmanship games! It has been...an experience knowing you. But I don't wish to know you further, okay? See you around." And I fled, quickly averting my own gaze from the quizzical expression of surprise and hurt that sprang into his.

What about the pragmatic stance I'd always adopted that romance was vastly overrated? Shouldn't that opinion keep me from being as upset, as...*crushed*... about this as I suddenly realized I was?

I don't remember my drive home in the Echo. I know only that, by the time I reached my apartment, the ache of sadness threatening to engulf me had given way to a sudden spasm of wrenching sobs.

# Chapter 16

A self-imposed ban on all further association with Damien Sparks meant purposely avoiding him at any of the functions I went to with Des where he happened to be present. There were more of those, it seemed, than there logically should have been. But I made myself steer clear. When the quizzical hurt in the flickering depths of those sea-blue eyes haunted me, I strengthened my resolve by recalling Rev. Connor's revelations. Those revelations increased my feelings of closeness to the man I was dating.

The night Des proposed, I was thinking about the little boy who'd spent weeks building a model airplane, only to have it smashed to pieces by his evil twin. That same little boy had spent his adult life watching girls he liked get swept off their feet by the smokin'-hot doctor. Whether or not Damien actually thumbed his nose at Des, it must feel to Des as though that was what was constantly happening.

You don't marry out of pity. Pity is no better a motive for marriage than is defiance of your elders who profess not to like your choice. I talked myself into believing that neither pity nor defiance had anything to do with my acceptance of Des' proposal. Today I'd say defiance was the stronger motive. Neither Mother nor Sarah liked Des any better than they had all along. It's also possible, if I'm being ruthlessly honest, that a perverse part of me convinced myself a union with Des would make Damien come after me. Hadn't Connor said that was how it worked?

Well, Connor was wrong. Damien honoured my determination to steer clear. The next time I had any contact with him at all was on the day I married his brother.

Lorne Salter assured me that, as long as my studies proceeded, neither marriage nor the possible starting of a family would affect my Hepplewhite standing. The support money would simply stop during any leave time I took and then start up again once I resumed classes. Abiding by the scholarship agreement to stay in town and pursue a profession that would benefit the town for at least five years fitted right in with my present plans. And staying in town by Des' side seemed only natural.

I was twenty and still naïve. When Des told me, just before our wedding day, that he had been promoted to assistant editor of the *Gazette*, I congratulated him and felt a genuine thrill—as though his promotion heralded rosy things for our future. When he told me he wanted a larger, more ostentatious wedding so he could brag to the world about his beautiful bride, I blushed and agreed. We were going to show the community of Barrett we had the world by the tail.

The wedding day was perfect: cloudless sky, radiant sunlight and a light breeze blowing that Sarah would have termed a *zephyr*—just enough of a zephyr to keep guests from getting too hot when they danced on the open-air terrace of the Barrett Golf and Country Club where we held the reception. Des was a member there, more for the sake of his image than his golf game. There'd been a full house at Pleasant Heights Church to watch Rev. Connor conduct the ceremony, with Mother giving me away and Sarah by my side as Matron of Honour. That same full house partied up a storm at the club afterwards, leading me to marvel that we'd ended up with so many guests who meant nothing at all to me. Mother was generous enough to foot a large part of the bill, but I felt guilt. Who *were* all these people? Should my mother's bank account pay the price of Des' need to show off?

I made myself shrug away my concerns. Not counting Mother, there were a few guests from my side: Sarah and Simon, Lorne and Lydia Salter, and some of my university classmates. But most came from Des' side: his drinking buds from the newspaper (whom I knew only slightly), his best man, editor Mike 'Hot-Wire' Peters (whom I knew not at all) and—at the groom's astounding insistence—his twin brother.

Damien's presence, I felt, must prove the truth of Rev. Connor's statement that Des loved his brother despite everything. My heart warmed toward my new husband—and also speeded up mutinously when I spotted Damien at a distance, with Joanna Farley on his arm. I was mortified that my wretched hormonal response to the man insisted on betraying me even on the very day of my marriage to his brother. It was shameful!

Inevitably, he and Joanna stepped up to us in the receiving line and offered their good wishes. Suit and tie made him handsome beyond measure, just as he'd been at Lorne Salter's party. Des shook his brother's hand with a small bow and a triumphant sneer he couldn't hide. Me, I tried to avoid being swallowed into the depths of those hypnotic eyes. His voice was deep and resonant as ever, though he said only, "Congratulations to the two of you. May you have many happy years together." He took my hand in both of his, applied brief pressure, and let go. His touch set the hand on fire.

Later in the evening we had one dance. He held me lightly, his gaze interrogating. "So are you ready to take on life with Desmond Sparks?" He kept the tone bantering. "Many would admire your courage."

I grinned back. "I've always been one for a challenge. I think I'm up for it."

"Good. Stay well, Mia. If there's anything..." He cut himself off, changed direction. "My brother is a lucky man."

"Thank you, Damien." His continued use of the pet name 'Mia' sent tingles through me. "Maybe it's time you two brothers made a start on trying to mend your differences."

"No." He shook his head. "Don't push it. Please. Some things are better left as they are, and this is one of them." He pulled me closer, brushed his lips into my hair. "But I thank you for your good intentions. Make him happy. And be happy yourself." Then, just as abruptly, he released me. "I'd better go find Joanna. She wanted to make an early night of it. Take care." He was gone.

Shortly afterwards, Hot-Wire Peters fetched his car and ushered Des and me into it. As best man, Peters was to drive us to a hotel near the airport where we were to spend the night before flying out on the following day for a week's honeymoon in Bermuda. "Maybe by the time we get back," Des ribbed his colleague as we got into the car, "you will have given us a decent wedding present by making good on that retirement you keep putting off. If you don't hurry up, I may have to speed things along by *really* electrocuting you!"

Peters chortled. "Des wants to be editor," he explained to me. "Not long ago, I nearly fried myself on a desk lamp he asked me to move. The cord was frayed. In my dissolute youth, I took a few joy rides in cars that weren't mine, plus, as a junior reporter, I got the jump on a few hot stories that came over the wire. So the nickname fits in several ways. But people around the office started using it constantly after that lamp incident. Everyone jokes it was no accident."

"Oh." Prickles went up and down my spine. I know he expected me to join his laughter, but I found the story creepy rather than funny.

Mother and Sarah both hugged me tightly while Simon threw confetti over us. They wished me happiness, and each, in her own way, echoed Damien's words, including the part where he stopped himself: "If there's anything..."

"There isn't," I assured them both. "Everything's fine!" And off we went on our lovely holiday.

I can't pretend Des wasn't considerate during our honeymoon. He was the soul of consideration. His manner was protective, very much that of the affectionate new husband. Making love to him didn't inflame me with passion, but then my stance on passion gave me only modest expectations. When expectations aren't unreasonably high, there can be no disappointment.

Our hotel was called Cambridge Beaches and was located on the westernmost tip of the island, away from the hubbub of Hamilton, the capital city, major port, and tourist centre. Hamilton was a place we could go to shop and sightsee; Cambridge Beaches was a honeymooners' paradise. Its units were separate and each had a name. Ours was 'Hibiscus South'. Besides the king-size bed and double-size shower, it had a glassed-in breakfast room facing the ocean, where we could sit and take our first meal of the day while looking out on pink-tinged Atlantic waters sparkling in early-morning sunlight. The coastline in this area was rugged and rocky, forming many little private coves rather than one large expansive beach. I adored it immediately. Optimism flooded me as I threw my arms around my new husband's neck and enthused about what a great time we were going to have.

Looking back, I can honestly say we *did* have a great time. We drank champagne, ate delicious and expertly-prepared meals, rented mopeds and rode them all around the island, and had our photo taken standing before several of the circular moon gates reputed to herald marital bliss. Des posted daily to his buds at the *Gazette*, and if he took pleasure in evoking their envy, so be it. Where was the harm?

Only one event occurred while we were there that was, for me, a little troubling.

No. Complete honesty forces me to dispute the phrase 'a little troubling'. Who am I kidding? 'Deeply disturbing' is a far more accurate description for the incident that took place just one day before we were due to return home.

# Chapter 17

Usual ideal Bermuda temperatures prevailed on that day: warm, rather than blistering hot. We rode our mopeds to a place we'd heard about called Lagoon Denizens, where a part of the ocean had been closed off to form a micro-environment for several varieties of marine life, including sharks and sea turtles. One could get a wonderful view of the monster swimmers simply by standing on a man-made bridge built out over the water and peering straight down into its clear blue depths. We paid the entry fee and proceeded onto the bridge, snapping photos with our phone cameras. The good-natured fellow who'd taken our money at the gate had urged us to 'go fishing' if we wanted a shot of a shark or a turtle coming up to the surface to grab a chunk of raw meat. Several lengths of coiled rope baited with that raw meat were tied to the bridge railing for the benefit of visitors.

"Watch this!" a fellow tourist urged us, grabbing a thick coil of baited rope and dropping it over the side of the bridge. Almost immediately, a hungry shark emerged to grab the meat, its massive jaws putting enormous pressure on the taut rope. In a trice the meat had disappeared, as had the diving creature. Now the rope dangled slackly in the water, waiting to be pulled out, re-coiled and re-baited.

An eerie light gleamed in Des' dark eyes. "Hey, cool! Mari, get a pic of me doing this so I can post it to the *Gazette*. The guys'll love it!" He seized one of the rope coils as he spoke and threw it into the water. His mistake was that, rather than letting go, he kept holding onto his end of it.

A huge sea turtle appeared at once, lunging upward to take the bait and swimming with it, still tied to the rope, back into the depths, dragging the rope downwards. It uncoiled so rapidly my husband was taken by surprise.

"Watch your hands...!" The first yelp came from our fellow tourist. A second yelp came from Des himself as the downward-moving rope burned his fingers before he had time to detach them. The remainder of the coil hit the water with a splash as he dropped it—and the shot I captured was of my husband moaning, rocking back and forth, and sucking on his painful fingers.

"There's a good one for your pals!" I couldn't help jibing after making sure the injury was minor. He glared at me with shockingly intense anger, seized my phone, and deleted the photo.

"Not funny, Mari!" That his rage continued to build bewildered and frightened me. "I could have lost my fingers! Would you have laughed then?"

"But you didn't," I soothed. "So let's try and forget it. How are your hands now?"

He ignored the question, gestured with a thumb towards the water. "Forget it, she says! *Forget it*? I think not, hon." The luminous glow of that eerie light in his eyes supplanted the fury. Through gritted teeth he whispered, "That fellow needs to be taught a lesson."

Why my skin began to crawl when he said those words I'm not precisely sure. It's not as though I'd never heard such words before. But I'd never heard them uttered the way Des uttered them that day. I can only surmise it was less the words themselves than the tone—the deadly, hushed tone bent solely on exacting revenge. Brighter than ever burned that terrifying gleam as I watched him—watched him in the same mesmerized way I'd watched him on the stormy evening seared forever into my memory.

Removing from his breast pocket a pair of driving gloves he'd been wearing on the moped, he pulled first one then the other on over his wrists with chilling deliberation. Then he took up a second coil of the baited rope and braced himself by jamming each foot between two posts of the bridge railing.

The tourist who'd originally recommended this pastime said, "I gotta go. Enjoy your day!" He waved and backed off. I sensed he found Des' manner as creepy as I did; his rapid exit betrayed panic. Scores of tiny needles jabbed my skin with relentless persistence.

A turtle's head broke surface. My husband had no way of knowing whether it was the same turtle, and he didn't care. The feral savagery of his demeanour made it impossible to wrench my gaze from him. Suddenly I could no longer control the wild beating of my heart or the rivulets of sweat drenching my armpits and running down my back.

Des dropped the rope coil into the water, again holding on to the other end with his glove-protected hands. Once more the turtle lunged. Des waited until its jaws had closed on the bait; then he yanked with all his strength in a steady sawing motion against its upper lip. The jaws re-opened to release the bait and I saw a crimson stain darken the water. Whether it came from the blood of the turtle or from the raw meat itself I had no idea. I knew only that a wave of nausea hit me so abruptly I had to turn away and run out of there as fast as possible to avoid being sick where I stood.

When my husband caught up to me, he looked like the cat in the adage—the one that has swallowed the canary. "You okay, Mari?" He tousled my hair. "I didn't mean to upset you, hon. Like I said, that guy—or *girl*—needed to be taught a lesson. Probably it was a girl!" He guffawed. "They're the ones that cause all the trouble, right? Maybe I shouldn't have done that, though. Let's forget it and go back to enjoying our day, okay?"

I nodded, trying to take comfort in the fact that the creepy aura had entirely deserted him now. This was the man I'd married, the urbane count who was dashing and subtly dangerous but irresistibly appealing. Nothing else took place to mar our pleasure in the rest of our last day. And by the following morning, when we flew home to take up our lives as Barrett's newest ideal couple, I had succeeded in shoving the whole unpleasant episode back into the recesses of my subconscious. Castigating myself as still immature and prone to over-dramatize, I decided I'd simply blown the whole incident out of proportion.

Very shortly afterwards, I was forced to re-think.

Hot-Wire Peters met us at the airport when our plane landed, slapped his pal on the back, and made a couple of crude jokes. "Still alive I see," Des kidded back. "And still not retired, right?"

"Right."

"Damn—on both counts!" The two men chortled. Des' boss dropped us, with our luggage, at Des' apartment where we were to reside.

I liked Des' place well enough but found it cramped. Even my student quarters had been more spacious. The kitchen was tiny and dark, having only one small north-facing window. The bedroom wouldn't accommodate more than a double bed and, because I'm a light sleeper, I wanted at least a queen size, so that my husband's tossing and turning wouldn't wake me. When I mentioned these things to Des after Hot-Wire had driven off, he laughed and slapped me on the behind. "Isn't that just like a woman—dissatisfied right away! Like I said when I caught that sea turtle, women are the ones who cause all the trouble!" He sighed. "Okay, hon, we'll look for a roomier place soon. It'll take a larger budget to afford it. I'll keep working on Hot-Wire to retire. Or I'll find a creative way to kill him."

"Des, please...I don't like that kind of joking."

He snorted. "Also just like a woman! Your gender is far too squeamish, hon." His eyes lit suddenly with that eerie glow at once fascinating and terrifying. "You belong to me now you know, oh squeamish female. You're *mine*! And you're the one who can pull it off where others failed." His gaze went momentarily blank, distant, and venomous. "Donna and Ingrid...pathetic specimens, both of them..." Then he shook himself as though coming out of a trance. "Look, we'll talk about where we want to move, and we'll start hunting just as soon as we get settled into marriage. I'm not sure, after all, how much I'm really into having a university professor for a wife—especially one who is going to bore her students with Voltaire and other philosophic non-relevant crap. Maybe a place closer to the *Gazette* offices would make more sense. But right now, let's just get unpacked and unwind from the trip, shall we? I'll run you a hot bath."

I could scarcely breathe. Where had his love of Voltaire and his enthusiasm for my career plans suddenly disappeared? He had never expressed anything but admiration for those plans—and for women in general—while we were dating. And what was he muttering that I could 'pull off' where the hapless 'Donna' had failed?—the same Donna, I presumed, who had lived in Mother's condo building and had taken a dive off her balcony?

And who the blazes was *Ingrid*?

I dared not ask.

لي

# Chapter 18

My mounting misgivings I kept to myself. Why? I think I now know the answer. Because, like battered or emotionally-abused wives, I was stunned at my own stupidity in ignoring all the warnings, and I was ashamed—even though I considered myself to be neither battered nor emotionally abused. It had become a matter of pride. I'd married Des at my own insistence, defying Mother and Sarah and wanting to be what Rev. Connor had begged me to be: the girl who loved Des for himself and was not going to be lured away by Damien. Admitting I'd made an error in judgment when I was supposed to be so smart would have involved a loss of face too humiliating to contemplate. Anyhow, Des remained mainly loving towards me as we settled into married life. It's not as though I had those misgivings every day.

Furthermore, we *did* find a new place far roomier and brighter, even if a greater distance from the university. The rent was considerably higher, which caused Des to joke again, in the way that made me uneasy: "That damn Hot-Wire needs someone to buy him an express ticket to the other side of the sod, so I can make enough to buy a place. He still hasn't announced when he's retiring. I'm going to have to push him over a cliff."

I gave a half-hearted smile and changed the subject. "I like that this place is within walking distance of Mother's. Maybe she and I can see each other more often now."

He gave a full wide smile. "*I* like that it's within walking distance of Barrett Medical Centre. There's a Family Practice Clinic on the ground floor. We should get ourselves a family doctor there. There's also an obstetrics clinic on the fourth floor for later on, when you become pregnant with my son."

"Des!" I couldn't help laughing. "I've heard of 'family planning', but I don't think that's quite what the phrase means. Wow! You *are* looking ahead!"

"It doesn't hurt to be prepared, Mari. My brother, by the way, is in that building as well. So is his friend, Joanna Farley."

He said it in such an offhand manner he might have been discussing the weather. And then he watched closely my reaction. I know I didn't imagine that. And, though my heart skipped a beat and then accelerated when I thought about Damien, I was careful not to betray anything. My self-imposed ban on contact with Desmond's brother I fully intended to honour to my dying day.

So I shrugged and made light of it. "Well, nice as that is, let's hope neither one of us is likely to need a neurologist or a psychiatrist!" And then I deliberately steered the conversation away by discussing plans for the evening meal.

Mother and I *did* start to become better friends after my move to the new apartment. Our monthly get-togethers became twice-monthly ones. When I commented on how Spartan our new place looked even with Des' and my combined furniture from our previous places, she and I visited a few furniture stores together and she helped me pick out a couple of new pieces. That led to our having more lunches out and to our starting to build—for the first time—a true rapport. Where I used to consider Mother's preoccupation with matters I termed 'pedestrian' to be beneath me as a lofty academic, I now saw that preoccupation of hers as a way of coping with the loss of a spouse she'd loved very much. Where I'd once condemned her lack of attention to his suffering during his final days, I now started to revise my opinion.

"Shopping with you brings back memories of shopping with

Paul." Her eyes glistened with nostalgia. "It was in our everyday activities together that I truly felt how much we loved each other. Your father and I were raised in very formal homes, Mari. When we were young and in love, both of us boasted about rejecting our parents' values and forging our own way in defiance of all of them. But as time went on, we grew to realize that turning one's back on one's upbringing is far easier said than done. A lot of who we turn out to be comes about because of the way we were raised."

I was listening—*really* listening—for the first time in my life. I said softly, "I always resented having to call you 'Mother' and 'Father' when my school friends mostly called their parents 'Mom' and 'Dad'. And I resented that you were so reserved with your emotions. You hardly ever hugged or kissed me."

"Did you feel like an unwanted child? Did you feel we didn't love you?"

They were questions I might have answered rashly even quite a short time ago. Now, I took the time to consider them more deeply. "No. No, I never felt unloved. I was angry that the two of you seemed so different from some of my friends' parents..." I shook my head, remembering Susie, my best friend in grade four, whose mom and dad had seemed perfect: cheerful, ever-affectionate, always feeding me treats and greeting me as though they were super-glad to see me. They'd divorced soon after Susie and I had entered grade five.

Mother gave a reminiscent smile. "The world is a circle, my dearest daughter. I felt exactly the same way about *my* parents. But as the years passed, I grew to love them and appreciate them for who they were. I hope the same thing happens to us."

To my astonishment, sudden tears coalesced in front of my eyes. "I'm...a reserved person in my own way, just like you and Father. I sometimes find it difficult to express affection or emotion of any kind—but that doesn't mean I don't feel it. I can be in turmoil inside and yet putting up a totally poised and 'together' front..."

Which was exactly what Mother had been doing at Father's deathbed. Why on earth had I failed to see that before now? More accurately, why on earth had I refused to understand it before now?

She read my mind, laid a hand on my arm. "Part of that is society's fault. Allowing oneself to fall apart is interpreted as weakness. I always remember how poised Jackie Kennedy was at her husband's funeral. Even right after he was shot and declared dead, she was waving at crowds with a sort of dazed smile. Reporter after reporter commented upon how admirably she conducted herself."

That was true enough. Though too young to have lived through President Kennedy's assassination, I'd read numerous accounts of his wife's self-possession in the midst of crisis. Never mind that he was a philanderer and maybe her love for him wasn't what Mother's was for Father; nevertheless, to keep her cool in the face of something so life-shattering was a feat that had evoked so much respect it had gone down in the annals of history.

I said, "I always knew how much you and Father loved each other, even though you weren't demonstrative. And I've always known how stubbornly you believe in romantic love despite the reality not living up to the expectation. Maybe that's a more admirable point of view than I've been willing to acknowledge in the past."

Her gaze became very penetrating. "For a newlywed, Mari, you're awfully cynical. Who says the reality doesn't live up to the expectation? It did for me, in terms of my romantic life. Being married to your father—at least until he got sick—was never anything but a beautiful experience."

My raised eyebrows challenged her. "Okay—I admit I've been wrong about some things concerning you two, but surely it's hypocritical to claim that you never found each other annoying and you never had disagreements in the whole of your married life!"

"I'm not claiming that." Her eyes continued to hold mine. "I doubt any couple could claim that, unless they were lying. But your father and I were lucky enough—and some of it *is* luck, Mari—to have an abiding love for each other that transcended all conflict in the end. We married for love, and we stayed in love."

I dared dip my toes in waters I doubted her prudery would allow me to wade into very far. "But didn't you admit to yourself fairly early on that 'love' is more a humdrum everyday thing than a hormone-driven pleasure trip? Didn't you realize quite soon that the 'hormone' part of it can be pleasant enough but is vastly overrated?"

She frowned, and the pause before she responded was so long I decided I was right: she was far too strait-laced to make any comment at all in this area, despite our newly-formed bond. But then she sent me reeling. In clipped, fervent tones she rapped, "No, Mari, I didn't. Your father and I believed demonstrativeness in public to be inappropriate. But in the bedroom it was quite a different story. We were passionate lovers. We couldn't keep our hands off each other." Again she paused. "If your experience is not the same—particularly as a newlywed—then maybe you're married to the wrong man."

I couldn't break my own stunned silence. And I couldn't even call to mind any comeback—other than to resort again to the juvenile and sometimes slyly dirty ones Susie and I used to think up when we were kids sitting together on her front porch after school and munching on her mom's fresh-baked tollhouse cookies. Now, those unvoiced comebacks rippled through my head like tinny tunes tinkling from a kid's wind-up music box:

*Well..., jab me with an open safety pin! Tar me into a gravel road! Sit me down on broken glass! Knock me over with a spiderweb strand!*

*Bite me on my bonny, bare, badass behind!*

# Chapter 19

The thought of someday securing a professorship at the university didn't just make me proud; it excited me in the way only an immersed academic can be excited. Hours spent with my nose in dusty volumes (more appealing, somehow, than the same online documents!) with a view to writing and eventually publishing my own papers gave me genuine satisfaction. Preoccupation with material such as *Candide, Micromegas*, and the *Lettres Philosophiques* might get me labelled a geek in the eyes of some; that didn't bother me at all. It didn't even bother me that my salary as a professor would be less than I could make teaching high school like Sarah. I basked in the university environment. Academia was where I belonged.

But dawning maturity had eliminated any feelings of loftiness. I came to realize I'd be but a cog in a machine—and not a particularly important cog to anyone other than my colleagues and the students I taught. I wasn't going to set the world on its ear. Fostering an interest in and a hunger for higher learning in most of those under my tutelage was going to be—I hoped—the difference I ended up making. So be it. That was okay by me.

Strangely though, my contentment with my ivy-walls destiny seemed to irk my husband. He had told me he wasn't sure he wanted to be married to a professor; yet I'd tried to tell myself his statement had come from a bout of ill humour and wasn't seriously meant. I was mistaken. When I seemed pleasurably immersed in my studies, he became increasingly grumpy about not having a family yet. "Let's start right away," he suggested only two months into our union. "We're on a single income anyway. The difference that scholarship pittance you get makes to us is more-or-less zilch. I want a son I can take fishing." Since the word 'fishing' evoked for me memories of that horrid incident in Bermuda, the line of conversation put me off.

"We're still building our nest-egg," I objected, swallowing my hurt at his demeaning of the scholarship. "Let's wait until we can afford a down-payment on a house with a yard that your future son can play in."

Des sulked and grumbled that we shouldn't wait long. In small ways he turned destructive when he sulked—crushing Styrofoam cups beneath his fingers and then methodically peeling them apart piece by piece, or regularly nicking and scraping away with his pocket knife the varnish on a small coffee table I'd bought at a garage sale, until it looked so ugly we had to dispose of it. These acts I didn't confide to Mother or Sarah, but I did to Rev. Connor. Connor told me I should nurture my husband with as much love and reassurance as possible at home, because job stress sometimes did cause Des to be that way. As a schoolboy he had occasionally acted like that just before a big exam. "He's impatient to get that editorship, Mari." Connor put a fatherly arm around my shoulders. "Try to be understanding. He'll calm down."

I nodded at his words, continuing to be uneasy and trying to talk myself out of that uneasiness. And then one day, without warning, I suddenly spilled my guts—and spilled them to the last person in the world I'd ever expected to confide in!

I was on my way to see John Watt, my physician at the Family Practice Clinic in the Barrett Medical Centre. On Des' advice, we had both become patients at the Clinic. Suffering from a mild flu bug that had me queasy and off my feed, I had made the appointment for right after school. As I was passing a bank of elevators that went to the building's upper floors, one set of doors opened and the man emerging nearly collided with me. He excused himself and then murmured, "Mia."

"Damien..." His gaze was mesmerizing as ever. "Hello. Uh... good to see you."

"How are you?"

"Fine. You?"

"I'm well, thank you." His smile lit the depths of those sea-blue eyes. It undid me.

He steered me out of the human traffic flow and toward a collection of utilitarian-looking armchairs in one corner of the lobby, asking if we could visit for a minute. I nodded and sat down. He lowered himself beside me.

"I knew you had your practice here. Guess I expected we might one day meet," I was chattering inanely, trying to calm my racing pulses. "You are...uh...you're looking good."

*You're looking more than good! You're looking great! You're looking...smokin' hot... as always...*

"So are you, Mia. Marriage agrees with you."

A high-pitched squeak of a giggle almost erupted from me. "Right! I'm coping as best I can." Why had I said that? "I mean, we're saving up for a house and both of us are very busy, so I'm learning to be soothing and understanding when Des gets grumpy..." I trailed off, amazed at what I'd just blurted.

His smile became a frown. Intensity darkened his eyes to indigo. He leaned toward me and, very softly, went right to the heart of the matter. "That sounds like advice Dad would give. Is my brother behaving like a gentleman? Are you all right?"

"Of course I'm all right! Why wouldn't I be?" My annoyance was with myself and my own failure to be discreet. "Des wants a son. He's a little cranky that I don't feel it's time yet, that's all." I was mortified that I didn't seem capable of keeping anything from him.

His frown remained. He said, "Des is a complex man. It's easy to cross him without even realizing you're doing it. Humouring him can be the easiest course of action if the issue isn't a vital one..." He shook his head slightly. "It's not my place to interfere between the two of you. But if I were you, I'd pick my battles very carefully."

"Says the man who did nothing but antagonize him when the two of you were growing up! Says the man who always stole his girlfriends, and who smashed his model airplane right after he'd lovingly finished building it! Who are *you* to give me advice?" Once more, I was stunned at what had just burst out of me. I covered my mouth with my hand.

For several moments he said nothing. Then he took that hand by the wrist, gently removed it from my mouth, pressed it between both of his, and rose to go. "It was good seeing you, Mia. Take care. I mean it." As suddenly as he had appeared, he was gone. My wrist was on fire where he had touched me, and an unuttered apology was still on my lips. I'd had no right to throw in his face things Connor had told me in confidence. After all, I really knew nothing of the circumstances. Maybe Des had somehow pushed Damien to the breaking point. Maybe it was more understandable than it might appear on the surface...

I would never know, because Damien was unlikely to speak to me any more, even if we did encounter each other again in this building. The subconscious part of me had huge regrets about that, though I consciously told myself that what had just happened was proof positive my self-imposed ban on contact with Damien Sparks was not just wise but imperative.

Rattled, I ducked into a nearby bathroom to splash cold water on my face and refresh my makeup before proceeding to my appointment at the Clinic. Thank heavens I'd been a bit early! Now I was exactly on time. And, to my relief, I had no opportunity to brood before I was called in.

Dr. John Watt was a pleasant corpulent man in his early fifties with ruddy cheeks and a ready, crooked smile. I was entirely at ease with him. When I spelled out my symptoms he said simply, "Well, you're not my first female patient to ask for birth control and then change her mind." He punched up my file on the office computer. "So you're twenty. That's a fine age to become a mother. Too many women these days leave first-time pregnancies too long, and the risk of complications goes up with age. Some couples keep putting it off until time runs out on them. You and Desmond are wise to start now."

I had thought my breast tenderness was due to the pill. That's how ignorant I was. I'd been all prepared for him to send me to the drugstore across the way with a prescription for an anti-nausea medicine or an antibiotic. What an idiot!

"We'll do the test to find out for sure, of course." Watt chuckled. "But there isn't much doubt in *my* mind! Yours either, I presume."

"Yes. I mean, no. Mine either."

"So, do you want a boy or a girl?"

"Yes."

"Good answer! I agree: a healthy baby is all that matters…" He began discussing the importance of exercise and good nutrition during pregnancy. Fortunately I didn't have to say much; he quite accepted that I was a bit overcome. He would refer me to the obstetrics clinic on the fourth floor. Shaking my hand, he congratulated me, adding that this was going to be very exciting for us both.

My walk home was a godsend. If I'd been rattled after encountering Damien, I was stupefied after my conversation with Watt. Walking gave me a chance to get my ducks in a row, to consider how I was going to approach my husband. Damien had advised me to pick my battles carefully, and maybe this should not become a battle. Maybe the fault was with the manufacturer of the pills: a defective batch. Of one thing I was certain: the fault was not with me. I'd been taking the pills religiously.

When and how had Desmond switched them? Had he ever for a second *really* agreed to wait for a short time until we were more financially stable?

I shouldn't think that way. I should start looking forward to being a mom. Publicly, I should attribute any blame that existed to my own carelessness: say I'd been too lackadaisical and was now reaping the reward, say I was happy I was expecting and perhaps I had botched up with the pills accidentally-on-purpose. Accusing Des was unthinkable.

So, I decided, was hoping for the boy Des wanted. Boy or girl, the new arrival would be welcomed with open arms. And nowadays a baby didn't have to mess up a woman's career aspirations; Lorne Salter had already told me that. I would adapt. I'd talk to Salter again, take enough time off to give the little one a good start in life, and then I'd go right back to my studies and my hopes of someday attaining a professorship.

I got home feeling cautiously optimistic. Things were going to work out fine for everyone concerned. When I broke the news to my husband, he would be thrilled. The sulkiness would end. He would sweep me into his arms and we would celebrate. There would be no argument or confrontation, only laughter and excited planning for our future.

I couldn't have been more wrong.

# Chapter 20

Mother, Sarah and Connor were the ones who were thrilled—and of course Simon, who *did* sweep me into his arms, lift me off my feet, and twirl me around several times. That was at one of our dinners at Sarah's, not long after Dr. Watt had given me the news. Now that Mother and I had grown much closer, she, too, was a regular guest at these. Connor had been invited as well, and had brought some of his famous homemade buns. Those buns, along with Mother's curried-chicken salad, my stuffed potatoes, and Sarah's ever-popular ham-and-asparagus quiche comprised the meal. Simon had fetched up something celebratory from their wine cellar and had poured a glass of pinot noir for everyone but me.

"You, young lady, get apple juice," he ordered. "No more alcohol for you until after that precious cargo you're carrying has been delivered!" I found I loved it when Simon got masterful.

Des was not present on that triumphant occasion. He had opted, instead, to attend a 'farewell to freedom forever' party thrown in his honour at a downtown pub by his buds at the *Gazette*. In light of how he'd behaved when I'd first told him, I found myself not regretting his absence.

I had stopped and picked up fried chicken—his favourite—on my way home from the clinic that day. For me it had no appeal, but this was about preparing him to be surprised and elated. Its aroma (a bit stomach-turning) was filling the apartment when he'd arrived home from work. Right away he'd suspected something. I mean, the man was not stupid. His eyes had turned cagey, a sneer had curled his upper lip, and he'd said, "So...to what do I owe this special supper? What's new?"

Since he was suspicious anyway, I hadn't minced words, just laid it on the line. "Seems you're about to become a father, Des. Dr. Watt says I'm three months along! Isn't that amazing?"

His sneer had become more pronounced. "Amazing is the right word! So...did you throw your pills down the toilet?"

"No. Uh...no, of course I didn't! I..."

"You figured you'd pander to the old boy after all? You figured it was time to put a *real* burden on me, make me feel even more stressed than I already am?" Blotches of red had splashed across his entire face and neck, as though he were hemorrhaging under the skin. I was mortified. All my happiness had stuck in my throat, where my unvoiced answer resided:

*This isn't on me! I've realized it makes me overjoyed, but I'm not the one who screwed up with the birth control; it has to be you! How did you do it? And why are you treating it like a punishment? Isn't it what you said you wanted...?*

I'd played it cool, recalling Damien's words of earlier. Des was a complex man. I should choose my battles very carefully. Hurling accusations could have been dangerous—yes, *dangerous*—both to me and to my unborn child. So I'd elected not to do it, not to say anything to fuel my husband's anger further. Ultimately, he had settled down, devoured the chicken, and called his editor, Hot-Wire Peters, to crow about his fertility and his success in putting the kibosh on the useless waste of time I called my studies. "Hurry up and die," he'd kidded as always. "Have an accident or something! Now I'm really going to need the salary increase of that editorship." He'd not made much attempt to keep his voice down during that conversation. Maybe I was supposed to overhear.

Revealing to anyone how he had behaved that day would have been an unwise move for more reasons than the danger of inciting him to further anger. No one would have believed me! By the time he'd ended his exchange with Hot-Wire, his mood had done an astounding about-face. He'd become the tickled-pink proud husband, almost giggling with glee. He'd become the Des I'd been expecting him to be when I'd told him the news in the first place.

Again, I was blown away. I actually began to wonder if I had imagined his initial reaction, or if he had been playing some sort of bizarre prank on me. Right after he'd hung up the phone on Peters, we'd gone over to Connor's, then Mother's, then Sarah and Simon's. Des had been the one to make the announcement each time, and he had expansively received congrats, handshakes and hugs from all of them.

Now, at Sarah and Simon's dinner, I allowed myself to relax and uncork my happiness—alongside Simon's wine—and to laugh giddily when our host swept me off my feet and twirled me. I let myself bask in Connor's and Mother's undisguised joy at the prospect of becoming grandparents. No one remarked upon Des being off at the bar with his buds instead of here with those closest to him. Maybe—even though none of them had any clue about his conduct when I'd broken the news to him—they still felt as relieved as I that he wasn't there.

We drank our toast and sat down to a meal I was only able to pick at. Mother assured me my appetite would return before long and Sarah echoed Dr. Watt's statement that, at twenty, I was just the right age to start my family.

And then Connor winked and unwittingly let slip something that caused the same prickles to go up and down my spine that I had experienced the day Des took revenge on that hapless sea turtle. He said, "My son will love fatherhood, Mari, no matter the gender of the child. They all say they want boys, but they're suckers for a girl if that's what they get! You'll see."

I smiled back as a bite of salad threatened to lodge in my throat. "So Des has been saying he wants a son and would have no use for a daughter?"

Connor chuckled. "Des is quite the kidder. He doesn't mean any of it. When he told me the two of you had decided to start trying for a family, I warned him that the more he wished for one gender, the higher his chances were of getting the other." The rest of the group—including me—echoed Connor's chuckle. Simon, the science teacher, called it 'the law of natural cussedness': a law no mathematical principle could explain. Me, I was able to mask my shock as witty comments flew concerning how things always went the opposite way from what you wanted. I let an expression of amusement remain on my face while the pins-and-needles in my spine dissipated and my stricken mind recovered its equilibrium.

*'When he told me the two of you had decided to start trying for a family...'*

This proved beyond the shadow of a doubt that *I* was not the one who had messed up with the pills. So why had Des lied to Connor—and to me? And—as I'd asked myself before—how had he switched them?

Again, Connor unwittingly revealed info that gave me the answer. Placing a butter pat atop his stuffed potato, he said, "If he hadn't told me you were trying to get pregnant, I'd have suspected him of pulling the same stunt he pulled last Christmas! That son of mine can be a real card. Sometimes I wonder if they ever do any work down at the *Gazette*, they're so busy playing practical jokes on each other. He and Hot-Wire bought some fake birth-control pills at Jim's Jokes and, at the staff Christmas party, put them in the stocking of one of their female colleagues who regularly carries on with guys in the back seats of cars. Unfunny as it is in my view, they call her 'the auto body'. Apparently the gift embarrassed her a bit, but she took it in good humour."

Simon sniffed. "It's harsh in my view too, but maybe not so bad if you know the recipient won't take offense. Our staff patronizes Jim's as well. Every September we draw names from a hat and each staff member is supposed to buy little gifts, from time to time, for the person whose name he drew. It's a way of improving morale around the workplace. Joke gifts are hugely popular."

"I've seen the fake birth-control pills," Sarah added. "They wouldn't be appropriate for my 'secret pal' this year; he's one of the male Phys Ed teachers. But they're good—hard to tell from the real thing."

I suddenly had to excuse myself to go and be sick.

# Chapter 21

Dr. Watt made me a referral to the obstetrical clinic upstairs. I arranged with the university to continue classes almost to my delivery date, take the minimum time off, and then resume my studies. Desmond put up no argument when I told him my plans, but I was on my guard now, cautiously braced for whatever might happen next to topple my complacency.

Two things occurred, one right after the other, at the start of my fifth month.

First, Charlotte Sabados, my obstetrician, ordered an ultrasound of my growing belly, and when I showed up at Blair Memorial to have it done, the cheerful technician who prepped me said, "Bet you can't wait to get a look at the little guy!" I asked if she could tell by my shape that the baby was male and she hastily denied it. "But you're pretty big already and boys tend to be larger." She seemed certain it was a boy. "You'll know soon enough."

"What if I don't *want* to know? What if I prefer to wait until the birth?"

She nodded. "Your choice, of course. Sometimes it can be hard to tell anyway—depends on the position of the baby." Her laughter bubbled. "More than one delivery-table surprise has happened!"

*My* surprise, though, was not destined to wait until the delivery table. I knew right away by the manner of those watching the screen that they weren't looking at a run-of-the-mill in-utero baby. No, they confirmed, I was quite right. They weren't.

They were looking at twin girls.

The attending doctor congratulated me, saying she wished my husband were here to 'meet' his daughters for the first time. No doubt he'd be thrilled to bits. I gave a weak smile and explained that Des was a *Gazette* reporter, away on assignment right now. I felt I should excuse his absence and the lie was harmless enough. In truth, he simply hadn't seen the need to interrupt his work schedule when I was going to tell him all about it later.

That I wasn't going to tell him what he expected to hear caused me some initial angst. I realized I, myself, was over the moon about the news, but would Des take it as though I had defied him on purpose? Would he be angry with me? Surely not. Yet my memory of how he'd behaved when I'd first told him I was pregnant—before he had fallen into line and assumed the socially-acceptable pose—haunted me. What if he flew into a rage? What if he was so disappointed it wasn't a boy he rejected the whole idea of parenthood and told me I'd be raising the children on my own?

Some instinct made me decide to pretend not to be as happy as I really was. Maybe if he believed I, too, felt tricked by fate, he'd be more accepting of the turn events had taken. Amazed at the thought of resorting to such deceit with a husband who supposedly loved me and was elated at the idea of impending fatherhood, I nevertheless decided this would be the safest course of action, both for me and for the girls.

The second complacency-toppling occurrence took place right after I'd revealed to him—with a convincing sigh—that perhaps I wouldn't be able to return to my studies so soon after all. I could sense he found that pleasing, even despite the dropped bomb of twin female fetuses. He made some muttered comment about my worthless studies being definitely down the toilet now, and

I honestly believe his satisfaction about that did a lot to stave off his anger. So my strategy had been spot-on.

And then, out of left field, he threw me the curve ball to end all curve balls.

"I'd like you to go and see my brother." He made the request with a coy little smile, as casually as though he were choosing which shirt to wear. "I think it would be a good idea if Damien examined you."

"What?" I gaped. "Damien? But he's a neurologist! And to say he's not your favourite person is a colossal understatement! Why on earth should *he* examine me...?"

"I'll make the call." He said it in a tone of finality. "You claim you've had a few headaches lately, and it doesn't hurt to have him check it out. You're his sister-in-law, after all. I'm sure he can clear a space in his busy schedule to see his own sister-in-law."

"But Des, I..."

"I'll take care of it, Mari. Don't worry." His voice was pleasantly reassuring. "Family should do things like that for each other, whether or not they get along. Don't you agree?"

I was completely befuddled. This was beyond comprehension. Yes, I'd had a few headaches off and on, but they weren't something I was particularly concerned about. Even if they *were* of enough concern to see a doctor, my family physician, Dr. Watt, should be that doctor. Bothering Damien made no sense whatever.

But protest was futile, and I knew it. Des had decided on a course of action, and he was bent on following it through. Whatever off-the-wall logic he was using I didn't dare try to fathom. Play along, I told myself. Don't cross him. Keep up the ruse of being mildly annoyed by the pregnancy derailing my studies—and the ruse of being hesitant and reluctant to go and see the smokin'-hot Dr. Damien Adonis Sparks.

Yes, my reluctance to see Damien *was* a ruse. The prospect of seeing him brought a rush of pleasurable excitement; it evoked the familiar hormonal response I'd insisted to Mother was overrated. Much as I castigated myself for having the gall to have such feelings while pregnant with his brother's babies, I could no more prevent the effect he had on me than I could prevent breathing.

Yet pervading that pleasurable excitement was something else very disturbing—the preposterous notion that both Damien and I were marionettes whose strings were being pulled by a hideous Machiavellian puppeteer.

# Chapter 22

Damien didn't see me during regular office hours. His receptionist, a Howard Green, called the following week to tell me I needed a referral from my family doctor if I wanted a consultation at the clinic, but Dr. Sparks would meet with me *un*officially that evening at six o'clock. Howard Green was very businesslike over the phone, but he broke into a grin when I later confronted him face-to-face, and he congratulated me on my upcoming motherhood.

"I'm finished for the day, but Dr. Sparks will be with you in just a moment," he beamed. "Have a seat." He was no doubt curious as to why I was there, but he retained his professionalism up to, and beyond, his gracious exit. I sat down and idly started to leaf through a magazine.

The clinic took up the entire eighth floor of the building, and the waiting room, flanked by windows on three sides, commanded a riveting aerial view of our picturesque town, with the confluence of the Blair and Barret Rivers at its centre and its abundance of park and recreational areas. I was still absently holding the magazine while trying to pick out various landmarks below when Damien emerged from the inner office, crossed the room, and offered a hand to help me to my feet.

"This way." He guided me into his consulting room and closed the door. I sat opposite him with a heavy oak desk between us, my hand tingling where his had held it. "Congratulations." His deep voice caressed the word. "I understand I'm going to be the uncle of twin girls. That's thrilling."

I nodded, feeling disturbed as always by his nearness, and starting to babble. "Yes. It is. Uh...the rent on this space must be humongous. Your office is gorgeous. Obviously, you're very successful."

He gave a deprecating shrug. "The rent is high. I'm in the normal amount of debt for someone in my situation. My earning power is capable of handling it. And none of that is remotely the reason why I do what I do. How can I help you, Mia?"

"Uh..." I shrugged back. "Des and I are extremely happy about becoming parents. Des wants the pregnancy to go perfectly. He thought I should come and see you about a few headaches I've had..."

He raised his eyebrows. "Has the onset of the headaches coincided with your pregnancy?"

"No. I'm not even worried about the headaches. This was all Des' idea...!"

His expression changed. "I see. Let me look at you all the same." He fetched a pocket light, came around to my side of the desk, and examined each of my pupils in turn. Unbidden, my heart fluttered like a wayward butterfly and my breathing grew ragged at feeling his warm breath close to my face, his exploring hand lightly push stray hair tendrils off my forehead. It was exquisite—and over far too soon. He pulled up another chair beside mine and lowered himself into it. "Was Desmond extremely insistent?"

"Yes, he was. I told him I'm fine, but he wanted to be absolutely sure. No harm in that, I guess. I'm...sorry if we've disturbed you for nothing."

His eyes, ink-blue in this light, searched mine. "How is the pregnancy going?"

"Like clockwork. I'm bigger than I'd otherwise be because it's twins, but I'm feeling just fine. I'm going to keep attending classes at the university as long as I can—maybe right up to my delivery day. Afterwards, we'll have to see."

"Is Desmond all right with that?"

"Why wouldn't he be?"

A shutter came down over those ink-blue eyes, turning them to slate. Very softly he said, "Is there anything else I can do for you?"

I came unhinged then. The power he had over me suddenly prevailed and unaccountably, I burst into tears. All my frustration, dread and confusion surfaced with a rush. Even as I frantically mopped at my face with the handkerchief he handed me, I continued to cry until I'd sobbed myself dry. I wished he would take me in his arms and comfort me, but I understood his reservations. Maybe he also understood mine.

When I choked to a halt at last, I apologized again. "Look, I'm very sorry. This pregnancy has my hormones all screwed up. I have no idea why I did that."

"It's the body's natural way of releasing stress. And I'm guessing you're under considerable stress at the moment."

"Why would you think that?"

He rose and began to pace, not responding for several seconds. When he did, he returned to sit in front of me and once more search my eyes with his. "Mia, there's no point at all to this exchange if you're going to be defensive. Either we really talk or we make our farewells right here and now and go our separate ways. Please choose."

I probed the depths of his eyes, hesitated a moment longer, then released the brakes on my anxiety. "There's no one I can confide in, Damien. Mother and Sarah are out, because they advised me not to marry Des in the first place and I ignored them. Connor is out, because Des can do no wrong in his eyes. And *you* are out because..."

He finished it for me. "Because I'm the bad brother who has always tried to ruin everything Des ever cared about. All right. I get that you have a problem trusting me. But why is Des intentionally shoving you in my direction? What is he up to? Have you asked yourself that?"

"I...yes. Yes, I have. I've asked myself why we moved to this neighbourhood where you have your office, why Des wants us to be patients at the particular Family Practice Clinic in this building, and why, when you and I aren't running into each other by accident often enough for his liking, he has found a non-existent excuse to throw us together. I've been asking myself these same things since even before Des and I married. Why did he make a point of seeking you out and getting you to dance with me at Lorne Salter's birthday party? And why did he want so much that you attend our wedding when the two of you don't get along? I...don't understand any of it."

He inhaled deeply, and I sensed his relief. Very quietly he said, "Thank you. I needed all your cards on the table. Let me put mine beside yours. Desmond harbours a huge grudge—against the world in general to some extent, but mostly against me. He has harboured it all his life. I don't think he can help it. Life is much easier when he and I steer clear of each other, but he doesn't always permit that. He thrives on the prospect of...taunting me. I can't describe it in any other way. He's willing to bide his time—for years, if necessary—for the eventual gratification of knowing that something he has is causing me to feel deprived. Does that make any sense?"

I stared at him, not knowing how to answer. What I eventually said was, "You don't like to speak—or think—ill of people. That makes you very different from Des. And yet, maybe you made him the way he is by your actions when the two of you were growing up: stealing his girlfriends, smashing his model airplane, et cetera. Why did you do those things to him? It doesn't seem to be in character with what I know of you today. If only you had acted more decently toward him when the two of you were children, perhaps now, he..."

Trailing off, I felt my own eyes widen as I perceived the expression in his. And I suddenly, unerringly knew my mistake, and wanted very much to hug him.

"The primary issue now, Mia," he said ultra-softly, "is that you stay safe. Knowing what makes Des tick is essential to maintaining that goal. I think you already realize that. The problem is Des' complexity. You know that it's possible to cross him without even realizing you're doing it. And if you cross him, he'll..."

I laid a hand on his arm. "He'll punish me. I do know that. Damien, I...I think I owe you an enormous apology..."

"Don't. I want you to focus with me on how you can avoid incurring his desire to punish you. What do you think he wants to achieve between us during this interview he has arranged? What does he want you to tell him when you get home about how things went today?"

I considered the question, feeling intense disappointment when he gently slid his arm out from under my hand. Cautiously I theorized, "He'd like to hear me say I...I sense you envy him being married to me and expecting not just one baby but twins. I think that would please him a great deal."

"Then tell him that. And tell him, as well, how much you love him, how I'll never compare to him in your estimation, and how you don't want to see me any more. I think that will hold him for quite a while."

I nodded, reflecting that a more bizarre turn of events than I had ever conceived possible had suddenly made us allies. I *would* administer to Desmond exactly the recipe Damien and I had just concocted—because Damien was right: my safety might be at stake. And I would continue my self-imposed ban on having no—or minimal—contact with my husband's brother.

I'd do it even though it ran absolutely counter to every rational and hormonal bone in my body.

೭

# Chapter 23

Labour began early, which was not unexpected. Weary of my lumbering heaviness, I viewed this as a definite advantage and, while I contacted first Mother, then Sarah, I was swept with a thrill I hadn't known since early-childhood exploration, if then. By pre-arrangement, my husband's office was called and he was notified, but he had declared himself quite content to make the acquaintance of the new additions after they were born. So his absence from the delivery room was no surprise. "New dads can be nothing but a hindrance if they don't want to be there," Dr. Charlotte Sabados told me. "You're smart to let him stay out."

Mother and Sarah, on the other hand, were outstanding coaches. They held my hands and kept me calm during the rough times—which, fortunately, were very brief. The twins— fraternal—were born at 4:08 and 4:12 in the afternoon, and they made their world entrance wailing lustily. Both were on the small side but definitely not preemies. The blonde one born first I named Carrie, which was Sarah's middle name. And the dark one I named Kathryn—Katie—which was Mother's.

"Lovely!" cooed one of the attending nurses. "Names of women in your family?"

"Yes—and in my honorary family. And also names my husband and I like."

Mother and Sarah exchanged glances. I think they both knew I was lying. Des had had nothing to do with selecting the names. He had told me from the start he didn't really care; I could name them what I wanted. Next time—when I produced a son for him—then he would get involved in name choosing.

He was, however, in an expansive mood upon their arrival and invited over a number of his co-workers to admire them. The *Gazette* staff came, bringing words of praise and beautiful gifts. Sarah and Simon had given us matching cribs; bedding for these appeared in abundance, as well as numerous cuddly toys. Mother and Connor put their heads together to throw me a sleeper-and-diaper shower at Connor's place.

And Damien made me bite my lip by sending a congratulatory card that had Des walking on air. It contained two generous cheques to start an education fund for each of our daughters. (Lorne and Lydia Salter, to my complete surprise, sent another two such cheques the day after, saying their neighbour had given them the idea!) Damien's card read, *Best to the new mom and dad, and to my nieces. I have no doubt they're lovely. And I'm very envious.*

Des tore into the card, read it with unnatural eagerness. "He means that!" he muttered before getting hold of himself and carefully readjusting his social mask. "It's great he's happy for us, isn't it, Mari?"

I nodded. "Great. Absolutely great." Gratitude toward Damien swelled up within me until it threatened to choke me.

He was buying time for me and for my new daughters.

"We should invite him over here to see them!" Des suggested. His eyes held that unpleasant onyx gleam. "They *are* perfect, aren't they?" Suddenly they were his pride and joy. True to the form Damien had described, Desmond was eerily turned-on by the thought of flaunting his prizes in front of his brother. Treading carefully, I shook my head.

"Send him a photo, Des. He'll seethe with jealousy when he looks at how pretty they are, but we'll deprive him of the pleasure of actually getting up-close and personal with them." I wondered whether I'd gone too far, whether he would become suspicious that I was onto his game and playing one of my own. But he nodded, brushed a kiss across my lips, and said I was a genius. He took several photos then and there, and he asked me to take a few of him holding one daughter on each knee. Even as he passed me his cell phone, the acrid dryness in my mouth told me how distasteful I found this whole thing.

Katie was a more restless baby than Carrie, but they were both fairly contented. I breast-fed them and supplemented with formula. Mother helped out with them sometimes, as did Sarah and Simon. Connor, too, loved being charged with the care of his granddaughters. In fact, on the day before I was due to return to classes, Connor said he'd take them for the night to give me a chance to sleep through till morning.

I was touched by the offer, though reluctant to leave them for a whole night. But when Connor insisted, I gave in. I was going to have to get used to leaving them sometimes anyway if I was going to resume my studies. Des made a joke about how having the night to ourselves would give us the chance to start trying for the boy we wanted. I laughed weakly, but my insides shrivelled at the thought of resuming our conjugal relations.

Des' blessing of my return to classes was something I'd accomplished by guile—just as Damien's guile had accomplished in Des a paternal pride in his daughters. Pretending I now found university somewhat annoying because it took me away from my babies (actually a partial truth!) and pretending I was now not sure I wanted a career at all, had achieved the desired reverse-psychology result. Des said I *should* go back! The eventual double income would be a great help after all; they were sure taking their sweet time at the *Gazette* about getting Hot-Wire to retire and promoting him to editor. Besides, I could always quit at some future time—after we'd had our boy.

On the night Connor looked after the girls and my husband and I were alone together in the bedroom for the first time since my delivery, I inadvertently gave myself away. I allowed Des to sense my aversion to what was coming—which made him all the more insistent. When he turned brutal, tearing off my nightgown and attacking me with the savagery of a caveman, I realized I'd messed up. He bit me hard several times, causing searing pain, and my pain seemed to rouse him further. In shock, I stopped resisting and lay prone and passive while he pounded into me. Afterwards, he turned tender, apologized, attributed it all to the deprivation during my pregnancy, and fell asleep.

For a long time I lay quietly, afraid to move. And while I lay there, I realized how careful I must be from this day forward. I was dealing with a man who found violence a turn-on, who would force himself on me without a second's hesitation, and whose psyche must be manipulated with kid gloves. I would have to learn about everything that pushed his buttons and then use that to my advantage. I would have to walk on eggshells, continuing to say my studies were onerous because they took me away from my babies and yet not betraying to him exactly how much joy those beautiful babies were really giving me.

Right now, he was pleased with the girls despite their gender because he thought they were making Damien jealous. If he ever sensed how all-important and precious our daughters had become to me from the moment they were placed in my arms—how much they had awakened my latent maternal instincts and how I now realized I'd be willing to walk through hell-fire itself to protect them—his pleasure would turn to a resentment that I knew might cause my babies harm. Their father, I told myself, could easily pose a threat to my babies, because...

Finishing that thought took some fortitude on my part. I forced myself to do it. Drawing in a breath to the tips of my toes, I reached into my mind and plucked from its recesses the rest of my unvoiced sentence:

*Their father could easily pose a threat to my babies because their importance to me placed them in the same category as Damien's model airplane!*

As though to underscore my stunned admission to myself, my husband suddenly stirred, groaned, and mumbled indistinctly in his sleep. Then he gave his eerie, bone-chilling smile and spoke up very clearly, his words stiffening my entire body in—I couldn't help thinking it—a horrible imitation of rigor mortis.

He said, "Poesie *had* to die, Ingrid. Yes, she *had* to die! You should have known that, you moronic little bitch!"

# Chapter 24

Connor's kind intentions of taking the girls for the night so I could sleep through were wasted. My mind churned for hours on end as I lay beside Des and wondered what to do. At times I dozed fitfully, only to dream of faceless monsters lurking in the shadows, ready to pounce on me as I approached. Then I'd wake with a start, an unuttered scream lodged in my throat.

As a child, I had never been inclined to nightmares. I was scornful of those who had them. Now, I suddenly knew what it was to feel trapped and helpless, an animal caught in a snare, staring impending doom in the face and powerless to escape its inevitability. What should I do? Marriage for the sake of preserving one's dignity has its limits. Could I afford to risk spending one more day with a man whose obscure and terrifying depths went far beyond my knowledge and understanding?

Endless as it seemed, that night ultimately gave way to dawn. And with dawn—as is often the case—things began to look less dramatic. Yes, I was very upset by a sexual encounter that had definitely been imposed on me by force, and yes, I was still horrified by the words Des had uttered in his sleep. But the first issue was dealt with almost at once when my husband woke: he repeated how genuinely sorry he was for several bruises—and a bite mark—he had inflicted, and he kissed each of them in turn.

"As I said, it was the deprivation while you were pregnant, Mari." He looked embarrassed and thoroughly regretful. "I don't know what got into me. It won't happen again."

Famous last words of the abusive husband? Perhaps. And yet abused wives accepted these apologies time after time, convinced their husbands really *were* going to reform. As with nightmares, I'd always been scornful in the past when I'd heard or read about downtrodden women staying with men who repeatedly abused them. What idiots! Didn't they deserve what they got? Now, for the first time, I felt some empathy for those poor women—even though I was still convinced I wasn't one of them.

The bruises and bite mark were not visible when I got dressed; my clothes successfully hid them. I could almost talk myself into believing they didn't exist. And Des was in such a contrite mood I decided I'd ask him about the second issue that had troubled me last night. Maybe we could clear that up as well, and I could start my first day back at university with no concerns at all. The morning sun was beginning to filter through our apartment's east-facing windows. Getting some sort of logical explanation for what he'd said in his sleep suddenly seemed very possible.

So I tackled it. And his explanation *did* ring true. I began to feel like a fool for making such a mountain out of a molehill.

"I sometimes babble when I'm sawing wood, hon." He gave a snort of laughter. "Just ignore it. It's total garbage. Ingrid is a girl I went with for a while a few years back. She even moved in for a brief period. Poesie was her little calico cat. You know: French for 'poetry' but also a play on 'pussy'. That was Ingrid's ingenious idea of wit. She loved the stupid name and she loved the stupid creature. Unfortunately, it got cancer and had to be put down. It was only a couple of years old, but those things happen. Not being very bright, Ingrid couldn't accept it. She cried about it for ages. Those constant tears were very frustrating. I kept saying to her, 'Move on. Get another cat'. But she wouldn't listen. She preferred wallowing in her grief over that one. I'm afraid I wasn't that sympathetic. Maybe I should have been more so."

"What happened to her?"

He shrugged. "She wasn't from here. She got laid off her job at Salter's textile plant and went back to where she came from. I followed the advice I'd given to her and I, myself, moved on."

I nodded. "You were wise. Thank you for explaining. I'd better get off to classes."

Desmond had mentioned Ingrid once before, I recalled, on the day we'd returned from our honeymoon. He'd mentioned her in the same breath as poor suicidal Donna Wooding. I didn't bring that up. I was afraid of seeming too pushy and paranoid, of asking too many questions at once. Someday I *would* ask him about it. And no doubt, I told myself, his explanation would be as reasonable as the one I'd just heard.

My husband had a brooding, tenebrous side to his nature. We all knew that. Learning to fly below his bugbear-detecting radar was eminently advisable for all who dealt with him. But some of the dread I'd been experiencing—the dread I'd confided to Damien—now seemed less dreadful than it had. I wanted everything to be all right, and I actually lectured at myself in the bathroom mirror that I had to stop being such an over-imaginative wimp.

I had two children with this man now. What kind of a wife would I be if I didn't stand by him?

So I returned to classes and I immersed myself again in my studies at the university. Mother was taking the girls during the day until they were old enough to go to a day home. Connor loved taking them when he could, as did Sarah and Simon. I counted myself blessed: Carrie and Katie were beautiful little girls who were growing up knowing they were loved and cared about. Their father largely ignored them, which caused me some heartache at first, but I decided to be thankful he had at least accepted them. Okay, so my marriage wasn't perfect. My husband had his warts. Who among us hasn't?

I'd been back at classes several weeks when I stopped by Mother's one day to pick up my daughters and found she had a visitor. Excusing myself for barging in, I was about to get the girls and leave when Mother's voice halted me.

"Don't rush off, Mari. You need to stay and hear this. The girls are asleep in the bedroom. Take off your coat and help yourself to a cup of tea and a dessert."

I thanked her, accepted her invitation, and eased into a chair at the kitchen table beside the guest, having no idea what I was in for. Mother introduced Bertha Baxter, a stoutish outdoorsy woman who looked to be in her early forties. "Nice to meet you," I greeted, biting into a sweet scone. "Please pardon me if I don't stay long; I have a term paper I need to get to."

"Bertha is the late Donna Wooding's cousin from out west," Mother interrupted. "She's the cousin who arranged for the sale of Donna's unit after that poor girl...um...met her untimely end." Mother cleared her throat. "It upset us all. But what Bertha has just told me upsets me even more."

Suddenly, I was on tenterhooks.

"I'm a private investigator," Ms. Baxter explained. "I felt I had some vacation time due. My original plan was an escape to Maui, not another trek out here to Barrett, beautiful little town though it is. But just recently I started reading my cousin's diary." She shot a meaningful look at Mother. "It's as you said, Louisa: sometimes fate steps in for no reason we can explain. I didn't even realize I had that diary when I stuck it in a box three years ago, along with a few other personal items of hers. They were all just little mementos. And then last week I was doing some tidying-up at home, throwing out stuff I haven't looked at lately. And I ran across this box, tucked away in my spare room. Next thing I knew, I'd cancelled Hawaii and was driving out here. The superintendent of the building said, 'Talk to Louisa Anderson'. And here I am."

Mother nodded. "My daughter is married to the man your late cousin refers to in the diary. I think you should read to my daughter what you've just read to me."

I swallowed a mouthful of tea, deciding I wasn't going to like PI Baxter. Private investigators did things like prove a spouse is cheating, or dig up evidence for wealthy parents that their son or daughter is dating an unworthy pauper. But I knew immediately that, like her or not, I had to hear whatever it was she was about to read.

"Right." Bertha Baxter opened the dusty volume and smoothed its creased pages. "This is the entry she made the day before she jumped off her balcony. In my opinion it requires follow-up. Have a listen:

*I realize now exactly what's happening. I didn't realize it before. This is all an elaborate game. I have failed to play by Des' rules, so I must be disposed of. But he can't punish me if I punish myself first! There will be far less suffering my way. If I jump, it will just be over. All I want is for it to be over!"*

Despite the moisture of the tea, I found my tongue was suddenly sticking to the roof of my mouth. When I spoke, my voice sounded foreign to my own ears. "So your cousin *did* commit suicide. This makes that quite clear. I would think the passage you've just read *removes* doubts, not raises them."

She shook her head. "I would disagree, Mrs. Sparks. Yes, my cousin had a fragile temperament. Yes, she took her own life. But why? The statements she makes here need to be delved into further. I have looked at the preceding pages, of course. It seems she and your present husband were hot-and-heavy for a while. She felt she had everything to live for. And then that suddenly changed. I'll be far more satisfied about laying this to rest when I understand more about the 'game' she refers to and what your husband did that caused her such despair she just couldn't go on."

I took another bite of my scone, ruminating before I responded. When I spoke, my tone was guarded. "Des can be moody. Donna was obviously that way as well. If she displeased him somehow, maybe he went from adoring her one day to breaking it off the next. Maybe he even said something mean, like that he had just been trifling with her and it was all a game."

Again she shook her head. "I'm not satisfied with that. I don't think you are, either. This investigation is unofficial but I intend to pursue it, with or without your help. I have a week in which to ask around. There's someone here in town, I'm sure, who can give me more information."

"Why not ask Des himself? Wouldn't that be the obvious thing to do?" I felt a hypocrite as I said it. After all, *I* hadn't asked Des himself. Her receptiveness to the suggestion was lukewarm.

"Possibly I'll talk to your husband at some point. But I'm not going to start there. The picture he'll paint will be a biased one. Do you know of anyone else I can talk to, someone who knew them both back then and might be able to give me a bit of history about their relationship?"

"Mm...no. No, I'm afraid I don't." Once more I began to lift my teacup to my mouth and stopped halfway, skewered on the gaze of the woman who was far more intuitive than I'd ever given her credit for being in my childhood.

"Yes, Mari," Mother contradicted. "You do."

# Chapter 25

It was presumptuous to expect that Damien would just drop everything and see us. I had no right to expect it. A lot of me didn't want it. But when I went ahead and contacted his office from Mother's place, I got Howard Green at the reception desk, who told me Dr. Sparks was in surgery and gave me his unlisted cell number. That surprised me. Obviously, Howard Green had permission to do that if I ever called.

I tapped in the number, got voice mail, and left a message. Then I looked at the pair of them and shrugged. "I've done all I can. Damien is a very busy man. I'm sure he'll get back to me when he has a chance." I outlined to Bertha the altercation I had witnessed in Mother's lobby the night before Donna's death. "Des was hurling accusations in anger and Damien was trying to calm him down. It didn't work. Des charged out of there like a mad bull."

Mother pursed her lips. "I seem to recall from the way you've told it before, Mari, that you had some concern about the accusations Des hurled. Didn't Des accuse Damien of having access to mood-altering drugs and being not above using them on Donna? And didn't Damien warn you not to tell anyone about what you'd seen and heard?"

Again I shrugged. "Des says things when he's angry that he doesn't really mean. He and Damien have been estranged since childhood. He's inclined to blame Damien for things that go wrong with his own life. Damien wouldn't have done anything to harm Donna. He's a doctor. I mean, 'do no harm' is part of the Hippocratic Oath he..." I stopped, realizing how my version of that night's events had taken on a very different slant since I'd got to know both brothers so much better. I was protecting Damien, making excuses for him at the expense of my own husband. I was being a traitor.

Bertha said, "Thank you for contacting Damien. There were no drugs of any kind in Donna's system, but I'd like to talk to him anyway." Her gaze was as penetrating as Mother's. "You have decided he isn't guilty of anything, and you're probably right. But now that you're family to them both, you're not unbiased any more." She gave me the name of the hotel she was staying at, her room number, and her cell number, which I keyed into my own phone. "Please contact me when he contacts you. I would greatly appreciate it."

I left Mother's place soon after, at the same time Bertha did. Mother hugged me hard; she'd been doing that more and more lately. I hugged her back, kissed her on the cheek, and told her to try not to worry about a thing.

Bertha helped me get the twins into my Echo. After I thanked her, I gave a rueful grin and said, "In your shoes, I would have picked Hawaii." She grinned back, agreeing she had probably been a dunce. I knew I'd lost the battle not to like her. When we parted company, we shook hands as though sealing a bargain.

My drive home gave me a chance to process these new events. Carrie and Katie slept on in their car seats, lulled by the vehicle's motion. I thought again about what Donna had written in her diary and wondered if it had really revealed anything that necessitated a meeting with Damien—or necessitated any investigation at all. I mean, hadn't Damien and I already discussed Des' 'game'? Even if Des had tried to flaunt Donna in front of his brother and Donna had refused to play, surely that gave neither brother motive for murder. Did it?

The prospect of seeing Damien again did its usual number on me. At least I wouldn't be alone with him. Bertha's presence would put a damper on the pesky hormonal response I couldn't seem to get over. And maybe a proper conversation about that night, once and for all, would clear up any remaining uncertainties for good. I hoped so.

Des was at home when I arrived and was uncharacteristically considerate. I had never seen him so cooperative, not even right after the twins were born when he'd taken such pleasure in showing them off and bragging about his fertility. He even handed me the diapers while I changed them, and he got out the baby food to heat up on the stove for their supper. Was it possible he was actually starting to take to the girls and to enjoy fatherhood? I would have loved to be able to buy that as an explanation—but I didn't.

"You're being very helpful tonight." I smiled at him. "Thank you."

He went around behind me and massaged my shoulders; then he kissed the back of my neck. "You're tense, Mari. You need to relax. Is that better?" The massage did feel good, and I nodded.

"Let's have a glass of wine, Des, while I get supper ready." I made the suggestion because I had a strong need to maintain the relaxed atmosphere. "There's an open bottle of Chablis in the fridge. Would you please pour us a glass each?"

"Gladly." He complied at once. "I need wine tonight, too. I'm afraid I have some news that could do with the dulling effects of alcohol."

"Oh?" Instantly, the benefits of the massage he had just administered evaporated. "What is it? What's wrong?"

The onyx in his eyes glittered as he sighed. "You're going to find out about it anyway. It's a sad way to come by the position.

I should never have joked about it. Hot-Wire Peters had an accident today at the office. One of the idiot data-entry girls pulled out the wastebasket to throw away her gum wrapper and didn't push it far enough back in. It was in the aisle where somebody could easily trip over it. And Hot-Wire did. He took a nasty fall—went headlong into the water cooler and gave his head a really hard whack." He shuddered. "I'll never forget that sound. None of us will. I think it shattered his skull. The poor stupid data-entry girl is kicking herself from here to Timbuktu, but of course what's done is done."

Saliva congealed in my mouth. I ran my tongue over dry lips. "Is he...dead?"

"As good as. He's in a coma and not expected ever to come out of it." He cast his eyes down. "As I say, I should never have tempted the fates by joking about it. But Mari, I think you're looking at the new editor of the *Gazette*."

# Chapter 26

How shall I describe the emotional war that began within me that night? To give way to panic would be to deep-six my entire world. To run screaming from the man I'd chosen as a mate, the father of my twins, would require far stronger and more tangible proof of malicious intent than anything I'd so far seen—or so I reasoned. Even despite my misgivings, I felt I was betraying Des by not trusting him. Does that make any sense?

My term paper assignment proved a heaven-sent diversion from what he'd just told me about Hot-Wire. While I flipped through reference books and made notes, sitting at a desk in the small study adjoining our bedroom, I could hear my husband in the shower, whistling. My phone buzzed, and Damien's soft-as-velvet voice said, "Mia. Are you all right?"

"Yes. I'm fine. I'm absolutely fine. But I left that message on your voice mail because there's something you need to know. Donna Wooding's cousin, who is a private investigator, is here in town and wants to meet with you. It has to do with Donna's death and a diary she didn't realize she had."

There was a beat's pause at his end. "Will tomorrow afternoon do, in the cafeteria at Blair Memorial? I have surgery all morning."

"Of course. I have classes all morning too, but my afternoon is free. I apologize for putting you out..."

"Don't. Three o'clock, in front of the coffee bar?"

"Perfect. See you then."

I spoke to Bertha next, said I'd pick her up at her hotel. Making these plans gave me a simultaneous sense of relief and disloyalty. After I'd terminated my conversation with her, I went back to my term paper. When Des came out of the shower and appeared in the study doorway, I was just reading the last paragraph in one of the reference books.

"I'd hate to think you're doing all that for nothing." He towelled his hair vigorously. "If I end up editor, I'll be well able to support us both."

"You know that's not the point. Geeky as it is, I love the world of academics, even these term papers. This particular assignment is quite fascinating because..."

"Mari, you're not angry with me, are you?"

I stared at him. "Angry? No. Why would you think that?"

He hung his head. "Because maybe I sounded a little too pleased about what happened to Hot-Wire. I'm not, you know. I'm as cut-up as you are. Hot-Wire was a friend, a bud..."

"Oh, Des..." I moved to sit on a couch in a corner of the room, patted the area beside me. "Come here."

He came into my arms. We held each other and then made love, right there on the couch. I was pervaded by guilt for ever having misgivings about him at all. It was taking him a while to get used to marriage and fatherhood, but he was learning. This was a sweet Des, a loveable Des whom I had no qualms about—a Des who held me for a long time after we finished making love and let me whisper to him words of comfort about poor Hot-Wire. There were still no fireworks, but it was companionable and nice. I stroked his hair, told him it wasn't his fault and reassured him we weren't going to let it bother us. In fact, by the time I saw

131

Damien on the following afternoon, I felt more disloyal than ever about going to Des' brother to talk behind Des' back.

As always with Damien, there *were* the fireworks. I had only to see the whiteness of his smile against his tanned face and the blueness of those almost-indigo eyes as they dwelt on me to feel my pulses quicken with the familiar response. I was glad Bertha was with me; it provided the distraction I needed. Bertha, too, seemed suddenly to develop a lilt to her voice and a flutter to her lashes when I introduced them, even though she got down to business right away. So I wasn't the only one.

"My cousin was not a strong woman emotionally." She read Damien the diary page she had read to me. "But, despite her mental fragility, Donna sounded very positive and full of life in the pages preceding that one. Mari tells me you know something about the 'game' Donna refers to and how she might have 'failed to play by Des' rules' and come to the conclusion she must be 'disposed of'. As I say, this is an investigation I'm conducting for my own sake only, but I would greatly appreciate any help you can provide."

Damien ran a hand through his abundance of hair. Soft and deep as always, the syllables he spoke were like pebbles dropped one by one into a tranquil pond. He said, "My brother is a many-faceted person, Ms. Baxter. I've been trying to understand him all my life and I have still not completely succeeded. I think I never will. Since we were children, his 'game' seems to have consisted of finding ways to taunt me. If he feels I want something he has, that will put him on a high for a very long time." A blush crept into his exquisitely-sculptured features. "I believe he wanted me to want Donna, and when he saw it wasn't happening, he decided to end things with Donna." His throat contracted in a swallow. "When *I* saw it wasn't happening, I was...concerned for Donna. Des can be hurtful. I went to have a talk with her." His gaze switched to me. "The night you saw us arguing, Des arrived at her place while she and I were talking. An argument ensued, which I insisted we take outside."

Bertha followed it up. "Your brother apparently made some accusations against you during that argument and claimed he'd caught you putting into my cousin's head exactly the thoughts I have just read to you from her diary. Is there any truth to that?"

Damien's blue gaze suddenly engulfed me. Ultra-quietly he breathed, "Desmond was playing to an audience when he said that. He knew we had one."

"That's not true!" It erupted from me before I could prevent it. "Neither of you had a clue I was there!"

His eyes held mine. "Desmond was aware of your presence the moment you entered the lobby from the stairwell—as was I. When I tried to terminate the discussion, he launched into those accusations."

"So you're saying your brother—my husband—deliberately lied in order to incriminate you in front of me, a total stranger? I find that very hard to believe."

The shutter I'd seen before came down over his eyes, and I sensed his withdrawal. He murmured, "I can only speculate about his motives. I admire you for standing by him. Believe what you choose to believe."

Bertha Baxter tapped him lightly on the arm. "What do *you* believe, Damien? May I hear your opinion?"

He did not respond immediately. When he did, it was with hesitation. He said, "As you've pointed out yourself, your cousin was emotionally vulnerable. What I believe, Ms. Baxter, is that she was afraid enough of what she thought Des was going to do to her that she preferred the alternative—which is exactly what she says in the diary."

"And you had no part in planting those ideas in her head? When you went to have your talk with her, you didn't perhaps lead her to think she might be in for some terrible punishment from Des? You didn't frighten her so much she felt jumping was her only means of escape?"

His eyes locked hers. "You don't know me, so I don't expect you to take my word, and there's no way I can prove it. I was encouraging her to alleviate her fears by taking positive action. But I'll give you the same advice I just gave my brother's wife, Ms. Baxter. Believe what you choose to believe."

Bertha nodded. "Okay, let's say I choose to believe your version. When you went to have your talk with Donna, what exactly did you say to her?"

"I suggested she move away immediately and leave no forwarding address. She told me Desmond had said he was going to destroy her 'slowly and by degrees'. The phrase was making her give way to terror. I couldn't soothe her out of being utterly petrified."

"How hard did you try?"

He sighed. "Obviously not hard enough. I don't need your help to feel guilt for possibly precipitating a situation I went there to prevent." His gaze continued to hold hers steadily. "But I'm not a martyr, Ms. Baxter. I didn't cause your cousin's death. As I've told you, I was trying to help."

Bertha gave another pensive nod. "It appears I may be chasing my tail on this one, but let me ask you one last question. In your opinion, is Desmond capable of doing what Donna feared— destroying 'slowly and by degrees'? That's an awfully chilling thing to say. Do you think my cousin could possibly have had legitimate cause for being so terrified?"

He shook his head. "Forgive me, but I can't give you what you're asking for. My brother can be...mean. I've seen vindictiveness in his behaviour. That doesn't make him a murderer." His right hand balled into a fist; I noticed the whiteness of the knuckles— and I realized how desperately Damien wanted to believe his own words.

"Yet you warned Donna to vacate her condo as quickly as she could and leave no forwarding address. Would concern about mere vindictiveness merit such a dire warning?"

"Concern is concern, Ms. Baxter. We all tend to follow our instincts. That's exactly what you are doing now by pursuing this investigation. My instincts made me uncomfortable about Donna's situation. I told her so. It's that simple."

The interview ended shortly after that. Damien shook Bertha's hand, expressed condolences about her cousin's death, and apologized again for not being able to offer more help. We made our farewells. He took my hand as well, applied brief electrifying pressure before letting it go. "Stay safe, Mia," he murmured.

And his tone when he uttered those words made me wonder whether he was as 'uncomfortable' about *my* present situation as he had been about Donna's.

# Chapter 27

We visited Rev. Connor next. It was an unannounced visit; I just took a chance that he would be in his office at Pleasant Heights Church. He was, and he had no one with him at the time. He was working on Sunday's sermon, which he gladly put aside.

But his initially expansive manner changed to wariness as soon as Bertha outlined the reason for our presence. His face clouded. "Look, I'm very sorry about your cousin, Ms. Baxter. But I don't see what I can offer here. All I can tell you is that my son grieved that poor girl's death."

"You mean your son Desmond."

"Of course I mean Desmond. Desmond was dating Donna. That was before he met Mari, naturally. Her death made him very sad, though he told me he'd been about to break things off with her anyway because of how unstable she was."

Bertha read him the page from Donna's diary. He commented that this proved exactly what he'd just said about Donna's instability. "As his father," she persisted, "would you say Desmond might be capable of exacting some sort of punishment on my cousin?"

"Punishment?" Connor shook his head. "My son was very fond the girl. I'm afraid your cousin was completely deluded, poor soul. At least she's now in a place where she's beyond all torment."

"Did Desmond tell you Damien was there that night—and that he, Desmond, accused Damien of planting those ideas in Donna's head and even of using mood-altering drugs on her to reinforce them?"

Connor looked tired. "Mari told me all about this some time ago—before she and Des were married. I advised her to forget about it. I'm sure neither of my sons had any direct responsibility for Donna's death. Really, Ms. Baxter, I think you should just go back out west and let sleeping dogs lie. No good can come of stirring all this up again. Honour your cousin's memory by letting her rest in peace."

Bertha smiled. "Thank you, Rev. Connor, for your input. Certainly I want my cousin to rest in peace." She rapped her knuckles against the diary. "For that reason, I'm trying to make sure I'm absolutely satisfied that the statements she makes in here are groundless. Once I'm convinced that is the case, I'll be on my way. I appreciate your cooperation in talking to me. Now, since I've already talked to Damien, it just remains to talk to Desmond."

He frowned. "I'd advise against that. Des was on the phone to me just before you arrived. His friend and boss, Mike Peters, died this afternoon. Mike was best man at Desmond and Mari's wedding. My son has offered to help Mike's family with funeral arrangements and they've asked me to do the service, which will be held here. So now is hardly the time, Ms. Baxter. But you can tell, from what I've just said, what kind of decent and caring man my son is. If I were you, I'd settle for the explanation that dear Donna had some serious mental health issues and just leave it at that. Don't you agree, Mari?"

I gulped. "Hot-Wire died? That's tragic!" Bertha Baxter's eyebrows went up, so I explained the reason for the nickname and continued. "Hot-Wire had an accident at work. Des told me about it last night. He was extremely upset." I rose, gave Connor a hug. "We'll be on our way. Thanks for seeing us. You're right: we shouldn't upset him further."

After Bertha and I had said our farewells to Connor, I echoed both Connor's and Damien's apologies about not having been of more help. Bertha quizzed me on the details of Hot-Wire's accident as soon as we'd left. She gave a low whistle under her breath.

"I completely understand, Mari, that you and Connor—and Damien—don't want me poking around and stirring this up any further. And yet I'm getting a sense of unease from all three of you, a sense of not wanting to believe certain things, and yet dreading, in your heart of hearts, that they're true. I especially got that sense from Damien when he told you to stay safe. Why, by the way, does he call you 'Mia'?"

So she hadn't missed that. He'd only used it once at the end of our meeting; yet she had caught it. I should have known better than to think she'd either miss or overlook it.

"It's the first letter of all three of my names—including my maiden name before I married Des: 'Marigold Iona Anderson'. He likes it better than 'Mari'."

"And you?"

"I...like it, too."

"It's a pet name of sorts, isn't it?"

I shrugged, feeling as though she were invading some private territory belonging only to Damien and me. "I suppose it is."

"Do you care for Damien, Mari? Because it's obvious to me, even as an outsider, that Damien cares a great deal for you."

"Why would you say that?" Heat suffused my face. "I mean, Damien cares for me as one would care for a sister-in-law. That's the extent of it."

"I see." She was looking right into my soul. "And does Desmond realize how much you two care for each other?"

I shook my head. "Look, Des is the father of my children! There's nothing going on between me and Damien. My marriage is just fine! Des is a great husband and father—and provider! Now that poor Hot-Wire has passed, Des will probably become the editor of the *Gazette*. It's a hell of a way of coming into the position, but he deserves to get it! He's very good at his job!" Embarrassment about her probing questions was disrupting my composure and I made a conscious effort to get hold of myself. "I'm sorry you've made the trip out here needlessly, but I think you were right when you told Damien you're chasing your tail on this one. Maybe you should just give up, go back home, and—as Connor suggested—let your cousin rest in peace. I've done all I can to help you. Anyhow, nothing is provable."

Her eyes narrowed. "It's interesting you should say that. Do you realize all three of you have said that? You've all made the point that nothing can be proved—which is to imply you all have your suspicions. Damien is the type who doesn't want to think badly of anybody, particularly his own brother. Connor can't bear to contemplate that any son of his could possibly have a cruel nature. And you, Mari, know Desmond best because you're his wife. You know he *is* capable of cruelty, even though most of you feels like a Benedict Arnold for thinking such things about the man you chose to marry."

I guess a person doesn't hang up a shingle as a PI unless that person has a well-honed talent for reading others.

I said weakly, "Hot-Wire's accident has shown me how unfounded my suspicions are. Poor Des is taking it very hard. He has wanted that editorship ever since we were married. He has even joked about Hot-Wire having an accident someday—and now he's kicking himself that he was ever tactless enough to say such a thing."

Bertha squeezed my shoulder. "I hope you keep listening to the part of yourself that wants answers—the part that is helping me, despite your own reluctance. I'm going to disobey Rev. Connor and go over to the *Gazette* office. Coming?"

Of course I was.

But some time later, upon hearing the tearful data-entry girl recount how awful it had been and how she was sure she'd pushed that wastebasket back where it belonged after she'd deposited her gum wrapper, I wasn't certain I'd made the right move. Des was angry and accused us—with some justification—of making things worse when the workplace atmosphere was already somber enough. He ushered us into his office, listened while Bertha explained why she was in town and read him the page from Donna's diary, then told her she had a fruitcake for a cousin and she should go back where she came from and try to remember Donna the way she used to be before she went nuts. Then he showed us both the door, saying he had a paper to get out and we'd wasted enough of his time.

"That went well." Bertha's voice was rueful. "I do hope I haven't got you in hot water at home, Mari."

"It'll be okay," I replied. "I'll apologize and comfort him. We should have listened to Connor."

"Mari...call me at my hotel if there's any trouble tonight. Promise?"

I laughed. "There'll be no trouble! I don't blame Des for being mad. In his place, I would have been mad too."

I won't pretend I didn't feel some trepidation that evening. But my anxieties eased as I fed and changed the girls before supper. Mother had had them for the day and—as always—had loved interacting with them, so they were tired and ready to be put down. Unlike on the previous evening, my husband didn't help. He maintained a stony silence throughout supper and only grunted in response to my apology. Later, as we got ready for bed, he finally spoke.

"That woman—is she leaving town?"

"Bertha? I think so. She just wanted some answers about her cousin's death. Her enquiries haven't really turned up anything, so I'm sure she'll go."

He grunted again. "I'm not as sure as you are. She's the nosey type—the type who can't help being curious. You know what happened to the cat that got too curious, don't you?"

My spine prickled. "Des, she has followed the trail to its dead end. No doubt she'll decide that poking around here any more is futile. She'll likely be gone by tomorrow."

"For her own good, let's hope so. Good night, Mari."

He turned away from me, and I heard the sound of his snoring shortly afterwards. I, too, eventually fell into fitful slumber, my dreams pervaded by Damien, whose deep soft voice whispered urgently into my ear, "Stay safe, Mia. Please stay safe!"

# Chapter 28

Carrie and Katie flourished the way weeds do in a flower garden. I'm not sure where the years went; I know only that I felt diligently compelled to keep busy, to bury myself in activities that precluded too much deep thought. A number of these were with the girls, who walked and talked early and were very precocious for their age. Both were bubbly and sociable, making friends easily wherever they went. They loved being left with Grandma Louisa and with Grandpa Connor, as well as with Sarah and Simon, who spoiled them rotten.

By the time they were four and in pre-school, I had completed my PhD and had accepted an assistant professorship at the university. By the time they were six and were starting regular school—and attending after-school care because my hours were longer than theirs—I felt well-established at the university, comfortable with the equilibrium of my professional life, and neutrally tolerant of my marriage and home life. Des, as expected, had become editor of the *Gazette*. No one in town who didn't know us well would ever have suspected we represented anything but the essence of what it means to be a completely fulfilled and successful couple.

Passing years had dulled my shock over poor Hot-Wire's fate. Connor had done a sterling job of the funeral and Des had done an equally memorable eulogy. Passing years had also dulled my uneasy astonishment over what had happened to poor Bertha Baxter.

Bertha had apparently been killed by the crazed wife of one of her clients only a few months after she'd departed our town. It had happened in Langley, where she'd been tailing the wife for evidence of infidelity. She must have bungled the job and somehow revealed herself because the wife turned on her out of the blue and shot her. Mother's neighbour—who'd discovered the article about it in a copy of the *Vancouver Sun* while visiting a daughter who lived in Langley—had brought the news (and the article) back to Barrett.

Initially, I had experienced those now-familiar pins-and-needles when I'd read that article, but I'd eventually laughed at myself for being paranoid. When I'd told Des, he'd simply shrugged and said, "Too bad. I guess a PI runs those risks daily. It's not a career I would have chosen." I hadn't told Damien at all—because I hadn't had any direct encounters with Damien in the course of the past six years.

How shall I describe my feelings for Des' brother as they had developed during that time? Perhaps I epitomized him because I only glimpsed him from a distance—sometimes with Joanna, sometimes with other women—and never had a chance to deepen further my knowledge of him as a human-being. The years had refined into maturity his breathtaking good looks. Hotter and handsomer than ever, he played escort to some of the town's loveliest. When I saw him, I was always with my husband at some crowded public event where I, the editor's wife, served as the usual 'arm candy'. The term made me wince when Des used it to introduce me to someone, but I knew, as I'd always known, that he meant it as a compliment, a tribute to my attractiveness.

Sometimes Des took pains on those occasions to signal a greeting to his brother across the crowd, to make sure Damien saw us—and it was then I realized Damien was right. Des was taunting his brother and was using me to do it. These across-the-crowd gestures of greeting didn't bring me the snide satisfaction they brought my husband. Instead, they awoke in me that always-lurking green-eyed monster, jealousy—of Joanna or of any other woman Damien was with.

No matter. The good doctor was the unattainable, as he had always been. 'Fireworks' with a man were something I felt destined never to have. At least the desirable and successful Dr. Sparks hadn't yet found anyone special enough to marry. Or maybe he and Joanna just had the sort of open relationship that didn't mind if either one saw other people. It was none of my business. I'm ashamed to admit it, but sometimes when Des and I went to bed, I imagined Des was Damien. It hurt nobody, and it was most likely the closest I'd ever get to those fireworks.

When the girls turned six, Des started scowling at me again the way he had before I'd become pregnant the first time. We should have had our boy long before now, he insisted. Why was I stalling? Was I using birth control behind his back? No, I told him truthfully, I wasn't. I don't think he believed me. And I began to fear that his anger, always smouldering, might be building up again for an eruption into a blaze.

I had become super-good, over the years, at 'managing' Des' anger. I never gave him cause to feel the girls—or anyone else—might be more important to me than he was. I continued to sigh and pretend university was humdrum and my position on the faculty there wasn't nearly as gratifying as I'd hoped it would be. That should hold him for a while, I'd thought—Damien's words. And I'd taught the girls how to say placating things that would 'hold him' as well. The fact we'd been achieving it for six years now was to our collective credit.

"I ran into Joanna Farley in the medical building this afternoon when I went for my physical," my husband reported one day, his mood almost jovial. "She said Damien has had a bad week. He lost two post-surgical patients who went suddenly south, and he lost another on the table after working on him in the OR for nearly seven hours. Shame." His tone belied the words. For weeks after learning that news, Des was a far more amiable man. And it occurred to me that perhaps Joanna had deliberately relayed the information in order to 'hold him for a while'. Perhaps she and Damien both were keeping tabs on us from a distance and were purposely supporting my efforts to 'manage' him.

The thought should have warmed me with gratitude. It didn't. It galled me. How *dare* they assume I couldn't look after my own marriage! What business was it of theirs, anyway?

As I ought to have known, though, 'managing' Des was something none of us could continue to do indefinitely.

If Damien had had a bad week on the occasion Des ran into Joanna, he had a very *good* week immediately afterwards—good for him, bad for Mallory Burgess, our town's mayor. Burgess keeled over at a town council meeting and was rushed to Blair Memorial where Damien found an acoustic neuroma: a huge but non-cancerous tumour growing in the left inner-ear and part of the brain. Surgery was long and complicated but ended in triumph. Burgess would take some months to recover, maybe even a year, but he would be all right.

Of course both the *Bugle* and the *Gazette* carried the story. Damien was praised to the skies, and there was even a short TV piece on the local news: Damien defining the term 'acoustic neuroma' and describing the current state of the mayor's health. That Damien wouldn't have been in the news at all if his patient weren't the mayor didn't appease Des. I mentioned it that same evening while my husband was glowering in front of the TV set and got a withering look. "Shut up, Mari." he snapped. "Just shut up!"

Our precious Katie piped, "Daddy, Mom says 'shut up' is a bad thing to say." I shoved my knuckles against my front teeth and frantically shook my head at her, but it was too late. Des' glare turned full upon my little one, and it contained pure loathing.

"Go to your room—you and your sister!" He thundered it. "This isn't your business, either one of you! Get out!"

"She's sorry, Daddy. She's real sorry," Carrie whispered. Grabbing Katie's hand she fled, tugging her sister after her. Young as they were, my training had taken root. They had become adept at saying the right soothing thing or simply retreating if soothing didn't work. It saddens me greatly to have to say that about my daughters. It shames me that I hadn't removed them by then from an environment where such skills were necessary for daily survival. But I hadn't. Mother and Sarah had taken to grilling me far too openly by that time. I kept telling them everything was absolutely fine—because I was still trying to convince *myself* that everything would be all right.

The night of Damien's appearance on the televised local news precipitated exactly what I'd been dreading. Des' rage, always smouldering, suddenly flared. Once the girls had left, he seized me by the arm, dragged me into the bedroom, threw me down on the bed, and tore off my blouse and bra. Terrified, I lay as still as I could, willing myself not to tremble.

The first time Des had taken me by force, I'd learned that struggling in any way incited more aggressive attack. So this time I lay prone from the start and waited for it to be over. I tried to send my mind out of my body as he punched and pounded into me. But I was aware enough to hear the words he hissed into my ear on the hot stream of his breath—words that forever eradicated further attempts on my part to tell either myself or the rest of the world that 'absolutely fine' in any way described the state of my marriage.

"Don't be a wuss, Mari!" His lips drew back from the pointed incisors in the feral snarl of that night in Mother's lobby. "You hear me? *Don't be a wuss!*" His hand shot out without warning and hit my cheek in a ringing slap. Through the slits of my own eyes, I saw the malevolent gleam in his. "Ingrid was a wuss. You don't *ever* want to be another Ingrid. She came to be very, very sorry. You hear me? You don't *ever* want to be that sorry!"

# Chapter 29

Contrition followed upon the heels of savagery, as it had the first time. He hadn't meant to get so rough, Des pleaded. He'd had a trying few days at the office. It wouldn't happen again. Would I please forgive him? I said I would.

But my head was out of the sand for good. It occurred to me that, by forgiving him, I might be proving I was indeed the 'wuss' he'd accused me of being. I had no idea what his definition of 'wuss' was, and he hadn't enlightened me, other than to liken me to Ingrid.

As before, the moment I'd forgiven him, he kissed me good-night and went to sleep. Me, I silently re-donned my clothes, crept out of our bedroom into the girls' room, and held a finger to my lips. They were sitting together on one of the twin beds, Carrie's, whispering. Carrie mouthed, "Is Dad still mad?" and I shook my head.

"Don't worry, darlings." I hugged them, planting a kiss on each of their foreheads. "Daddy had a bad day at work. He shouldn't have yelled at you. He's sorry he did. Would you please brush your teeth and get ready for bed? You've got school tomorrow."

They loved school, as well as their after-school care centre. They were soon giggling together and feeling entirely safe again.

Above all, I wanted them to keep feeling safe. For tonight they'd be all right. In fact, all of us would probably be quite all right now for several days. The contrite Des would behave himself for at least a week before the smouldering anger reappeared. That was the pattern. It gave me time to plan.

Both my daughters brushed their teeth quickly and climbed into their beds without any argument—a non-typical situation that proved their sensitivity to tonight's vibes. I tucked them in, read them Shel Silverstein's *The Giving Tree*—one of my own favourites as a child—and left them to drift off while I went into the kitchen and warmed myself a glass of milk.

From the breast pocket of my blouse, my cell phone pinged. I removed it and read the text: 'r u ok? D." Surprise gave way to tears. For several moments I wept silently before I texted back a sad-face emoji.

The phone buzzed. I went into the hall closet to talk to Damien. As though the six-year hiatus had never existed I said, "You and Joanna have been playing watchdog. You've been keeping him pacified by making sure he thought you'd had a run of bad luck. You knew your success story today would set him off!"

"Mia, you're not safe with him. You have to leave. I've been in denial far too long. Joanna has finally talked sense into me. I don't think you're in immediate danger. He'll be sorry for several days; he always is. Use that time to plan your escape. Pack a bag for yourself and the girls; then let me know and I'll come for you."

"Better if *I* come to *you*. I can pack my own suitcase right now and stow it in the trunk of my car; he sleeps heavily. The girls are asleep too. I'll throw some of their things in another case..."

"Do you want to come right now? Joanna is nodding. She thinks it's a good idea."

Oh...Joanna was there with him. I swallowed. Now they *were* living together. The thought nudged to life the green-eyed monster, despite my having no right in the world to harbour it. I said, "No. It's okay. I don't want to put you guys out. Sarah and

Simon would make room for us. Mother would, too. Or maybe I should just move into a hotel."

"No. He'd find you and you'd have no one to protect you. Come here. Come as soon as you can."

I made a quick decision as he gave me directions for getting there. "Okay. I'll come tomorrow. I'll put the cases in the car tonight; then I'll go back to bed. I'll be okay; he won't wake. In the morning I'll take the girls to school as usual and I'll go off to work—as will he. He won't suspect a thing until I don't come home in the evening."

"Agreed. Once I'm finished morning surgery..."

"Don't disrupt your surgery schedule or your clinic hours on my account. I'm still not sure I should be imposing on you at all."

"You're not imposing, Mia. There's plenty of room for all of you. And the Salters live close by. Lorne and Lydia have a new dog now, Chimo, a very protective Rottweiler. I think Chimo and the girls should get acquainted."

I swallowed again. "And Joanna is definitely okay with all this?"

"Joanna feels as strongly about it as I do, maybe more so. I'll talk to Lorne and Lydia ASAP. They'll be onside as well— guaranteed. Try to get some sleep, Mia. Keep your phone beside you in case you need to call me—or 911."

I nodded, attempted to shift the lump in my throat. "Thank you—for worrying. I'll be okay. See you tomorrow. Try to get some sleep yourself. You need to be alert to operate."

"Joanna is warming milk in the microwave as we speak. Good night, Mia."

"'Night, Damien."

It comforted me somehow that they were having warm milk as well. I finished mine and crept back into the master bedroom to grab an armful of my clothes out of the dresser and closet. Holding my breath, I dragged out two suitcases from where we kept them in a curtained-off recess adjacent to the pantry, opened up the first, and began throwing things in. I did the same with the second case for the girls. Still scarcely breathing, I disarmed the alarm system and wheeled both cases out the door. Not until I'd put them into the trunk of my car did I breathe normally.

As I re-armed the system and re-entered the bedroom, I heard Des talking and froze. *No!* My finger hovered over 911, but then I relaxed. Loud snores interspersed the words. My husband was babbling in his sleep again.

And the things he said converted those prickles previously going up and down my spine to stabbing-cold pellets of ice.

"Sunshine, you and Ingrid are so *absolutely* alike! D'you know how *she* paid? *D'you know how she paid?* 'Slowly and by degrees' is *exactly* right, my little sunshine wuss. *Slowly.* And by *degrees...*" He enunciated the words with chilling crispness, then mumbled something else unintelligible, chuckling with rapture. What the 'something else' was, I knew I would have dreaded to hear even more than the words I *could* distinguish.

It took all my self-control to move on muffled footsteps across the room to the bed. Des had rolled over and was facing away from my side. Silently I slipped under the covers and willed myself to stop trembling.

Despite my intention to try and get some sleep, I couldn't even close my eyes.

# Chapter 30

Des was especially considerate the following morning while I was supervising Carrie's and Katie's preparations for school. He poured their juice, shooed them off to brush their teeth after breakfast, and gave us all a good-bye kiss and hug before we departed. An objective outsider would have called *me* the crazy one for leaving him.

"I'll be home late tonight, hon," he told me. "Things are piling up at the office as usual. Don't hold dinner."

I nodded. So much the better.

Looking at myself in the hall mirror just before I made my exit, it occurred to me that the same objective outsider would think I was crazier than ever to claim Des was physically abusive. Not a sign of a bruise or scar—except for very faint finger impressions on my cheek that I'd managed to cover up with a concealer stick—was evident anywhere outside my clothes. The first time he'd taken me by force, I'd considered myself fortunate that nothing showed. This time, I knew suddenly that good fortune had nothing at all to do with it. That cheek slap had been a slip, a letting-down of his usual guard against leaving any visible marks. Des was very cunning and deliberate—and clever—about the way he inflicted harm.

Mentally articulating for the first time what that meant, my mouth went dry. The man was a sadist.

Naturally I said nothing to the girls when I dropped them off, other than to wish them a lovely day as I hugged and kissed them. Carrie assumed an important air and announced, "*We* get to serve snack today!" Their insouciant resilience warmed my heart.

Lectures and the post-lecture discussions I had with students kept my mind well occupied right up until it was time to pick them up from after-school care. And when I got there and they clambered into the car, they were full of stories about the day's events and didn't even notice right away that we weren't headed home. When they did notice, Carrie nudged her sister and said, "Mom's taking us for treats!"

Katie squealed with delight and I made the instant decision not to disappoint them. I stopped at *Lucy's Fifty Flavours*, a favourite locally-owned ice-cream shop, and bought them a small cone each while I texted Damien we were on our way. He texted back a few minutes later: Joanna was already there and would meet us. He would be home ASAP.

My feelings about Joanna would have to be put aside for the moment. This was a matter of our safety—mine and my daughters'. Applewood Grove, as I've mentioned before, was an upscale neighbourhood of beautiful estate homes on large lots, where people with Damien's and Lorne Salter's earning power could afford to live. As I drove there—in the grey Echo I'd bought as a starving student and still owned—I reflected ruefully that, even as *Gazette* editor and even with my assistant professor's salary to supplement our income, Des could never bring in what it took to belong here. No doubt it helped foster my husband's bitterness toward his brother that Damien's economic bracket was beyond his own achievement. But I somehow now understood that economics had nothing to do with it. Desmond would have hated his brother no matter what.

To say I found Joanna a far more dislikeable person than she'd been when I first met her at Lorne Salter's party would give me tremendous satisfaction. To say she turned out not to be good with children would give me even more. I can't say either one. I was still parked in the circular drive, awed by the spacious grounds and the grand-looking brick-and-stucco ranch-style home in front of me when she emerged through the wide front doors and approached us. She was lovely as ever, her voice full of warmth and welcome.

"I'm so glad you've come! Don't worry about the cases; Manuel will bring them in for you. He's out back; I'll call him." She whipped out her cell, tapped the screen and spoke briefly before turning her attention to my daughters. "Hi, guys. I'm Joanna." She shook their hands solemnly. "And I think you guys are going to love Chimo."

"Who's Chimo?" It came from Katie. "Why are we here? What is this place, Mom?" My eyes conveyed to Joanna that I hadn't explained at all, and her voice became gentle. She told them what I should have told them before now: daddy could be scary sometimes. He needed help to control his anger before he hurt someone. Until he got that help, they and Mommy were going to be staying here, where it was safe. Chimo was a big friendly doggy who could protect us all. Carrie's serious little face broke into a tentative smile and her hand sought her sister's. I mouthed a grateful 'thank you' to the one who'd uttered aloud things I hadn't dared tell even myself before yesterday.

The house was set on two acres, its nearest neighbour being the Salters' place which was set on five. The Salters, Joanna informed my girls, were Chimo's owners, and they had a stable. She lowered her voice to a confidential whisper, placed a hand on each small shoulder. "Two ponies, Dolly and Jasmine, live in that stable. The Salters' grandchildren ride them when they visit. But when the grandchildren aren't visiting, those two ponies get lonely because they don't have anyone to ride them."

Carrie's eyes lit, and her tentative smile blossomed into a full one. She said softly, "Do you think maybe *we* could ride them?"

153

"I bet they'd really like that. You'd have to ask the Salters nicely. Let's get all of you settled in, and then we'll see."

There were five bedrooms in the house: a master suite with its own hot tub and fireplace, and four spacious guest rooms. Joanna introduced us to Consuela, Manuel's wife, who was not much older than I and was obviously second-generation, with no trace of an accent. "Manuel and I work mostly for Mr. and Mrs. Salter," Consuela told us. "We live over there as well. We work just one day a week for Dr. Damien. I've made up one of the guest bedrooms for you and a second one next door for your girls. Is that all right—or would they prefer separate rooms?"

"It's quite all right," I assured her. "They've always slept in the same room. They're company for each other. Thank you very much."

She inclined her head. "No thanks needed, Dr. Mari. It's my job."

"Thank you anyway. And please—I'm an assistant professor, not a medical doctor. Just call me 'Mari'."

She nodded again, smiled. "You're nice—like Dr. Joanna and Dr. Damien."

"But she won't listen to you," Joanna laughed. "Damien and I have been trying for ages to get her to drop the 'doctor' bit. She won't do it."

"It feels more comfortable," Consuela said. "Let me show you around." As I followed her, Joanna took Carrie and Katie outside to meet Chimo. The hospitality was overwhelming.

And after Damien arrived home, my gratitude swelled within me until I felt I would burst. The girls took to him right away and began to call him 'Uncle Damien'. Young as they were, his white smile and Adonis good looks held them entranced—those traits in him that had always held *me* entranced. He hugged them and swung them up into his arms, the way their own father had never done. And he listened while they chattered excitedly about Chimo; he gave them his whole attention—which their own father had never done either. It was clear to me while I watched him with them what a wonderful parent he would make. Something inside me dangerously close to love—which I fought down—bubbled up and threatened to break surface.

Manuel, the soft-spoken handyman and groundskeeper, eventually entered through the back door to pick up his wife and take her home for the evening. More introductions followed. Like Consuela, Manuel was second-generation but with a charming old-world manner of politeness and respect. Also like his wife, he insisted on addressing me as 'Dr. Mari'. When my daughters shook his hand, he said he'd be glad to find out if the Salters would let them ride the ponies.

"There's a snack for you in the fridge, girls," Consuela told them, shrugging into her coat. "Supper will be later on. Be good! See you soon."

Carrie frowned, looked from Consuela to Joanna to me. "But... who's gonna make the supper?"

Damien laughed, stroked her hair. "I'm making it, sweetheart. I love cooking; it relaxes me. You can help. Both of you can. Mia, you too."

"Joanna too!" Katie declared, but Joanna shook her head.

"Thank you for including me, honey, but the kitchen and I never got along that well." She grinned. "Damien is the cook. If pressed, I can melt butter and boil water, but that's about it for my culinary talents. Besides, I've got paperwork to catch up on. I should be going."

"Going?" echoed Carrie, frowning again. "But...don't you live here?" Her words were a replica of my own thoughts, her surprise identical to mine. I felt my heart do a sudden strange flip-flop inside my chest.

"I do, practically," Joanna admitted. "I certainly spend enough time here. And yes, I stay over sometimes. But home is in a high-rise across town, not far from your mother's place, Mari. Occasionally I need to stop by there and tend to a few things. Carrie and Katie, I'll see you both soon, and that's a promise!" She hugged them and me, then exchanged a long embrace with Damien. "Be safe, you guys—all of you."

So they still weren't living together permanently. But they almost were. Isn't that what Joanna had said? From time to time I had seen Damien with other women. Was he still insisting on dating others besides Joanna, despite how close the two of them were? Did other women ever spend time at this gorgeous home or 'stay over', as Joanna had put it? I longed to ask him, but of course it wasn't remotely my business.

What *was* my business was getting unpacked in my room and helping the girls do the same in theirs. After that, I helped them get their snack, and then we all set about preparing dinner: delicious little crepes with an egg, ham, and green-onion filling. The crepes had been already made, and Damien peeled wax-paper sheets from between them, set them out and whisked eggs while my daughters and I carefully diced ham and chopped green onions. That we'd all had a hand in creating the finished product made the girls visibly proud. After the cooking was complete, we sat down together to an elegant dinner in the kitchen nook.

"This is so cool!" Katie piped. "I love it here! Can we stay, Mom?"

Damien laughed again and stroked her hair. I adored the sound of his laughter: as deep, rich, and musical as his speaking voice. "You're welcome to come here any time you want to, sweetheart," he said softly. "All of you are." His blue eyes, soft as his voice, dwelled on me briefly before he averted them. "Let's dig in before things go cold."

Yet when he averted those eyes, they flickered with a shadow of anxiety, and I suddenly knew why. They had come to rest on my bare arms. Without thinking, I'd pushed up the long sleeves of my blouse while engrossed in the food preparation. Now, I hastily pulled the sleeves down again, realizing it was already too late.

The concealer stick I'd applied in the morning still successfully hid all facial evidence. But on both my wrists, etched in bruises, had appeared clear patterns left by the obviously vise-like grip of cruelly-squeezing fingers and thumbs.

# Chapter 31

It took longer than usual to get the girls off to sleep. Not the least of their excitement about this stimulating new environment was the queen-size bed they got to share. When Katie asked if Uncle Damien could read to them tonight instead of Mom, his blue eyes lit and his deep voice, as he responded, was almost reverent. "I'd be honoured, sweetheart." And again, my gratitude—*or was it love?*—threatened to choke me.

Then Connor's call, two hours after they were settled and dozing, sent me crashing to earth with the speed of the mythical wax-winged Icarus. It was Damien's cell that trilled first and it was Damien my father-in-law blasted first—but second-hand, I could read clearly enough the gist of the conversation. Damien's entire body stiffened with defensiveness—a self-protective pose he'd probably learned to adopt since early childhood. Deadly in its quietness, his deep voice was taut as a whip. He said, "None of that is true, Dad. Mia *is* here with me and I *did* advise her to leave Desmond. No. I'm a full adult and I don't owe you justification of my actions. What Des has told you is a lie...I don't care what you believe...No. If you try to do that, you're going to have to go through me. This conversation is at an end." He broke the connection. My cell buzzed moments later. I drew a deep fortifying breath, squared quaking shoulders, and said, 'Hello, Connor."

With me he was calmer, but cold. "I thought you were different from the others, Mari. Des has been so happy with you. You're breaking his heart! And you're breaking mine. I'm shocked and very disappointed. Until last Friday, I thought you had more substance to you than to be wooed away by looks and money."

I almost didn't hear the insult. *Last Friday? What had happened last Friday?*

Damien made a move to take the phone; I caught his arm. "Connor, *I'm* the one who is shocked and disappointed..." I braced myself, summoned inner strength before continuing. "I've tried hard to make it work with Des, but I'm scared to stay with him any longer. The girls are getting old enough to understand and to be afraid of his moods and his cruelty. One day that cruelty is going to be directed specifically at them. They'll say or do the wrong thing by mistake and he'll turn on them and...hurt them." I swallowed. "It nearly happened last night. I want my daughters out of harm's way. I...want myself out of harm's way."

I heard his snort of disbelief. "You're using that as an excuse. You've gone and fallen in love with Damien; that's the truth of the matter! At least, you *think* you're in love with him. It's the same old story as it always is with poor Des. Damien's wealth and good looks have got to you. Don't deny it!"

Again I swallowed. When he put it like that, I wasn't sure I *could* completely deny it. Instead, I evaded it. "Damien is a good person, Connor. I don't know why you're condemning him. He doesn't deserve your condemnation. He has never been anything but a gentleman to me." I swallowed a third time. "I'm afraid I can't say the same for Des. My daughters..."

"They're Des' daughters, too," he broke in. "And they're *my* granddaughters! I've just been telling Damien there's a very new congregant at Pleasant Heights, a Theodore Kelly, who last Friday happened to reveal something rather interesting about his past—a racy past of consorting with prostitutes and what he terms 'sluts'—that he now regrets to the bottom of his heart.

He revealed it quite openly in a discussion group or I wouldn't be disclosing it at all. In fact, I tried to interrupt and stop him from naming the first 'slut' who started him down this road, but I was too late. The name he gave was yours, Mari." Connor cleared his throat. "Apparently, you brazenly seduced him. Have you brazenly seduced Damien as well? You say Damien is a gentleman—but you, I'm stunned to find out, are no lady."

I was appalled. My shaking hands gripped the phone as though it were a lifesaver in a pool where I was drowning. Damien moved beside me, wrested it from my clenched hands at last, his jaw set iron-hard. He said, "Dad, *this* conversation is also at an end. I mean it: if you and Des do anything to try and discredit Mia as a fit mother, you'll be dealing with me." He disconnected, handed the phone back to me as though it were something unclean.

We were sitting in a little alcove just off the kitchen, on a butter-soft stretched loveseat that I loved for its enveloping comfort. He rose from his position beside me there and began to pace, the way he always did when upset. I watched him silently, my heart hammering. Teddy Kelly! Who'd have thought a stupid incident from my Teddy Kelly days would rear its ugly head now to destroy my image in the eyes of my father-in-law? And who'd have thought Teddy Kelly would blame *me* for the apparent path his life had taken since our association? I clenched my hands together, filled with frustration at how unfair all this was.

Had Connor's words destroyed my image in the eyes of Damien as well? —in the hypnotic, sea-blue eyes of the man I...yes, *loved*?

I opened my mouth to speak, not even sure what I was going to say. What came out was, "They can't do this! The girls are my life! Des doesn't even know how to take care of them! He...!" Damien stopped in mid-pace, held up a restraining hand.

"They're angry and hurt, Mia." His voice was a murmur. "Dad is being abnormally judgmental and he's making threats he wouldn't make under any other circumstances. So much of his life has been devoted to protecting Desmond that he can't seem to stop it. The moment Des gets into trouble, he still runs straight to Dad. You, Mia, are to be congratulated. You've kept him from doing that for years."

"Damien, I was nineteen and stupid and so was Teddy Kelly when..."

"Don't. You don't owe me an explanation any more than you owe one to Dad."

"I *want* to explain. Please! I...didn't seduce Teddy. We were a couple of bookish nerds who got drunk one night and decided it was time we made our relationship more intimate. It didn't happen. He had no protection with him, so I put the kibosh on the whole thing and he agreed. He spent the night in my apartment, sleeping it off on the couch. I...guess his manhood was more fragile than I realized, because afterwards he went around saying he didn't want to date me anymore because I was a tease and a slut. It was a lie!"

For several moments Damien was silent. And suddenly, I sucked in my breath with a gasp because I knew what he was thinking. Carried back to that night on the balcony at Lorne Salter's sixtieth birthday party, I remembered his whispered words while I waxed triumphant over having put him into a state of arousal. He had said I was what the Victorian romance novels termed a 'vixen'. When his own experience told him otherwise, how could I expect him to believe me about Teddy Kelly?

Very quietly he said, "Nineteen and in doubt about one's manhood can be a difficult place to be. While I have a certain amount of sympathy for Teddy Kelly, I can't condone his choosing to slander you in order to get even. And the lifestyle he pursued afterwards was strictly his own doing. Dad knows as well as I that you're not to blame."

My eyes filled with hot tears that spilled over before I could stop them. Frantically I mopped at my wet face with the heels of my hands. He handed me tissues from a side table adjacent to the love seat, and again lowered himself beside me. "Thank you," I sniffled. "Damien, I...I'm sorry for what I did to you that night at Lorne's party..."

He shook his head. "You didn't do anything to me, Mia, except be lovely and alluring. It was Des who threw us together and Des who wanted me to want you. The behaviour pattern was entirely predictable, and I know you understand it much better now than you did then. Don't apologize."

"I shouldn't have used seduction as a weapon. You were right when you said I didn't fight fair."

He smiled. "You can seduce me without trying, and 'fair' never really entered into it—unless you're being unfair by being beautiful." The smile faded and his expression grew serious. "We need to be clear about what has been going on all these years. Des has always wanted me to envy what he has—especially his women. He has made a career of choosing girlfriends he thinks I'll lust after. If you're going to tell me you think I'm an egocentric jerk for believing that, I'll stop talking right there."

"No! No, I *don't* think you're an egocentric jerk. I'm sorry I ever thought that. I believe you. Please continue. Please!"

I wanted him to go on—not just because I wished more information but because I needed time to hug and hold close to me his delicious words. *'You can seduce me without trying'*, he had said. *'Fair never really entered into it'*, he had said, *'unless you're being unfair by being beautiful'*. I wanted to treasure those words, to savour the knowledge that he found me desirable—even if the love of his life was Joanna.

"I've tried not to believe Des' games were anything but harmless." His eyes riveted mine. "Thinking of him as a...an individual who deliberately inflicts hurt and takes pleasure in the pain of others...was something I couldn't bring myself to deal with."

I plumbed the depths of those marvellously blue eyes, knowing mine were equally grave. I laid a hand on his arm. "Damien, I have already forced myself, in my own mind, to call Des what I think he is. He's a sadist."

Damien did not avert his gaze—though, as he'd done once before, he gently slid his arm out from underneath my hand. He said, "We tend to think of a sadist as a monster like Jeffrey Dahmer, not an everyday, if slightly vindictive person like Desmond."

I shook my head. "People who knew Jeffrey Dahmer said he seemed like an everyday person who couldn't possibly be capable of doing the horrific things he did. Jack the Ripper is reputed to have been urbane and charming..."

Urbane and charming. Just like Des. I shivered.

Damien's white smile reappeared; it was rueful. "We can be aware of things academically, yet we purposely turn away from considering them applicable to someone we know well, someone we grew up with." His sigh was agonized. "Mia, he's my twin brother!"

I squeezed his shoulder. "You're fraternal twins. You're nothing like him, Damien."

His spectacular gaze continued to explore mine, then softened. He breathed, "I'm going to risk getting personal, even though it's none of my business. I can't get it out of my head and I need to ask. How many times has Desmond raped you?"

I gulped. "*Raped* me? Uh..." Hadn't I acknowledged I was through burying my head in the sand? Weren't we in the process of calling a spade a spade? By not labelling my husband's acts of force by their actual name, I was doing exactly what Damien was struggling against doing—retreating into denial. At the moment, the two of us were engaged in the act of helping one another stop doing it—forever. Moistening dry lips, I retched out my answer. "Only a couple."

In the now-familiar gesture of agitation, he ran a hand through his abundance of hair, making it stand on end. For a moment I had a glimpse of the disillusioned little boy he must have been when his brother repeatedly tried to hurt him all through his childhood—tried and succeeded. And I had to fight the urge to take that endearing little boy into my arms, to soothe him and kiss his forehead and murmur consoling words. His gentle gaze still held mine, its depths now agonized. "'A 'couple' is an *unforgivable* 'couple', my precious girl!" When he whispered that, I wanted more than ever to hug him.

But we didn't hug. This wasn't the time. There was work ahead. We needed to decide how to set about tackling what our ever-increasing awareness made us realize we were up against.

# Chapter 32

Within the next few days it became obvious that Damien had had a frank talk with Lorne and Lydia Salter. Lydia invited me and the girls to come and stay with them. Part of me felt hurt that Damien himself urged us to accept the offer—though I knew he wasn't rejecting us. He wanted us away from what he termed 'the direct line of fire'. Now that we'd faced what we were dealing with, he was convinced Des was going to come for him first. He didn't want me and the girls anywhere near when it happened. Joanna agreed with him.

"Desmond is simultaneously furious and exultant that you have run to Damien," Joanna told me. "In my professional opinion, Mari—off the record—your husband is actually a sado-masochist. He revels in feeling furious that his brother has yet again victimized him—and yet that is precisely what he wanted his brother to do. It gives him reason, in his own mind, to seek Damien's destruction. All his life, in various ways, he has sought Damien's destruction. You, Mari, have brought things to a head."

"I'm very frightened for Damien," I admitted. "I...actually think Desmond is capable of trying to kill him."

"Lorne has responded to that possibility," she agreed. "At Damien's request, he has talked to the police, and he has several friends who are retired police officers. They'll be keeping unofficial watch—on Damien, and on all of you. Carry on with your regular activities. Keep teaching your classes at the university, and keep taking the girls to school. Know that you're under surveillance—as are your mother, and Simon and Sarah."

I gasped and pressed her hand, wishing my jealousy of her wasn't standing in the way of our total friendship. Fervently I said, "You and Damien are the best! I'm lucky to know you both!"

"Ditto." She pressed back. "Damien has never been anything but honest with me about his turmoil surrounding his brother. But he *has* been less than honest with himself about the extent of the problem. His fears for your safety—and the safety of Carrie and Katie—have finally brought him square up against issues he should have faced before now."

I nodded. "Like Donna Wooding's death. And Ingrid's leaving her position at Salter Textiles and running away. I hadn't faced those issues either."

"And Hot-Wire's death. And Bertha Baxter's death."

I gasped again. "Bertha, as well?"

Damien suspects. I agree with him."

"But how...? Bertha died far away from here!"

"A former *Gazette* employee used to be a drinking buddy of your husband. He and his wife—one of my patients—moved to Surrey several years ago. She was flamboyantly sex-crazed, had severe mental-health issues, and could turn quite violent at times. I'm not sure why they moved, but I remember referring her to a colleague of mine there. Apparently she never made the appointment. Des is capable of having gathered all that knowledge and used it to achieve his own ends."

I bit my knuckles. "This is all speculation. We can't prove a thing."

"That's what Damien has always said. Up to now, though, he has never *wanted* to prove a thing. Now, he has arranged to go to Caldwell next Tuesday. He has re-scheduled both his surgery and his clinic hours that were originally booked for that day. He's meeting with Ingrid, who now lives there with her aunt."

Caldwell was our neighbouring town, half a day's drive north of Barrett. I said, "I'm going to clear next Tuesday on *my* calendar as well. I want to go with him."

"Talk to him. He's trying to protect you. Tell him you want to be involved."

Damien and I *had* been talking. But Damien had also been attempting to spare my emotions and let me carry on my life as normally as possible. Joanna told me he'd had Lorne Salter ask the manager of Salter Textiles' accounting department—where Ingrid used to work—to look into what had become of Ingrid after she'd left Barrett. There'd been enough of a paper trail to trace her to Caldwell. I didn't want Damien going there alone.

When I texted him I wanted to come, he texted back it wasn't necessary. I responded it *was* necessary—to me. Mother would look after the girls. Enough of not being in the direct line of fire! I was not some helpless female who could only tremble and hide behind the macho he-man! I could almost see his smile as he finally texted back, 'u win'.

Tuesday morning, his Volvo SUV arrived at the Salters' in time to fetch his nieces and drop them at school before he and I set off. "Nice car," I said of the Volvo. "But shouldn't it be a Porsche or a Lexus, Doctor?"

"No. I'm into transportation, Mia, not status symbols."

I felt chastened. "I like your style."

It was a lovely early-spring day with a cloudless blue sky. Recent rain had turned the countryside a rich emerald green. Despite the grisly nature of our mission, I felt supremely content riding beside him in the front passenger seat. When the girls clambered out at school, they each in turn put their arms around his neck and kissed him good-bye. "Love you, Uncle Damien," Carrie piped, and Katie echoed her sister.

"I love you too, muffins." He kissed them both back. When he called them 'muffins', they always dimpled and giggled that they were *not* muffins. But I could tell they adored his pet name for them—as much as I adored his pet name for me.

Watching him in profile as he drove, I dared reflect on how dear he was becoming to me. His strong surgeon's hands grasped the wheel with a compelling mastery, and yet they were gentle hands. The hardness of his jaw when troubled spoke of strength and courage; yet when his white smile shone and the compelling blueness of his eyes held me in their thrall, I saw only kindness and an intensity that—if I didn't know his love was already committed elsewhere—I might be tempted to read as something more. Both Sarah and Mother had said I was married to the wrong brother. How clearly the difference between the two men came home to me now! And how stupidly immature my attraction to Des' flashy charm looked in retrospect! It was with the glitz and glamour of being Des' 'arm candy' that I had fallen in love, never with the man himself.

Caldwell, as pretty a town as Barrett, was considerably smaller. We found the tiny cottage of Ingrid's aunt without difficulty. The lady met us at the door and stepped outside with us for a moment, finger to her lips. She looked the broody-hen type, with a figure that reminded me of a plumped-up pillow and a manner that said she was used to interceding in her niece's behalf. "Ingrid isn't well," she warned. "Talking about those days upsets her extremely. I'm not sure I should have let you come here at all. If she can't or won't talk, I'll have to send you away."

"We understand. And we so appreciate your seeing us, Mrs. Lindstrom." Damien's deep voice caressed. She gave a half smile and made a quick tidying motion to her iron-grey hair. His masculine charisma was not lost on women of any age.

"Call me Freda." Her laughter trilled. "You seem a nice young man, and you're quite a treat to look at. Come on in, both of you."

Damien blushed and thanked her. Freda showed us to a sofa

in a quaint little room she called the parlour, went to fetch her niece, and bustled about the kitchen making tea. Ingrid was the antithesis of her aunt in appearance: beanpole thin with platinum blonde hair, delicate features and enormous grey eyes. She looked frail enough that a strong gust of wind might carry her off. Tottering unsteadily, she installed herself in a rocking chair directly across from us, staring hard at Damien and raising a fluttery white hand to stroke her chin. Throughout our brief interview, she never ceased to rock.

"I remember you." Her left hand gripped the arm of the chair. "You're Desmond's brother. Desmond always wanted to...show me off...to you. I was a failure because I didn't attract you."

"No." Damien trod carefully, his tone warm. "You weren't a failure, Ingrid. Is that why you left our town and your job—because you thought you were a failure?"

She shuddered. "I...don't like to think of those days. I feel safe here now with Aunt Freda. She protects me. We bake together. In the summer, we tend the garden. We grow all our own vegetables, you know? We're always very busy when it's canning time—too busy for visitors." She was breathing heavily, as though the effort of speaking so many sentences at once had utterly exhausted her. My heart contracted with pity.

Whatever Des had done had destroyed this woman as surely as if he had actually taken her life. *She'll never be a functioning member of society again*, my inner voice lamented. *The poor lady is a basket case!*

Sipping my tea, I ventured a careful question I wasn't sure she'd be able to deal with; yet I had to try. "Ingrid, you used to have a little calico cat named Poesie, right? Would you mind telling me what happened to that cat?"

Ingrid had just taken hold of her own tea mug. The sudden wobbling of her hand sent its contents slopping into her lap and onto the carpet. With a small shriek she rose, shaking out her skirt. The aunt moved quickly to hold the skirt away from her legs and usher her off to get changed. With a sinking feeling I turned to Damien and said, "This was a mistake. I doubt she'll reappear—and if she does, I don't want to put her through any more. Des says the cat had cancer and had to be euthanized. I don't believe that. But I don't think we'll ever know."

Damien rose, went into the kitchen and came back with a wet sponge and a roll of paper towels. Together, we began mopping at the spill on the carpet. When the aunt returned alone from Ingrid's bedroom, I knew I was right: our conversation with Ingrid was done.

But about the other thing, I was wrong. We *did* succeed in finding out—much as I was repulsed and sickened by it—what had happened to the little calico cat.

# Chapter 33

"Ingrid sends her apologies," Freda said. "She's very tired. She's taken one of her pills and is going to have a bit of a lie-down. But please don't rush off. Stay and finish your tea." She took the sponge and the paper towel roll from Damien. "What a treasure you are! Good-looking *and* domestic! You're a keeper!" He blushed again. "I'm going to close the door to this room so she can't hear us. There! Now let me sit myself down and see what I can do for you." She poured tea into a fourth mug and lifted it to her lips.

"Please forgive us for upsetting her," Damien murmured. "Whatever trauma she endured was probably at the hands of my brother." He drew a breath. "We have reason to believe my brother capable of more than just meanness. We were hoping Ingrid might be able to shed some light on that by telling us about her own experience while she was living with him."

Freda Lindstrom nodded. "I don't doubt your brother was unkind to her—but, as you see, she's not made of very stern stuff to begin with. One of the few times I saw her take on a sparkle was when your brother was first dating her. She said he made her feel like a princess. When he asked her to move in with him, she was thrilled. I was thrilled as well. The timid wallflower at last showed promise of blooming! She had just managed to land herself a job at Salter Textiles and now she'd landed herself a boyfriend. Her phone calls to me were all giggly and excited. I couldn't have been more pleased for her. I would have liked to see Desmond propose marriage before they lived together, but then I'm old-fashioned. The important thing was that she was happy." Freda's shoulders slumped. "The happiness was very short-lived. She started telling me he was throwing her at...at *you*. He was trying to get you to steal her away from him. I wasn't sure I believed her. It seemed so far-fetched, and sometimes her imagination can run a little wild."

Damien shook his head. "She wasn't imagining it. It's a bizarre game my brother has always played." He drew another breath. "What I have finally had to face, Freda, is that it might go beyond bizarre. And it might go beyond a game. Ingrid said she felt like a failure for not attracting me. Des made her feel that way. I think it's probable he punished her for it."

Freda's eyes grew wide. "I was sure she was exaggerating things in her own mind. She has always tended to do that. You're telling me that what she said might actually be *true*?"

"I don't know." Damien's voice was ultra-soft. "What did she say?"

"She said he was rough with her. I'm not sure if she meant in bed or all the time. But I never saw any marks on her."

"They may have been under her clothes," I whispered. The poor woman stared at me in shock. "He is very calculating about the way he inflicts punishment. Like Damien, I've been in denial for much too long. Desmond is a dangerous man." I had to pause for a moment to seek the fortitude to carry on. "He talks in his sleep sometimes. One night he talked to Ingrid. He said something like, 'Poesie had to die, you moronic bitch.' When I asked him about it the next day, he told me the cat had cancer and had to be put down." Again I paused before doggedly continuing. "Ingrid would tell me a very different story, wouldn't she?"

Freda winced as though she herself had been struck. Quite

deliberately she lifted the teapot and freshened up all our tea while she gathered her composure. Replacing the flowered cozy that covered the pot, she dusted her hands together before she spoke, as though to rid them of something odious.

"Ingrid mentioned that Desmond had started to call her a moronic bitch. It undermined her self-confidence something terrible. I mean, she'd never had much to begin with, right? Fool that I was, I asked her if maybe it was just an affectionate type of kidding. I so wanted her to be happy, you know? You aren't the only ones who've been in denial. Then one day she showed up at my door in a state like I've never seen her. God help me, I thought it was histrionics. But of course I took her in and comforted her—and made her an appointment for counselling. She's been seeing a counsellor ever since. She had run away—from both the boyfriend *and* the job. She said Desmond had killed Poesie. He'd done it to punish her, she said, because she'd failed to attract Desmond's brother. I repeat: it all sounded so fabricated, so far-fetched...!"

"Did she say *how* he had killed the cat?" Damien prodded gently. Freda bit trembling lips and gave the barest nod.

"She said he'd done it with a carving knife. He'd cut the cat up, torturing it and making her watch while it screamed and writhed in agony. He'd told her she was going to see it die 'slowly and by degrees'. When she got sick, he made her clean that up, along with the cat's blood." A spasm shook Freda. "It's just too horrible a story to credit. As I say, Ingrid isn't well. Your brother may be a cruel man, and maybe he *did* kick the cat and hurt it, but this carving-knife story has to be a product of her tendency to over-dramatize. I still don't believe it." Her hands, gripping the mug she held, turned white at the knuckles. "Please don't say *you* do!"

Damien started to respond; I clutched his sleeve. I said, "I wish I could honestly say I don't. I *can* honestly say I don't want to. But I'm Des's wife of several years, Freda, and I've come to know him well. In my opinion, the truth of Ingrid's story is...is not beyond possibility. Just the other day, he talked in his sleep to another of his past girlfriends. He called the girl a 'wuss' and said she was going to pay just like Ingrid: slowly and by degrees. That girl is dead today. She took a dive off her balcony. He's my husband and the father of my children, Freda—and I'm terrified of him. I, too, have run away."

Replacing his mug on the side table, Damien reached up to take my hand, the one still clutching his sleeve, and sandwich it between both of his. Blue gaze continuing to dwell on Freda, he breathed, "I've never wanted to believe. Through my entire childhood and much of my adulthood I convinced myself that, with the right influence—maybe a strong loving wife—Desmond would stop being so mean. When he married Mia and the marriage seemed to be going well, I congratulated myself on not losing faith in him. My biggest present regret is that I've been purposely blind for so long." That compelling gaze switched to me. "Desmond specializes in 'slowly and by degrees'. The B-52 fighter plane I built from a kit when we were twelve was very intricate and took me countless hours to put together. While I was working on it, I kept it hidden on a high shelf in the closet because I'd planned on giving it to Dad for his birthday. Dad had just seen a documentary on the B-52. Fighter planes, along with trains, are a fascination of his. As intricately as I'd put it together—piece by piece—Des took it apart. One day, when I reached up to get it down off the shelf, it just crumbled to nothing. Des gave a macabre grin and ran to tell Dad *he* had built the plane and *I* had smashed it. Dad bought the story, and I was too shocked to contradict it. Until that day, I hadn't realized the full extent of Des'...meanness. No. God help me, I can't call it that any more. Meanness doesn't begin to describe it."

My other hand that held my mug had turned icy. "Didn't you eventually correct Connor's impression?"

"It was too late. Dad lit into me with such cold fury I couldn't say anything. I should have more consideration for my poor brother who'd had a rougher go of life than I'd had. I was to get out of the house and not come back until I was ready to apologize.

I left. I went walking for a long time, alone. By supper, I was cold enough and hungry enough that I did go back, but I wouldn't apologize. He sent me to my room without supper."

"Damien…!"

"It's not pity I'm after, Mia. That ship sailed a long time ago. Dad was protecting his wounded cub, just as he always does. His actions that night made me realize the uselessness of trying to change his attitude. Dad sees me as the son who can cope on his own—and his perspective is an accurate one. By seventeen, I had earned the academic standing to apply for the Hepplewhite—which looked after my living expenses—and I moved out."

"And you never apologized?"

"No. Dad stopped asking me for an apology. I think part of him knows I don't really owe him one, but he can't bring himself to tell me that. I'll never demand of him any such admission. Our relationship is what it is. We're two stubborn men, destined to be estranged."

I shook my head. "Not necessarily. I used to think Mother and I were destined to be estranged, but we're okay now. If I talked to Connor…"

"We're straying from the point, Mia—which is that Desmond *is* capable of destroying 'slowly and by degrees'." His gaze switched back to our hostess. "As I've said, Freda, I'm with Mia. Though it's not 'beyond-a-reasonable-doubt' provable, I, too, think it's possible, maybe probable, that my brother *did* do exactly what Ingrid says he did."

Freda's face crumpled. Tears flowed freely down her cheeks. "That poor darling girl," she choked. "That poor darling girl…" Then she glared at Damien with new venom in her expression and spat, "He deserves to die! He deserves someone to do to *him* exactly what he's done to my niece—and to that pitiful defenseless little cat!"

و

# Chapter 34

The drive back was relatively silent. I sat with my hands folded in my lap, the fingertips of the left one stroking the knuckles of the right—the one Damien had held between both of his. When he'd held my hand that way while we talked to Freda, I'd been grateful the crucial nature of our conversation had distracted me from the response flooding me head to toe. The gesture was merely a symbol of our alliance in this common mission. It surely meant nothing beyond that. Getting my hopes up that it did would be an exercise in futility. Even if they weren't yet living together, he and Joanna were serious. She spent nights at his place. The intimacy of their bond was unmistakable. As I'd said to myself before, they were obviously a modern couple who didn't need the formal vows of marriage to cement it.

Lorne and Lydia Salter owned a gracious Tudor-style manor with its own guest wing. On the grounds were tennis courts, an Olympic-size pool, and the stables Joanna had told us about that housed Dolly and Jasmine, the two lonely ponies—lonely no more, because of Carrie's and Katie's frequent visits. Manuel, who looked after them, had already given my daughters several riding lessons and they loved it. With the resilience of the young, they were adapting almost seamlessly to their new life, which included being closely watched by Chimo and a couple of retired police officers. Two officers surreptitiously guarded me, as well. Such thorough security measures greatly eased my concern about our safety.

It was Damien's safety that had me on tenterhooks.

I shared his certainty that Des would come for him first. Not knowing when or how the attack would occur made the tension that much worse—like waiting for the other shoe to drop. I told him so as the Volvo, headed back from Caldwell, reached the outskirts of Barrett, and we stopped for a bite to eat just before picking up the girls from after-school care.

"Like the three of you, I'm being watched," he reassured. "And I'm careful, as you are, to stay in public places. Try to relax, my precious girl. There's nothing to be gained by being up-tight all the time."

I nodded, suppressing my thrill at being called his 'precious girl'. It was the second time he'd called me that, and it made me realize how much I longed to *be* that. But I strove to make my tone betray nothing of my feelings. "Easier said than done."

"I know. He's with Dad, and my hope is that Dad will calm him down."

"Even though Teddy Kelly has convinced Connor I'm a slut? Won't that feed Des' hatred even more, rather than calming him down?"

"No. I don't think Dad really believes you're a slut, Mia. He's just single-mindedly obsessed with protecting his wounded cub. He gets angry when he hears things that might hurt that wounded cub. He'll gradually calm down himself and he'll question the truth of what Kelly has told him. And he'll calm down the wounded cub in the process."

"What if he doesn't? Does it occur to you that *Connor* could be in danger?"

"It occurs to me. I don't think it's the least bit likely, but there are two retired officers watching them, as well."

"Damien...I owe you such an *ocean* of apology for what I thought when we first met, and for the way I've treated you, and for the things I've...!"

"Don't, Mia. We need to keep our heads clear. This brigade of retired police is Lorne's doing, not mine. Once I drop you and the girls at Lorne and Lydia's, I intend to go home and take a long and relaxing shower. I'd recommend you do the same. We both have to work tomorrow and we're going to find keeping our minds off what Freda has told us harder than we anticipate."

I nodded. "It makes me quake all over every time I think about it! It also makes me want to talk further to that poor data-entry girl at the *Gazette* who thinks she caused Hot-Wire's death."

His hand pressed mine, released it quickly. "Don't do any investigating on your own. And, given the circumstances, it might be best to stay away from the *Gazette* offices for the moment."

My phone buzzed; it was the after-school care centre. "Mrs. Sparks?" The child-care worker's voice was steady but contained an anxious note. "You asked me to let you know if your husband ever came by. Well, he did. Just now. He tried to pick up the girls. On your instructions, I refused to release them to him."

I almost dropped the phone. "Thank you. Thank you very much! I'll be right there to get them!" Damien guessed without having to be told. We left the rest of our meals uneaten and drove there as quickly as we could.

"Dad wasn't mad or anything," Carrie told us. "He said he was going to buy us treats. But Miss Barbara wouldn't let us go with him."

"Miss Barbara was right." Damien swung them both, in turn, up into his arms and kissed them. "Tell you what: I have ice-cream back at my place. We'll stop there on our way to the Salters'. Last one in the car gets only a half-scoop!"

They squealed and climbed quickly aboard. Laughing, I followed suit, joking it was no fair; *I* wanted a treat, too. Katie, ever generous, promised to let me share hers. And again, my gratitude to Damien bubbled up until it threatened to break surface.

It was as we were sitting at his kitchen table facing bowls of hot-caramel drizzle atop French-vanilla ice-cream that Joanna called. He excused himself to take it in the adjacent alcove, but I could overhear his voice—overhear the deep caressing note in it as he talked to her with excitement about 'the plans'. Intentionally I fussed with the girls, warning them to be careful they didn't burn their mouths on the sauce, doing my best to drown out what was definitely none of my business. But I feared I had already overheard too much. When a person talked about 'the plans' with that much excitement, it had to be wedding plans.

And even as I was grappling with almost overwhelming sadness at that idea, he clearly said, "Lorne and Lydia have invited us over for a celebration party Friday night. We'll have to let them know if that's all right. Joanna, I haven't told a soul. I already promised you I wouldn't. We'll Skype Melanie. She can join us by computer."

Melanie must be Joanna's mother, who was bound to be overjoyed by the news. I went back to my ice-cream—for which I suddenly had no appetite—and to my conversation with the girls. That they, too, had overheard came home to me when Carrie said, "Mom, do Uncle Damien and Joanna have a secret?" I shushed her, saying it was very rude to listen in on other people's conversations. But the questions didn't stop there. Katie wanted to know if *we* would be invited to the Salters' party, since we were living there now anyway. Once more I shushed them both and warned them not to ask him.

My sleep that night was fitful and punctuated by many sudden starts followed by spells of wakefulness. As Damien had predicted, I found it hard to stop thinking about what Freda had told us—but found it even harder to come to terms with my new knowledge of his and Joanna's engagement. Why was I surprised? Hadn't I already acknowledged in my own mind the intimacy of their bond? When they ultimately did make the news public, as they were sure to do soon, I'd best prepare myself to offer hearty and sincere congratulations.

Wetness on my pillow from hot angry tears I hardly knew I'd shed, was a situation I had to get under control, and fast!

# Chapter 35

The following morning, as Damien was backing out to drive to work, the spring on his heavy garage door gave way and the door came crashing down, crushing the Volvo's front end. He had it towed and acquired a courtesy vehicle while it was being repaired. Connection to Des was without evidence. If my husband had tampered with the spring, he'd been clever enough to evade notice.

Later in the week, one of Damien's patients named Philip Bradshaw suddenly went berserk in the consulting room and began smashing things—including a display of model planes that had formed the centrepiece of the heavy oak desk. The man had a massive cerebral tumour that could certainly have been the cause of such a behaviour anomaly. Damien summoned help and the perp was carted off by security, a distraught wife trailing in his wake. Again, connection to Des was without evidence.

Being non-superstitious, I tried to dismiss the notion that things happen in threes. But my subconscious forbade it. In dreams I kept seeing Des looking down and laughing—the Machiavellian puppeteer who had already orchestrated two upsetting incidents and was gleefully planning a third. And I was *so* scared for Damien—despite that he was not mine to be scared for!

By Friday evening I was exhausted, and I wasn't lying when I used the excuse of a headache to decline attendance at the celebration party. The girls came to my room and we three spent a quiet evening watching TV. At one point Damien tapped on the door and brought in a tray of food for all of us. Carrie and Katie squealed delight and hugged him. I thanked him quietly and sent my best to the celebrants.

"Are you all right?" The intensity in those blue eyes of his made me want to answer honestly. I wanted to scream, *'Of course I'm not all right! I adore you and you're marrying someone else!'* But I said simply, "I'm fine. Don't trouble yourself about me. A good sleep is all I need."

"I wish it for you." He placed his hands on my shoulders, exerted brief pressure. "Let me know if the headache gets any worse."

I couldn't help laughing. "Always the neurologist! Go away! Have a good time!"

I had the impression he stood outside my door for several moments after I'd closed it, but I decided I was being foolish. He had his fiancée and his group of well-wishers—including Joanna's mother on Skype—to return to. The girls were already wolfing down the food he'd brought, so I joined them and did my best to put thoughts of the party completely out of my head.

Consulting a lawyer and taking divorce action was something I'd been shying away from dealing with; yet it had to be done, and soon. Connor had no doubt used the threat of claiming I was an unfit mother to make me re-think my position on leaving Des. Connor was gambling, or hoping, I'd decide the slightest risk of losing the girls was too great, and go back. I knew I wasn't going to do that, not ever. I also knew Connor was grasping at straws, making a last-ditch attempt to restore what he'd thought was—at last—a stability and happiness in the life of his wounded cub.

Knowing these things ought to have been the catalyst that impelled me to take the immediate offensive. If I didn't file citing cruelty, Des might well file first, citing desertion and maybe infidelity. That would make things look much worse for me. And yet I continued to delay. It was almost as though I had a sixth sense about another factor coming into play that was going to alter the playing field entirely.

Damien was the one I mentioned this to a few days later when he came down to the Salter stable in the late afternoon to watch the girls ride. My heart did its usual flip-flop at his appearance, and I had a quiet chuckle to myself about the stable being the appropriate setting for the figurative reining-in of my feelings. More than ever, now that he was an engaged man, I was strictly forbidden to love him.

He was wearing a blue open-necked polo shirt that accented the amazing blueness of his eyes and showed the fine matting of blond hair on his muscular chest. As he lounged against the corral fence beside me, those eyes dwelled on me with definite tenderness, and the whiteness of his smile held me captivated.

He said, "Are you feeling better? Headache gone?"

I nodded. "I was right. A good night's sleep was all I needed. Damien...may I ask you something?"

"By all means. Fire away."

"Do you think I should see a lawyer and start divorce proceedings against Des? I keep thinking I ought to get on with it, and then I procrastinate."

Something flickered in his eyes; then he cast them down and didn't respond for several moments. When he finally raised them to meet mine, the flicker was gone. He said, "It's not my place, Mia, to encourage or dissuade you. I'm not an objective party. What is your heart telling you to do? Can you still be in love with him after all this?"

"No! No, that isn't it at all! I don't think I was ever really in love with him in the first place. I'm not sure what I was trying to prove by marrying him. But I can't shake the feeling that legal action against him on my part might perhaps be...superfluous."

He frowned. "Are you saying you think Des means *himself* harm, as well as the rest of us?"

I shrugged. "I don't really know *what* I'm saying. I know I no longer want to be married to Des, but I...I don't want to be a divorcee either. Does that make any sense at all?"

"None. But then vague intuition frequently has no rational basis. My advice to you remains the same: follow your heart."

Inwardly I replied, *'How can I follow my heart when it leads right to you, an engaged man? I don't dare follow my heart!'* But outwardly I was able to play it cool, even to sound offhand. "I'm already an expert at making foolish mistakes, aren't I? Sometimes following one's heart can hurt oneself and others. One has to be very careful how one follows one's heart."

He quirked the teasing eyebrow. "Is that your thought for the day?"

"It's my thought for my life."

His arm brushed mine. I had the distinct impression that it wasn't accidental. When he spoke, his deep voice resonated. "Mia, you're an intelligent and resourceful woman, as well as a beautiful one. I would never presume to tell you what to do. You'll have to decide that on your own. But I don't want to see you making decisions that end up hurting you or the girls."

I leaned on him, allowing myself to revel in the contact, in the pleasantness of his masculine scent—in what might well be my only opportunity, before Joanna claimed him, to fantasize that he could actually be mine. Impulsively I breathed, "Thank you. Thank you for your concern, Damien. You're a dear and wonderful friend."

He turned toward me, pulled me roughly against him for one delicious moment, stroked my hair and brought his lips to my forehead, branding it with electricity. I was engulfed in the lights of those spectacular eyes. In that moment his heart thundered against mine and I felt the urgency of his male desire pressed exquisitely against me. I wanted nothing more than to respond with everything I possessed. But he didn't allow it; his hands moved quickly yet gently to my shoulders and he put me from him with a determination that brooked no argument. It was over in a split second, before I'd had the chance to savour any of it.

"Mia..." His voice shook. "You're entirely too attractive for your own good—or mine." He inhaled deeply. "Please give the muffins a hug for me when they've finished their ride. I have to go." He touched the fingers of his right hand to his lips; then he touched those fingers to *my* lips. "Be careful, precious girl. When you're not with Lorne and Lydia, continue to hang around in public places only. Stay safe."

"You too, Damien." My own voice shook as much as his.

It was a mundane parting, an anticlimax to what had just preceded; yet it had to be, and I knew it. I was his brother's wife. And now he was Joanna's fiancé. I hadn't a choice in the world but to resign myself to the bitter inevitable truth that too many circumstances prohibited our love.

He had exhorted me to stay safe and to hang around in public places only: a warning I wouldn't have dreamt of ignoring. Even with Lorne Salter's security people on the watch, it was best I restrict my comings and goings, as well as those of the girls, to crowded areas like the centre of town, where Des wouldn't dare try anything. I counted myself fortunate that their after-school care centre—where he had already shown up once—was in just such an area. Nothing he might try was likely to happen there. Besides, absurd though it was, I still waited for the third mishap to befall Damien: an occurrence I dreaded, yet almost wanted to hurry up and be over with, so that I could stop worrying about him.

And it was for all these reasons that I was totally off my guard and thoroughly unprepared for what happened next.

# Chapter 36

I attribute some of my distraction to the turbulence of my feelings for Damien, to my sadness about the impossibility of my love for him, and to my own lingering naiveté about the extent of my husband's rash and self-destructive psychosis. And definitely I was also naïve about how safe you are in public places.

The morning of the Friday following our conversation at the stable, I accepted Damien's invitation—one that included the girls—to join him and Joanna at four o'clock for a late-afternoon tea at Robert's Bistro. They were kicking back after a tough work week, he said, and the tea might well stretch into supper. His treat. Smiling into the phone, I realized I hadn't even congratulated the two of them yet on their engagement. I said I'd be there as soon as I could, after I'd picked up the girls from after-school care. Maybe, I thought, Carrie and Katie could help me choose a suitable card if we stopped off at a drugstore en route.

"You're sure we're not intruding?" I asked him.

"You could never intrude, my Mia. I invited you, didn't I? See you at four."

My last lecture ended at three. There was time to do it all comfortably: fetch the girls, get the card, put our three signatures on it, and drive across town to Robert's. When I arrived at their after-school care centre and explained the plan, the girls were excited—even despite Katie's rueful comment: "I wish *you* were marrying Uncle Damien, Mom. I want him for my dad." I shushed her, bundled them into the Echo's back seat, and pulled out into traffic.

While I drove, I mentally composed a short note to the happy couple that would in no way betray my own misery: *'May married life be all you want it to be—and more.'* Would that do? Was it too terse? *'Wishing you both the best of everything.'* Was that too bland and mundane? *'Hoping you find joy in each other forever.'* No. That was a lie—a blatant lie. I hoped for no such thing.

It was Carrie who spotted the flashing red-and-blue light on the dashboard of the car behind us. So absorbed was I in brooding that it took me several seconds to focus where she pointed in the rear-view mirror and to register that the plain-clothes officer was instructing me to pull over. Great! I groaned, realizing I hadn't been watching and might inadvertently have sped through Barrett's only playground zone located on a main street because of the park at the town's centre. We were coming up on Robert's at the intersection of Rembrandt and Sterling, and I turned right onto Sterling, which I'd been going to do anyway. The drugstore where I planned on getting the card was just a couple of blocks down this way. Behind me, the police officer gestured I turn right again onto Placid Road: much quieter and more residential. I obeyed and pulled over. Immediately behind me, he exited his vehicle and approached my driver's-side door. With a sigh, I lowered the window.

There was no time to react, no time to depress the gas pedal and escape before he was upon me. Too late, I noted his dark brows and his Count-Dracula features, but by then he had already wrenched open the door, undone my seatbelt, dragged me out by my left arm onto the sidewalk, and levelled a pistol at my temple. I'd had no idea Desmond even owned a pistol.

Not a soul was anywhere close by. Where were the security people who were supposed to be keeping an eye on me? To whom could I turn for help? My hand crept into the right pocket of my jacket, touched my cell phone. Des' hand, right behind mine, grabbed the phone and threw it to the ground, ripping the pocket in the process.

"Good afternoon, Mari." He said it as though uttering a pleasantry at a social event. "Kindly move around the front of the car and get in on the passenger side; there's a good girl." He adjusted the pistol's aim to my chest. "I'll stay here until you've done it; then I'll get in myself. I know you're not going to run off on me with your precious daughters in the back seat. Move."

I had no choice but to do as I was told. Trying not to succumb to terror, I watched him ease himself behind the steering wheel and close the door. A grin creased the corners of his mouth, partially revealing his pointed incisors. He buckled up and gestured at me to do the same.

"What...about the car you were driving?" My voice was a pitiful squeak forced from a fear-closed throat. "Are you just going to leave it there?"

He chuckled. "Borrowed. Couldn't risk your recognizing mine, could I?" Laying down the pistol for a moment to shift into 'drive' and pull away from the curb, he took it up again in his right hand before I could gather my reflexes to grab it. "You know, Madam Straight-A Scholar, you're remarkably stupid. Did you really think you could escape me? Lots of things go on in the public streets all the time and are just ignored. No one wants to get involved. I could rape you here and now, and people would just walk by on their merry way without even slowing down." He gave another pleasant chuckle, the way he chuckled when someone had just told him a good joke at a party.

Painfully I swallowed through the dryness of my mouth, clasped together palms wringing wet with sweat. "Desmond, we're being tailed." I couldn't see a sign of anyone when I said it, but I hoped desperately it was true. "There are security people following me. You...won't get away with trying anything. In a moment they'll move in and it'll all be over."

"Right." Eyes gleaming, he shoved the pistol's cold metal against my temple. "Sure they will! A moment, my dear girl, is all I need. A moment is all it takes to press this cute little trigger, isn't it?" His laughter, no longer pleasant but maniacal, assaulted my ears; the pitch of his voice turned joyful. "I have to hand it to you, Mari. You have finally accomplished what I've been trying for all my life." We were back out into traffic and picking up speed as I listened, mesmerized with horror. "I knew there was a way to bring my brother to his knees, but I could never find it. Wrecking that B-52 model he built when we were kids came close—especially when Dad was so mad at him—but he didn't even cry. Then we both started dating and I saw the way: find a girl he would fall deeply in love with and then kill her before his eyes. The idea was so beautiful it kept me happy for ages." A plaintive whine entered his voice. "But the girls wouldn't cooperate, and neither would he!"

A low moan came from Carrie in the seat behind me. Young as she was, I'm sure she recognized this—as did I—to be what psychiatrists would term a full-fledged 'psychotic break'. No, she couldn't have put it into those words, and I couldn't have either, at the time. But that moan said it all. The man she'd thought of all these years as her daddy had suddenly morphed before her stunned eyes into a hideous monster.

Hardly realizing what I did, I pulled down the sun visor on the passenger's side where a makeup mirror was attached. In the mirror, I managed to catch her petrified gaze and warn her not to make another sound. Mutely, she clasped Katie's hand instead. It was critically important—in order to buy us more time—to keep him talking.

"How...?" I gulped, tried it again. "How wouldn't your girlfriends cooperate, Des?"

He seemed unaware I'd pulled down the visor. His eyes stared straight ahead and his voice continued to whine. "They wouldn't play the game. I'd introduce them to him and yes, they fell for him, but not in an all-consuming way. Know what I mean?" I nodded, pretended I did. "It wasn't good enough. And he would like them all right but not *love* them. So destroying them wouldn't have hurt him at all! He couldn't have cared less!"

"But you *did* destroy Donna." I spoke carefully, mindful of what havoc this might wreak. "And you destroyed Ingrid as well."

He sighed. "Both were worth a try. Damien actually went to warn Donna about me. I thought that might indicate she meant something to him, but no such luck. It was easy to go back to her place after our little altercation in the lobby and talk the poor sick idiot into taking a leap off her balcony. She was so scared she practically ran over the edge, railing and all!" His face fell. "But Damien wasn't a bit cut-up by her death—worried, maybe, that I had caused it, but not cut-up. Again I'd failed! As for Ingrid, she asked for it: getting so goopy over that stupid cat. I didn't have to arrange her death at all; all I had to do was destroy the cat! I had thought, when I was dating her, that Damien was really interested in Ingrid, but it turned out he wasn't. And by then she'd moved in with me—along with that smelly feline—and had become a royal pain. So I got rid of them both. End of story."

I tried not to let the trembling in my body enter my voice. "Did you kill Donna's cousin Bertha as well?"

He arched the heavy black brows I'd once thought so intriguing. "She asked for it by snooping around, didn't she? And she wasn't about to quit snooping; I could tell. How was she to know I had a pal with a crazy wife who lived in the next town over from hers? Frankly, I wasn't at all sure that little gambit would work. I was highly delighted when it did."

Once more I nodded, realizing that, at this moment, his vanity superseded all fear of consequences. "And it was you, not the data-entry girl at the *Gazette*, who tripped up Hot-Wire with the wastebasket, right? You said it yourself: you were getting tired of waiting for him to retire and let you have the editorship of the paper. Finally, you lost patience."

Again he sighed. "Editor of a two-bit rag doesn't equal wealthy neurologist, but at least it beats lowly reporter. Some people are such saps! They make it super-easy for the rest of us. Of course I didn't assume he would die—just be badly enough hurt to step aside. I feel for his widow, poor lady."

"Did you have something to do with the malfunction of Damien's garage door, and the mad smashing spree of his patient?"

He puffed out his chest. "There's a whole slew of stuff to my credit—more than most people would suspect. Yes, I tampered with that door—almost under the noses of those goons who call themselves security! As for Philip Bradshaw, I bought him a drink and told him some lies about my brother that drove him absolutely wild—wild enough to mess up Damien's office, if not his handsome face! That was too bad." Suddenly, he jammed the pistol hard against my forehead. "But let's talk about *you,* sunshine. Let's talk about the huge accomplishment that is to *your* credit!"

I stared at him. "*My* credit?"

"Yours, and yours alone. You have achieved what I have been trying to do all my life. From the moment my brother clapped those baby-blues of his on you—that night in the lobby of your mother's building—he hasn't been able to take them off you, has he?"

"Uh..." I had to continue stalling for time, and yet not say anything that might antagonize him and cause him to pull over and shoot the three of us on the spot. It was critical to keep feeding his ego, keep him bragging about all the clever things he had masterminded—keep him feeling he was the one running the show. If I let him crow on long enough, maybe I could somehow signal through the window for help. Maybe a car would eventually pass by close enough for someone to notice the pistol. And with all the confessing he had just done—in my presence and in the presence of our daughters—there was no further doubt he'd be going away for life.

But what he said next jolted me as though he'd been reading my mind. "No, Mari hon, I'm not headed for the slammer—or the loony bin." It was a whisper. "If I thought it existed, I'd probably figure I'm headed straight to hell. But I won't be going anywhere until this grand game is finished. You see, *you* are my triumph, sunshine! At last I've found the girl he *has* fallen in love with—the girl whose death will break him in half! I read him super-well, Mari, and finally, the girl he wants is the girl I have! So when I kill you, he'll never recover from the heartbreak, will he? Even when I kill myself as well, it won't matter, right? He'll never, *ever* get over losing you. He'll eat himself away, slowly and by degrees. He'll rot from the inside out! His good looks will become a thing of the past. He'll never be successful again, or attractive to women again." My husband was panting, slobbering. I could only continue to stare at him, every muscle of my body paralyzed by horror at the extent of his insanity.

But then, blessedly, my tongue loosened as I heard a retching sound from Katie in the back and strove, with every ounce of will left in me, to keep him distracted from my babies. "No, Desmond. You're wrong. You're making a huge mistake. Damien isn't interested in me at all. He's engaged to marry Joanna Farley. They just haven't announced it officially yet. *Joanna* is the one he has loved forever!"

Again the black brows arched and he burst into raucous laughter. "Farley? That's rich, hon! *Farley*? Not in a million years! Now I think the time has come to quit talking. When I pull over, it'll be the girls who go first—so you'll get a chance to watch them die, just before you, in your heart-warming maternal distress, join them..."

And that was when I closed my eyes and decided it would be no use to plead with him for my daughters' lives—for *his* daughters' lives—because Des hated all women and had never really forgiven me for having girls. That was when, for the first time ever, I began to pray, on a personal level, to a God who, till that moment, had been a total stranger to me.

That was also when, with the gun's barrel jammed against my temple, I retreated into an emotional stasis that had me re-living it all, right up to this terrible moment, plunging myself back into a past world beyond his reach, where my mind was immune to all torment...

Sirens in the distance wrenched me out of it—and then they weren't so distant after all. Numerous black-and-white police vehicles closed in around us, instructing Des to pull over, their red-and-blue lights strobing my face in harsh, garish reality. My gaze darted to the girls, still holding hands in the back seat. Praise God, he hadn't hurt them—yet. In the visor's makeup mirror I recognized Damien's courtesy car directly behind us, with Damien at the wheel and Joanna beside him. Was this a wishful fantasy? Had I finally lost my own sanity? It was entirely possible.

"It's over, sunshine." Pleasantness again pervaded Desmond's tone. "The confessions I just made are about to die, right along with you—and with these girls I never wanted. No one will be any the wiser, right?" He nosed the Echo into the curb and braked to a stop, his upper lip lifting in a half-snarl. "Looks like I may be running a little short on time. I might have to skip the girls. They won't be believed anyhow." From the corner of my eye, I saw in the mirror the barest hint of movement by Katie towards his forearm—the forearm of the hand in which he held the weapon. He let out a blood-curdling whoop. "It's just you and me, sunshine! Here we go!"

And then he fired.

# Chapter 37

Scattered images flashed into my consciousness, bathed in gyrating red and blue. I sagged with relief to see my daughters, safe but in tears, helped from the Echo's back seat. In a moment of bliss, I saw Damien as well, above me, and also in tears, his hand gripping mine, his deep broken voice whispering, "*No. Please God, no!* Mia, my love, stay with me. We're getting you help. Stay with me..."

Was I dead? Had Desmond killed me? Was I looking down on all this from somewhere else? If so, in what world did I now reside?

There was no pain, only crescendos of noise interspersed with nothingness. A few times I seemed to surface and realize I was in bed somewhere and Damien was still by my side, still holding my hand, blue eyes cloudy with tears. But I couldn't stay in that world. Blackness rose up to swallow me and swirl me down into its bottomless depths. I tried to hold onto Damien, but—as always—he was beyond my reach.

Time lost all meaning in this new world. Huge gaps of nothingness persisted. Once, I thought Mother was with me, then Sarah and Simon, then Lorne and Lydia Salter, then Joanna Farley, then Carrie and Katie, then even Connor. They were all beyond my reach. The moment had come to bid them farewell...

Yet I couldn't do it. Too much of me wanted to stay—especially with Damien. I had to stay because I knew now that he *did* love me—maybe not the same way I loved him, and not the way Desmond had insisted he loved me—but perhaps as a dear and trusted friend. I had heard him call me 'my love'. No matter how he meant it, that would have to do. I would have to make it do.

Getting my mouth around his name took all the effort I could summon. In a half-gasp, half-whimper I forced out, "Damien..."—and found myself looking into Mother's anxious face.

"Mari...!" Her eyes teared. "Sarah, she's awake!"

Sarah's beaming face appeared beside Mother's. And Sarah said something quite wonderful. "Welcome back, honey. Everything's going to be okay now. You've been recovering bit by bit. You've turned the corner, they say."

My lips were parched. I asked for water and Mother lifted a cup from the bedside table and held it while I took a few sips through the inserted straw. "I...thought I died. Am I in hospital?"

"Blair Memorial."

"The girls...?"

"They're fine. Right now they're with Grandpa Connor. They know you're getting better. Connor and Sarah and Lydia and Damien and I have been taking it in shifts."

I nodded, managed a shaky, "Thank you." Then I gripped her wrist and again uttered the name I so loved. "Damien...?"

"He's been with us all the way." Mother wiped her eyes with a tissue she held in her free hand. "He has taken a temporary leave—got a colleague to fill in for him at the clinic—so he can spend as much time as possible by your bedside. He really is a sweetheart, Mari. Aside from your father, I've never met a more loveable man!"

I tried to nod, even though it made my head hurt. "I...never have, either. Mother, I've been such a..."

"Shush! Enough of that. He's gone home to shower and shave.

He'll be back soon."

"Des...?"

A momentary shadow crossed Sarah's face, erasing her smile. "Des is dead, honey. Right after he shot you, he turned the gun on himself. Thank God, he did a better job on himself than he did on you!"

I wept—whether with sorrow or relief I can't say. Mother held one of my hands, Sarah the other. The nothingness came again, briefly. And when I woke they were gone. Joanna Farley was sitting in the chair Mother had vacated. Despite what a lovely kind person she was, I had mixed feelings seeing her there.

"Joanna..." My throat was parched again, and she helped me sip some more water. Gazing at her, I realized I could never bring myself to resent her, even though, as the holder of Damien's heart, she was the black cloud on my horizon. There was nothing in her beautiful hazel eyes but concern for me.

"Just rest, Mari." Her voice was soothing. "Rest is critical right now. You'll be back to your old self in no time."

"You and Damien...were following us in Damien's courtesy car. Damien was driving; I saw you both in the makeup mirror. Or did I imagine it?"

She laid a hand over mine. "You didn't imagine it. We had just arrived at Robert's when Damien got the call on his cell from one of the security people tailing you. Thank God, you were so close it took us hardly any time to get to you."

"Hardly any time...? But it was *ages*!"

"No, sweetheart. I'm sure it seemed like ages, but Damien acted instantly. The police acted instantly as well. All protective measures failed to provide for how rash and heedlessly neurotic Des had become. Thank God, also, that your husband got too rattled, when they were closing in, to aim properly. The bullet went pretty wild. Removing it, I understand, was relatively easy."

I stifled a sob. "I...think the bullet went wild because Katie deflected his arm just as he fired. I think I owe my darling daughter my life!"

She squeezed my hand harder. "That could well be. Those girls have been through an awful lot. They're bound to have some PTSD after this. I'll be there for them, Mari. I'll see them regularly—as a friend."

Unable to stifle sobs any longer, I gave them free rein at last. "You guys are too much! Did... Damien do the surgery on me?"

"No. Damien is too involved. A colleague, Chad Winthrop, did it—the same colleague who's going to take over his clinic temporarily. But you can bet Damien has kept an eagle eye on things. We're all involved, Mari."

I felt a smile tug my lips, in no way sardonic. A wave of renewed fatigue was fast encroaching, but before I succumbed I had enough strength left to blurt, "Inside as well as out, Joanna, you're beautiful. No wonder Damien loves you!"

Recovery was quick after that. Ten days later I was released. Damien was with me almost all of the time. He bantered with Mother and Sarah, took Carrie and Katie down to the cafeteria for meals when they visited, and made my room fragrant with fresh flowers—insisting to the disapproving nurses that I wasn't allergic and the blooms would disappear promptly if any nearby patients were. All those closest to me hugged him constantly, as though he were family. When Joanna dropped by, they hugged her as well. I told myself the pain of Damien and Joanna's being together was just something I'd have to learn to live with. Damien had already given me far more than he owed me—which was nothing. I had no right to any feelings for Joanna other than affection. But it took many stern talks with that ugly green-eyed monster to force it to retreat into a corner.

The day of my release, Damien took me and the girls to his place where he had prepared a lovely lunch of butter chicken on rice, broad beans (the girls were dubious but liked them) and fresh bread.

I ate sparingly, knowing my appetite would soon return. Carrie and Katie ate with relish and seemed completely their normal happy selves. After lunch, they asked if we could get Manuel to come over and take them to visit the ponies. Damien complied, and it warmed my heart to see the bounce in their steps as they ran off in company with the handyman.

"They act as though they're over it," I told Damien while I helped him load the dishwasher. "I don't think they're suffering any after-effects."

He shook his head. "Not true, Mia. They *will* be all right, but they'll need Joanna's care. They have to work this through their systems, just as we adults do. Lydia says they've been having nightmares and Carrie wet her pants at school yesterday." His hand closed over my wrist. "Let me finish this alone. You still need to rest. Talk to me while you're sitting down."

"That's not necessary..."

"Doctor's orders. Sit."

I obeyed reluctantly, adoring him. "Damien...am I right that Connor had a turn looking after the girls while I was in hospital?"

He nodded slowly. "He did. And so he should have done. He's their grandfather."

"How *is* Connor?"

"I think he's devastated. It honestly never entered his head that Des would try to kill you. He's been forced to make some very uncomfortable admissions to himself about the way he has treated you, Mia. I know he's extremely sorry. But he has also got his pride, and I know how that feels as well." He smiled ruefully. "I'm his son."

"I should call him. I'm sure the dear man is in terrible pain."

Damien's smile softened. "I could have predicted you'd say that, my precious girl. You're as dear a girl as he is a man. The rift between you two will mend. I can feel it. And I want it for you both."

Meeting his gaze, aquamarine in this light, I said, "Damien, what about the rift between *you* and Connor? Is there a chance that *that* will mend?"

The gaze became very tender. "This isn't a fairy-tale, darling Mia. You can't solve everything, my love."

"I can try. Because I want that for *you* both! When I talk to him..."

"Don't. Please don't try to force anything. Dad and I have been estranged for a very long time." He pressed the 'start' button on the dishwasher, came to lower himself beside me again on the butter-soft stretched loveseat in his kitchen alcove. He took my right hand between both of his. "One thing at a time. Talk to Dad in your own behalf, not mine. Promise."

"What if Connor initiates a conversation about you?"

"He won't."

"Damien, I can see how much you love him...!"

"Promise, Mia."

I made a gesture of resignation. "Okay. I promise."

He exerted brief pressure on my hand and released it—but not before stroking the back of it with feather-light fingertips and then lifting it lingeringly to his lips. They were cool and velvet-soft; yet they branded the hand with fire. I very much wanted them on my own lips—and the need was strong enough that I had to push it from me by summoning up a disapproving imaginary Joanna.

I loved him so enormously! When he addressed me with phrases like 'my love' and 'darling Mia', I found it hard not to tell him so. My mind kept harking back to the day I was shot, the day I'd seen his tears and heard him say, '*No*. Please God, *no*! Mia, my love, stay with me...' Dwelling on those words, I could almost convince myself he loved me as much as I loved him. Yet smack in the middle of that road stood his fiancée—as beautiful and as dear a person as he was.

And the next time that dear fiancée of his spoke to me was the same day she slammed me with news that crushed forever any hope I might still be clinging to that Damien and I could ever be together.

# Chapter 38

Once lunch had been cleared away, an invitation was extended to me and the girls to stay the night. Consuela had made up the guest bedrooms yesterday, Damien told me, in anticipation of the possibility. When I replied that we were perfectly comfortable at the Salters', he insisted. "Do it for me tonight only—because you've just been released, and I'm a doctor. I'll go over there and pick up overnight things for all of you if you'll give me a list. Humour me, Mia."

I laughed. "Humouring you is very easy. And the girls love staying here. But will it be...proper?"

"I swear I'll behave."

I laughed again, shaking my head and shoving away the thought that the last thing in the world I wanted was for him to behave! "Okay. You've talked me into it—on condition I get to make supper!"

"You've got a deal."

Lunch had been more substantial, so supper was a light salad. As day moved into evening, the girls began to yawn. They had school the next day, and Damien was returning to work. Bundling them—and ourselves—off to bed early was a wise move. Even though I still had more leave time remaining and could take it easy tomorrow, my first day up and about had taken its toll. I was bone-weary.

Eagerly the girls washed up and prepared to turn in for the night, Katie saying, "Uncle Damien's going to read us those stories again and make all the different voices!" He ruffled her hair and replied, "Only if you have your teeth brushed – thoroughly—in less than five minutes." They yelped and dashed off again to the bathroom, leaving me in unhappy contemplation of a future without his adored presence in my life.

Despite my fatigue, I had expected to have trouble falling asleep. I had envisioned brooding in the guest bedroom next door to the girls and longing to be in the master bedroom beside Damien. Instead, I crashed right away. But I hadn't slept more than two hours when I was roused by a cry of terror from the girls' room. Almost as a reflex action, I bolted out of bed and down the hall to the adjacent doorway. Damien was already inside, holding Katie in his arms while she clung to him, sobbing.

When he saw me, he breathed, "It's all right, Mia. She had a bad dream. Don't worry." With his head he gestured toward Carrie, who still slept. "The bad dreams will stop, sweetheart." His words were for Katie. "It's your mind's way of getting rid of the fear you felt that day. They'll go away. They will. I promise. Your sister is dealing with it as well. Time will heal both of you. Look. Your mom is right here."

She continued to cling to him. She said, "Carrie wet her pants, you know."

"I know. Both of you are going to have some sessions with Joanna. We'll talk about it very soon."

She rested her head on his shoulder. "I love you, Uncle Damien. You don't treat me like a baby."

"I love you too, sweetheart. You're *not* a baby, so why would I treat you like one? Try to get back to sleep. Leave the bedside lamp on if that will help."

She nodded, detached herself from Damien to hug me. Against my ear she whispered, "Mom...can Dad ever come back as a zombie and hurt us again?"

"No, darling! No." I could not hold back the tears. "Dad will never, *never* hurt us again—any of us! There *are* no zombies, Katie. They're just made-up creatures. Do as Uncle Damien suggested and leave your bedside lamp on."

She nodded again, eyes already re-closing. "I love you both," she murmured. "Uncle Damien, I wish *you* had been my daddy..."

We tiptoed out, leaving the door ajar. It was only then that I let my own tears flow freely. Yes, children are resilient and get over trauma quickly—maybe more quickly than adults—but I couldn't help blaming myself and my bad decision to marry Des in the first place, for the fact that my daughters were enduring any trauma at all.

Until Damien responded, I wasn't aware I'd mumbled the last thought aloud. His arms came around me and he breathed into my hair, "If you hadn't married their dad, Mia, they wouldn't be. Point of logic, my love." Successfully he turned my tears into laughter, which he joined. For several moments we just held onto one another laughing, aware this was a release we needed.

Ultimately he again breathed into my hair, "If I don't stop holding you like this, I won't be responsible for my own actions. Go back to bed, Mia, and get some rest. I've got clinic hours all day tomorrow but I should be back here by four. Joanna's last appointment is at three. Why don't I text her to come over here when she's done and we can all talk? Stay here for the day. My first appointment isn't till nine, so I'll run the girls to school on my way in to the clinic. Are you okay to pick them up?"

"Of course. I should probably drive the Echo again anyway, as soon as possible—like getting back on a horse after it has thrown you."

He kissed my forehead. "Maybe we should do something about getting you another car."

"Damien..." Pressed against him as I was and dressed only in a flimsy nightgown, the hardness of his male desire was unmistakable. He wanted me. And that knowledge was exquisite as ever, even though he was an engaged man. I drew a deep breath. "Damien, I...I'm not sorry I excite you. I can't pretend I am. But I'll never again be that obnoxious nineteen-year-old who used it at Lorne's party to take advantage of you. You've been wonderful to me and the girls. I don't want to burden you with our troubles much longer. I should be taking steps soon to vacate the apartment Des and I occupied and find ourselves a new place to..."

"Stop it." His smile was tender, his eyes compelling. "There's no hurry. You're welcome to stay as long as you want. I swore to you I'd behave, remember? And again: you weren't obnoxious at Lorne's party; you were desperately attractive." Once more, he kissed my forehead. "You still are. I...need to break this contact. Good night, my Mia." He drew away. "Please try and go back to sleep. I don't think Katie will wake again until morning."

"The way I feel about your attraction to me..."

"Don't." He closed his hands over mine, applied pressure. "I'm fighting very hard, my Mia, and I'm asking you, please, not to make it any more difficult for me." He swallowed; I saw the motion in his throat. "You're still recovering from physical trauma. You're also recovering from the scars of abuse, both physical and emotional. You need gentleness and kindness and respect. You need time and space."

My eyes searched his. Yes, I did need all those things. But I also needed *him*. And he was not mine to have. Isn't that what he was so diplomatically telling me? My ache for him was almost physical pain; yet he belonged to Joanna Farley. After they were married, would she be as generous as he was being? Would she tolerate my seeing him so often and including him in the girls' lives? Wouldn't she want to start her own family with him? Wouldn't she ask me—probably super-nicely—to please back off? I knew *I* would, in her place.

I did return to bed, and the next thing I knew it was morning. I woke to the sounds of the girls' voices in the kitchen, mingled with Damien's. He was preparing them breakfast. Their laughter joined his and I clearly heard his deep voice warn, "Last one to sit down at the table gets two less strawberries on her cereal!" Sounds of a giggle-filled scuffle ensued. With a cleansing sigh, I closed my eyes tightly and wished for the millionth time that *he* were their father. How happy they sounded—happier than they'd ever sounded when we lived with Des! Part of me wanted to retreat again into the sleep cocoon, where a world without storms existed—a world where the huge Joanna Farley cloud had dissipated, leaving only clear-sky serenity.

Yet life demanded I not only contend with Joanna Farley's existence, but also look to her professional expertise to help my children. I needed Joanna as strongly as I needed Damien. Washing up and getting dressed, I shook my head at the irony. No doubt Carrie and Katie would soon grow to love Joanna as much as they already loved Damien.

They were ready for school, I saw as I entered the kitchen, and their bowlfuls of strawberry-topped shredded wheat were fast disappearing. Damien turned from the sink to give me a brief hug and a light kiss full on the lips. It was over before I could enjoy it. He ruffled my hair, said, "Good morning, sleepyhead. We're off to school and work in a few minutes. Rummage and enjoy your breakfast. I'll contact Joanna from the clinic—or I might even take a short break and run down to the fifth floor to see her at *her* clinic. We'll get a meeting arranged to organize those sessions."

"I like Joanna," Carrie grinned, a milk mustache on her upper lip. "She's so nice." Her words should have lightened my heart, not made it heavy as lead.

Pouring myself a glass of orange juice I said, "I hate to presume on your relationship with her."

"No presumption, my Mia. Purely a labour of love." He fetched his coat from the closet. "Girls, you need to brush your teeth and get into your jackets *yesterday*, if you want to hear the end of my story."

They gave me a hug each and scampered off. Once Damien had left with them in the Volvo, now back from the repair shop, I turned the problem over and over in my head while I nibbled on bagels and cream cheese. Maybe I should just confess to Joanna that I couldn't live without him and beg her to release him from his proposal. I laughed aloud. Fat chance! Could I appeal to her nobility, or possibly her pity? It appalled me to be considering such ideas, even half-jokingly.

I made up my mind that the next time I spoke to her, I would offer my sincerest congratulations—something I hadn't yet done—and wish them both much happiness. I'd do it without losing my cool or betraying anything other than happiness equal to theirs. And maybe, once my five-year obligation to stay in Barrett had elapsed, I might consider moving out of town, going someplace where I wouldn't have to see them every day, try for the rest of my life to keep the green-eyed monster at bay...

Startled out of these unpleasant ruminations by the trill of Damien's land-line phone, I squared my shoulders and picked up. I would be completely efficient and businesslike, I decided, as I took whatever message the caller had for Damien. Enough with the moping around like a fool! Self-pity was the last thing I should be nurturing!

My resolutions nosedived the moment I pressed 'talk' and realized it was the cloud herself! Mortified at even thinking of her that way, I forced lightness into my voice. "Joanna! Hi! Good to hear from you. Damien is at the clinic. He..."

"I know. He told me you're over there. I just texted him that I can't make it this afternoon, and I wanted you to know as well. I've got a doctor's appointment. I'm sorry, but I'll set up a schedule to see the girls first chance I get."

"Of course. I'm the one who should be apologizing. You're not sick, are you?"

"Oh, I'm absolutely fine! We both are."

My heart did one of those flip-flops. "*Both...?*"

"Me *and* the baby. This is just a regular obstetrical checkup."

I heard a gagging sound coming from my own throat before I could stifle it. "You're...pregnant?"

"You didn't know?" I heard her sigh. "That's what we were celebrating at the Salters' the Friday evening you had the headache. Men! I can't think why Damien didn't tell you—though he's not one for gossip and I guess I *did* swear him to secrecy. But that was only until we had made our Skype call."

"I see."

So it hadn't been an engagement party after all. It had been a joyous announcement of the news that Joanna was carrying Damien's child.

My world tilted on its axis.

# Chapter 39

"Where are my manners? Congratulations to you both! How lovely!"

There! I had managed to say it—and with as much sincerity and fake cheerfulness in my voice as when I'd picked up. I deserved a pat on the back for my abilities as an actress.

But I couldn't maintain it. I had to get off the phone *now*, before the pose crumbled. As politely as I could, I excused myself, said I was on the way out to see my mother. Of course Joanna had to go as well; she was in the middle of her work day and had made a quick call between patients. With renewed congrats, I hung up—and gave in to another onslaught of hot angry tears.

When the attack subsided, I changed clothes, gathered up my own and the girls' stuff, and loaded up the Echo. Now that it was unquestionably obvious that Damien's kindness to us *was* only kindness and nothing more, I should leave without delay and stop being a burden to him. I'd go back to the Salters' for now and dump our things; then I'd do what I'd told Joanna I was going to do: call Mother, go over to her condo (if she was home) and enlist her assistance in searching for another apartment of my own. The sooner I started forging a new life for myself, the sooner I'd be able to put all this behind me.

She answered on the third ring and reacted to the neutrality in my voice by inviting me over right away. I don't know how I'd ever thought Mother to be insensitive. It even turned out she'd cancelled lunch with a friend just to be there for me.

And as much as I'd decided not to cry in her presence, the tears flowed again as soon as she came to her door. Gathering me into her arms, she ushered me in and listened while I regaled her with reasons for not being a bother to Damien or Joanna any more. She gave me a squeeze, sat me on her sofa, and brought a box of tissues.

"I didn't know about Joanna." Her expression was sad. "It complicates things, of course."

"No." I sniffled. "Actually, it simplifies things a great deal. Will you help me find an apartment? I'd like to move to the other end of town as quickly as I can. And after my five-year obligation to stay in Barrett is up, I'll pull up stakes here and look for another university town where I can transfer."

She shook her head. "I think you're jumping the gun, Mari. I think you would devastate Damien by making a decision like that."

"Mother, I owe it to Damien to get out of his way now! If I had known sooner about Joanna, I would never have imposed upon his hospitality in the first place!"

Again she shook her head. "Damien's feelings for you are as deep as yours are for him. I'm not sure where or how Joanna fits in. Sure, I'll help you find an apartment. But don't run away from Damien. He's the best thing that has ever happened to you."

"He...doesn't care for me at all!"

"How can you say that? Mari, he hardly left your side while you were recovering. He very openly cares for you a great deal."

"All right then, he doesn't *love* me! He loves Joanna."

She chewed a thumbnail. "Maybe he *used* to love Joanna before he loved you. I admit I don't know. And I admit I wish she weren't pregnant."

"Mother, if their relationship were over, I think Joanna would be disturbed about the pregnancy. She isn't; she's ecstatic. She and Damien were celebrating the other night at the Salters.'"

Mother spread her hands and admitted to being stumped. "I understand your dilemma, Mari. Just...don't run away. Things have a way of becoming clear eventually. Sometimes one needs to be patient." She gave a wistful smile. "I'd love to have that dear man for a son-in-law."

"Mother, there's no way that's happening!"

"Let's go for a drive and scout out 'for rent' signs, shall we? Just getting out and about will make you feel better."

I nodded. Searching the old-fashioned way—making an outing of it—was exactly what I wanted. Maybe I could put my 'Jane Henry' on the dotted line before the afternoon was over.

To text Damien and tell him I'd left his place and gone back to the Salters' seemed too impersonal. I chose to leave a message on his voice mail instead: "Damien, you already know Joanna can't make this afternoon, so I've moved back with Lorne and Lydia—temporarily. Mother and I are going apartment hunting today. I'll be out of everyone's hair very soon." Hesitating for a beat, I plunged on. "Thank you for hosting us last night—and for being there for me through all of this. It has...meant everything. Goodbye."

When I broke the connection, Mother made a 'tsk, tsk' sound, but didn't comment. She fetched her coat and we took my car. Several places we looked at would have done the job quite nicely, but I didn't commit. Even a cute little townhouse within walking distance of the university campus I passed up, knowing someone else was bound to grab it if I didn't act immediately.

We stopped for a bite to eat just before picking up the girls from school. It warmed my heart to hear Mother tell me to quit fiddling with my food and get some decent nourishment down me. How I would have loved to be a carefree kid again! This time I would have gratefully appreciated the ministrations I now knew had always been motivated by love and caring. Even more comforting was her reassurance that Connor was profoundly sorry for the way he had spoken to me when we'd last talked.

"Has Connor confided in you?" I asked it in some surprise.

"Yes. We've had coffee together a few times and commiserated about how neither one of us has been the best of parents."

My eyebrows rose. "You've been fine, Mother. *I'm* the one who hasn't been the best of children." I reached for her hand; its clasp was warm and strong. "Why does it take the human being so long to grow up? A foal can stand almost as soon as it's born and has made most of the journey towards being an adult horse within the first year of its life. A lot of the animal kingdom is like that. And yet we humans still have the arrogance to think we're superior!" My eyes misted again. "Please forgive my stupidity, Mother, at ever thinking I was superior!"

The pressure of her hand in mine increased. "We all need to learn, Mari. We all need to make our mistakes along the way. And because we well remember our own mistakes, we tend to be much more sympathetic of them in our children."

"Thank you." I squeezed back. "I...want to make things up with Connor. The poor man has been hurting for a very long time."

"He has."

"Do you think he'd be receptive to a visit from me?"

"I think he'd be very receptive. He's a proud man, Mari, and he has spent far too long being a deluded one, but I guarantee you he fully recognizes that he has behaved like an ass." Tenderly, she brushed at an unruly lock of my hair. "Both you and I know, though, that Connor certainly has no monopoly on asinine behavior."

My smile was tenuous. "I want Connor and Damien to make things up between *them* as well."

She nodded. "Someone just has to make the first move, that's all. I have already smoothed the way for you—by giving Connor the gears and telling him he should know his daughter-in-law better than to believe some maladjusted unfortunate like Teddy Kelly."

"Mother!"

"It had to be done. He took it very well. And he agrees with me."

"Mother, you're...amazing!" I couldn't seem to stop sniffling. "A reconciliation between me and his father is what *Damien* wants. I'll call Connor. I'll do it today, this evening." I swallowed. "I'll... do it for Damien."

She raised her teacup to mine in a salute. "Good girl! Now let's finish up here and go get my lovely granddaughters!"

It was the first time the girls had ridden in the Echo since Des had commandeered it and threatened to kill us all. I saw the look they exchanged before getting tentatively into their car seats and doing up the seatbelts. Katie said solemnly, "We love you, Grandma, but we want Uncle Damien. He can protect us from zombies." And when both Mother and I reassured them once more that there *were* no zombies, Carrie added, "Jill Bates, who sits in front of me, said the souls of people like Dad don't go to heaven or hell. They live in a place called limbo. And their tortured souls can leave limbo any time to go torture other souls. She said we should sleep with the lights on, so Dad doesn't come back to torture us."

And while Mother was shushing them and telling them Jill Bates spoke pure nonsense, I was brought face-to-face with the realization that—cloud or no cloud—Joanna Farley and the help she represented was vital right now, both to me and to my dearest daughters.

Connor could wait a few more days. The person I had to speak to again without further delay—and despite my own considerable qualms—was Joanna.

As it turned out, Joanna herself felt exactly the same way about speaking to me!

Shortly after the girls and I had arrived back at the Salters' and Manuel had offered to take the girls down to the stable and give them another riding lesson, my cell phone buzzed. Dispensing with time-wasting pleasantries, Joanna dove straight to the point. "I've just finished with the obstetrician. She'd had a cancellation right before my appointment, so I'm earlier than I'd expected to be. Damien says you're back at Lorne's. Don't move from there. I'll be over in twenty minutes. It's vital that we talk. I mean it, Mari. Don't go *anywhere*! I think something's terribly wrong."

# Chapter 40

They were twenty of the longest minutes of my life.

All sorts of dire scenarios reared up on my mental horizon: the diagnosis of a grave defect in Joanna's baby, Joanna herself on the point of miscarrying, Damien threatened by one of Des' evil machinations—maybe a delayed-action time bomb about to detonate...? Nothing made any logical sense.

If it were to do with the baby, surely Damien would be the one she was desperate to contact. If Damien were threatened, she'd be seeking out the police. If a ticking Des device posed imminent danger, she'd be calling the bomb squad. So why was it so imperative Joanna talk to *me*?

I was still pacing and stewing when she arrived. Breathless, she enfolded me in a quick hug. "Good girl! I'm glad you stayed put. Where are the girls?"

"Down at the stable riding the ponies. If you want to see them, I can..."

"No. Not right now. It's good they're out of the way so we can talk. I wanted us to be alone. Mari, I've been troubled all day! The way you reacted to the news of my pregnancy leads me to believe you've gone down a completely wrong road."

"Oh... So the baby is all right? Damien is all right? I'm afraid my imagination has been running totally amok..."

"Come and sit down." She took both my hands gently in hers, guided me to a sofa, and placed herself beside me. "For someone who is supposed to be an expert on human feelings, I've been pretty dense. I assumed you knew things you couldn't have known. If you *had* known them, you wouldn't have drawn an erroneous conclusion. Listen to me. Damien and I have been close friends for a number of years. We tell each other our problems and we act as sounding boards for one another. It's a beautiful relationship. But Mari, it's not sexual. This baby I'm expecting is not Damien's."

Once more my world wobbled. I could only gape at her stupidly, mouth wide open.

She said, "My significant other is a drilling engineer and is away on the oil rigs a lot of the time. Now, with the baby coming, that's going to change. Melanie has found an office job much closer to home."

"Melanie... *Melanie* is the person you Skyped! I thought Melanie was your mother."

She shook her head. "My mother died when I was quite young. Melanie is my same-sex partner. We don't particularly hide it, but neither do we go trumpeting it about town. These days most people are open-minded, but there are those who still have issues. That aside, Damien has been the one who helped me find a fertility clinic, the one whose shoulder I've cried on through all the disappointments. Melanie and I have been dying to be parents for quite some while. We're both on cloud nine about this."

"But...Damien takes you out on dates..."

"Damien has been kind enough, while Melanie is away, to escort me to functions where I would otherwise be a fifth wheel. They aren't really dates. In the past, Damien has done some dating, yes—but not lately." She lowered her voice. "Not since you, Mari."

I was unable to reply.

"Mari..." Her voice was earnest; she echoed Mother's words. "Whatever you do, don't run away from Damien. It's obvious to me how much you love him. As for Damien—remember that night at Lorne's birthday party, the night Desmond did the usual and threw you into his brother's arms? That night, Mari, I swear you bewitched Damien. And he has been crazy, out-of-his-mind in love with you ever since."

I heard a low guttural sound coming from my own mouth. My words fell over one another in a stammer. "He...has told you that?"

"OMG, no. He would never tell me before he declared himself to you. Even though he and I confide in each other a lot, Damien is all about ethics. But I'd have to be blind not to see it. He calls you 'Mia' and he uses endearments to you all the time; I've heard him. He didn't so much before Des' psychotic break, but when Des shot you, he was beside himself..."

"I know. But I'm his brother's widow. He's bound to be concerned about me. He's that kind of giving, generous person."

"He *wants* you, Mari! Haven't you seen it? He can't hide it. I think he's fighting it very hard because he's afraid of losing control and taking you as passionately as he's dying to take you."

*'I'm fighting very hard, my Mia, and I'm asking you, please, not to make it any more difficult for me...'*

My God! Was it possible...?

Damien's deep voice intruded then, startling us both. Consuela had ushered him inside and she now quietly retreated. Neither Joanna nor I had heard them enter. At this moment, there was a rare sternness to his tone as he confronted his friend and confidante and breathed, "Joanna. What are you doing? You have absolutely no right..."

"I'm sorry, Damien." She faced him, unabashed. "No, I take that back. I'm not sorry at all. Under normal circumstances I'd agree with you wholeheartedly, but these circumstances are anything but normal. Mari didn't know I'm pregnant. And when I told her, she thought the baby was yours. I had to do what I had to do."

The iron-hardness of his jaw relaxed slowly. The frown faded from his handsome features. Very softly he said, "I apologize. You're a true friend. But I...need you to go now, please. I need you to let me be alone with Mia."

She grinned. "Your wish, my command. I'm outta here! Mari, call about setting up some counselling sessions for the girls."

I hardly heard her. Neither of us responded.

My gaze held his transfixed; I was lost in the indigo depths of those amazing eyes. Even so, I finally goaded myself to speak, and what I whispered was, "Please don't resent Joanna. She didn't mean..."

"I love Joanna." His deep voice caressed. "I love her like a sister. Mia, you've misunderstood for far, far too long. And I haven't made any attempt to enlighten you, have I?  Subconsciously, I may have done that purposely in order to hold you at arm's length. I apologize to you, too."

"You don't owe me an..."

"Desmond wanted me to love you." His eyes riveted mine. "And what Desmond wanted spelled danger for you." He drew a deep breath. "Desmond's attempts to get me to love his women were an aspect of his psychotic game I've always refused to play. You know that. He tried to draw me in again and again— unsuccessfully. I always feared for the women but I never became emotionally involved." In a gesture I had grown to love, he ran a hand through his abundance of hair, standing it on end. "I was impervious, my Mia. I made it my business to be impervious. Until you."

"Damien, I know I've caused trouble..."

"Shush, please." He took my hand. "Come with me—to my place next door. The Volvo is parked outside; I came straight here from the clinic after I listened to your message on my voice mail. Let's check with Manuel that the girls will be riding for a while, and then let's go where we can be truly alone and private." He swallowed. "What I want to say to you, my Mia, needs to be said someplace where Consuela won't walk in on us."

My own breathing was ragged—but in a glorious way. My hand, on fire in his, felt as though it had always belonged there. We did exactly as he had suggested: found Manuel and my daughters down at the stable and verified the girls would be occupied with the ponies for at least the next hour. Manuel's curious glance strayed to Damien's right hand, still holding my left. He broke into a beaming smile, gave a little bow, and chuckled, "No worries, Dr. Damien, no worries! Take as long as you want."

Damien blushed, thanked him, and then murmured into my ear, "Privacy can be difficult to come by around here. Come on, my love."

And, as we crossed the grounds and he led me toward the Volvo, parked in the Salters' drive, I can honestly say that the world around me—lit by skies containing no trace of a cloud—was suddenly bathed in the resplendent sunlit sheen of burnished gold.

# Chapter 41

He drove swiftly, with almost tangible impatience. Beside him in the passenger seat, I revelled in our closeness—physical and emotional both. He loved me! It was a chorus inside my head, a symphony. And yet it was still too new—and too phenomenal—to believe.

Joanna had known it. Mother had known it. Me, I'd been so cynical about romance for so long that I'd tried to deny in my head what my heart and my hormones had been telling me unerringly for what seemed an age.

Damien loved me. Could it be true? I hugged to me the knowledge, lingering over it—as I had lingered over and held close my success at arousing him that night at Lorne's birthday party. And I kept pinching myself, sure this must be a pink-sugar-candy dream from which I never wanted to wake.

When we pulled into his drive, he came around and opened the door for me, his arm about my waist as he ushered me through the front entrance to the house. It was a house I already adored as much as I adored its owner. And yet I hesitated on the brink—just in case all of this was nothing more than some divine fantasy.

He led me to the small alcove just off the kitchen, installed me on the buttery-soft stretched loveseat, and lowered himself beside me. His blue eyes were two profound pools into which I felt I might sink and drown. If I did drown, it would be a heavenly way to go.

"Mia..." Husky with emotion, his voice sensually stroked the pet name that was ours alone. "Just to be accurate, I need to correct something Joanna said. She told you you've bewitched me since the night of Lorne's party. About that she's quite wrong."

Again, my world threatened to tilt. "Oh. I...see."

"No. You don't see at all. Shush and listen to me. You've bewitched me since long before that, my precious girl. You've bewitched me since the night I saw you step out of the shadows in the lobby of your mother's condo building. And Des knew it. Psychotic he was, but also very astute. That's why he decided he had to marry you."

I inhaled deeply. "Des also knew you and Joanna weren't lovers. He said as much that day he was holding me and the girls hostage in the Echo. I argued with him. He said, 'Farley? That's rich, Mari.' Somehow he had found out Joanna was in a same-sex union and not involved with you."

His arm came up behind me on the loveseat. "He would have made it his business to find out. Studying and ruining my relationships had become his obsession."

"That's so sad...!"

"Don't. We've closed that chapter of our lives, my love. I want it to *stay* closed."

For the first time, I dared raise my hand to touch his face and tentatively stroke the five-o'clock-shadow roughness of his chin. "So Joanna's statement is inaccurate. You deny I bewitched you on the night of Lorne's party. But...is she accurate about the rest of it? Are you really 'crazy, out-of-your-mind' in love with me?"

His profusely tender smile became a resonating laugh as he pushed stray tendrils of hair off my forehead. "I'm crazy, out-of-my-mind, over the moon, to the heights of Everest, to the depths of my soul, in love with you, my darling Mia. And, if you don't believe that, I'll find more ways to say it. There aren't enough words, my precious girl, to describe the depth of my love for you."

And only then did my world truly burst into bloom. Only then did I allow my fingers to trace and memorize every contour of his beloved face. "Damien..." I murmured it. "I think I fell in love with *you* the day you came to Lorne's rescue during that lunch I had with him in Robert's Bistro. Of course I resisted my feelings, and my immature delight at shocking people drove me straight into Desmond's arms. If I'd only known then what I know now...!"

His hands were stroking the nape of my neck, lighting fires. Ultra-softly he whispered, "I was in torment because I knew how much he must be hurting you. As I live and breathe, Mia, rough sex will never be a part of your love life again!"

Comprehension dawned. Widening the circles of my caresses to include his muscular shoulders, I brushed my lips against his neck. "Des was right about one thing. For a supposedly smart girl, I've been abysmally dumb. *That's* why you're repressing your desire for me—because you're afraid I might think of it as rape. Damien, I don't believe I carry any emotional scars. I have a confession. My marriage bed was enhanced sometimes by envisioning *you* as my lover instead of Des. Please, don't fight it any more. I want you as much as you want me."

He blushed to the roots of his hair. "I...very much doubt that, darling girl. It isn't possible to want any more than I want you. You're exciting me far too much, and gentleness is imperative. The last thing in the world you need is even a hint of roughness..."

"*Passion*, Damien, is what I both need and want! Honestly. Passion with you is what I have dreamed of! I've seen *your* passion, and it lights me up." I made my voice purposely coy. "So...shall we make our way to the bedroom?"

He shook his head, voice shaking as well. "I can't. I won't make it as far as the bedroom. Come here..."

Our lovemaking was frenzied. His urgency inflamed me as nothing in my life ever had before. Right there on the stretched loveseat, I was encircled in his embrace, held close against his thundering heart for mere seconds; then, balancing his weight on his forearms, his chest came against mine and lowered me to a lying position. His kisses moved from my forehead to my eyelids, to my cheeks, to the hollow of my throat, and then our mouths met. The kiss deepened instantly, deliciously, and I wanted it to go on forever. When he suddenly broke away and groaned, "My love, forgive me. I...need to be quick, or I won't hold on!" his urgency roused mine to a fever equal to his.

We were ready together—and together we scaled heights such as I had never before known. He gasped and sobbed endearments to me that brought me to multiple peaks, until I was gasping and sobbing in my turn and never wanting it to end. For the first time, I felt catapulted almost to the stars, and I rode the thermal draft of our throbbing ecstasy over mountain after mountain. He was with me all the way, his passion fuelling mine. And when we descended at last, slowly, reluctantly, he continued to caress and kiss me all over as his panting gradually subsided. With infinite tenderness, he pushed the hair off my forehead, his sea-blue eyes exploring my own as he murmured, "Are you all right, my love? I so wanted to be slower, more attentive to your..."

"Damien...!" I buried my hands in his abundance of hair as I had longed to do for a seeming lifetime; then I pulled his head down against my breast, cutting off the rest of the sentence. "Damien, it was everything I have imagined in my wildest dreams. *You* are everything I've ever imagined and wanted in a lover, and more. I can still hardly believe that *I* am the one you love!"

His soft laughter vibrated against me. "Ditto, my sweetheart. I have to be the luckiest man alive." He raised his head to meet my eyes once more. "Be patient with me, please. I can learn to be as slow and gentle as you want me to be."

"Damien, I adore you! I already know how gentle you can be."

I felt his sigh of contentment as he quirked the teasing eyebrow. "Now shall we go to the bedroom?"

I sucked in my breath. "Again? Already?"

He kissed the tip of my nose. "I have faith, love, that what you've always done to me you'll do again, very soon. I've wanted you for an eternity, and I can't get enough. And this time I'm going to undress you, being as deliberate as I can, and kissing the whole of you as I go."

I giggled. "Do *I* get to undress *you*, as well?"

"I wouldn't have it any other way. Sex is a mechanical act, my precious Mia. You and I are in the process of *making love.*"

Exquisite contentment filtered through me. I teased, "I'm glad Manuel understands. And I presume it may be a good couple of hours before we get in touch with Joanna."

He stood, took both my hands in his, pulled me up beside him, kissed me long and lingeringly as we moved together down the hall toward the master bedroom. He said, "Joanna reads me far better than I wish she did! If we don't delay getting back to her for quite a while, I have a feeling she'll be moderately disappointed."

And again we laughed together, abandoning ourselves to pure joy.

# Chapter 42

Slow and deliberate was luscious. In no time, his kisses had me gasping and drowning again, begging for more. He was an impresario, a maestro of a lover. As he finished undressing me, touching and stroking and kissing, I was amazed at his renewed arousal, and I said so. In wonder I stammered, "This is...unreal. Des could never..." He placed the feather-light hand over my lips.

"Des, my dearest love, is gone from our lives. I definitely want him gone from our bedroom. This is our party—yours and mine. Let's throw Des out and lock the door."

I nodded. "Amen! Damien, I have never really even...touched a man before. My love life in the past..."

"Shush, sweetheart. Shush." He nibbled my ear, shedding the shirt he'd been too hasty to remove till now—or even to unbutton all the way—and exposing a washboard chest, with that fine matting of hair the same ripe-wheat colour as the hair on his head. Already his breathing had dramatically quickened. "The past is gone forever." He took my hands, guided them to rest on that chest and then to stroke it tauntingly. "We're going to make changes to your previous love life, my beautiful darling." His breathing increased further. "We're going to teach you not to hesitate to touch as much as you want. Your touch is magic. It sends me into orbit!" He drew a tremulous breath. "

And we're going to teach *me* to control myself and let you explore."

"Can I undo the belt and take off the pants?"

"I thought you'd never ask."

"Damien, I...hope you don't find me too forward, or too clumsy..."

"Stop it. I'll eagerly volunteer, Madam Professor, to give you as many tutorials as you need. My only concern is that I won't be able to wait."

"Again?"

His deep laughter reverberated. "Always with you, beautiful Mia." He traced a path across my breasts with the fingers of his left hand, sucked each erect nipple in turn, as his right hand guided mine to his belt. Softly he said, "I'm not at all in control. I apologize in advance that I may...want to explode before you're done. If that happens, I can only promise that the more we make love, the better I'll behave."

"You're behaving beautifully. I am...captivated!"

"Thank you, my Mia."

"That I excite you like this is thrilling beyond measure! It has been since that night at Lorne's party. I can't *believe* how much I've missed! I used to think the whole romance thing was so vastly overblown..."

"You hadn't found the right lover." He helped me undo the belt, peel the pants, stroke and kiss his muscular thighs. My eyes moved to the jockey shorts and the bulging mound there that I suddenly longed to caress. But his hands closed over mine and he sobbed, "Forgive me, love! I need to be quick again...!" And then I was once more gliding over those magic mountains of ecstasy.

We descended together as though wafted down on gentle breezes. Our breathing slowed. Damien's eyes were closed, his head resting on my breast. Stroking his hair, I whispered, "Is it all right if I touch you now? There's no risk of starting any new fires, is there?"

Once more his laughter vibrated against me. "Don't bet on it! Mia, my darling, touch me to your heart's content. I long for your touch. And again I'm asking you to please be patient with me. I'm not used to having such a...hair trigger. It's a state *you* induce in me." He guided my hands to the shorts, helped me remove them, let my eyes have their fill; then enquired almost shyly, "Do I pass inspection?"

"You are Adonis, Damien. I've always known that. I repeat: you're everything I imagined, and more!"

"Thank you again, my dearest love. Touch. Stroke. Kiss. Just don't expect me to stay on this planet while you're doing it. If my eyes roll back in my head, don't call the paramedics; I'm all right. I'm better than all right."

"You are...amazing!"

"I'm madly in love. It's a beautiful place to be. We're going to have to come back to earth eventually—but not quite yet. Not quite yet, love of my life. I want your hands on me, my Mia, and your lips. Please!"

I obliged him, thrilled at my own power to make him groan with pleasure like that. Ultimately, we again made love—this time with all the slow gentleness he had promised—and it was every bit as wonderful as the urgency. And finally, when we re-donned our clothing, we dressed each other and we kept looking into one another's eyes and laughing in wholly unrestrained rapture.

"*Now* I'll call Joanna and we'll set up some counselling sessions for the girls." He made a teasing show of sobering his demeanour; then he surrendered to renewed laughter. "Mia, I think I might need you out of my sight while I'm doing it, so I can maintain some semblance of professional dignity."

"I can't be out of your sight. I'm the one who knows the girls' schedules." There was nothing at all funny about that; yet it provoked still more laughter from both of us.

"We're drunk on passion. We have to sober up." Damien tickled me in the ribs, his teasing having just the opposite effect. "Mia, we have to get serious or I'm going to get aroused again."

"I dare you!"

"Don't dare me, or we'll be here the rest of the afternoon!"

"I love you so very much, Damien..."

"I mean it, love. I'm going to boil a kettle and make us a mug of tea each before we call. Are you in?"

I nodded. "Of course. Let's get the girls some help."

We toasted that with our tea mugs. And then Damien brought his mug against mine in another toast: "To *us*, lovely girl. To our future. To all that is so thrillingly beautiful about being in love!" His eyes lit with a mischievous glow. "To having my hands occupied holding this mug so that, for at least two seconds, I can keep them off you." With a sensual sigh, he reached into the breast pocket of his shirt for his cell. "I'm calling." Tapping the phone's screen, he began a conversation that ended with Joanna's inviting us all over to her place on the following afternoon. Just before Damien terminated the exchange, I saw him blush and heard him murmur, "How about you keep that uncomfortably keen perception of yours out of my bedroom?" And I could clearly hear Joanna's tinkling laughter at the other end.

Naturally, I moved out of the Salters', giving Lorne and Lydia each a huge hug of gratitude for being so gracious and kind to me. Lorne said, "Dear girl, it was nothing if not a sound strategy on our part. We began to be quite certain that you were soon to become our neighbour." Lydia hugged me, nodding affirmation. Everyone but I, it seemed, had been unquestioningly confident that this outcome was inevitable.

The girls whirled about like exultant dervishes when told we were moving in with Uncle Damien forever. Katie's sagacity made us all giggle. "You sure took long enough, Mom!" It warmed my heart to watch the two of them becoming more carefree and secure by the day. Joanna's sessions with them—and Damien's gentle paternal manner with them—were effectively expunging all fearful or negative associations.

Such legal details as cancelling the lease on my former apartment with Des and going through the thousand trivialities that required copies of the death certificate, I handled in as orderly and matter-of-fact a fashion as I could. Damien helped me just by being at my side. When the *Gazette* requested I clear out my late husband's office to make room for the new editor, I gritted my teeth and got it done at first convenience—again, with Damien at my side. "Let's close each chapter as promptly and completely as we can, my love," he advised, "so we can put all unpleasantness behind us."

Transferring my possessions into Damien's gracious home was something that held all the *pleasantness* I could wish for. When I kiddingly began carrying my things into the guest bedroom, he frowned. "What are you doing?" I played demure.

"Maybe we should give it a decent interval. What do you think?"

"I think you're being a vixen again. I want you to marry me just as soon as we can arrange it, my love. I know this town will understand and forgive us the hurry. But don't deny me your bed unless you want me to climb walls! I've been doing that for eons already."

"Shouldn't I be traditional and wait until after we're married? What would you say if I insisted on that?"

He kissed the tip of my nose. "I'd take sixteen cold showers a day and abide by your wishes. I'm praying you're joking."

"Of course I'm joking."

"Mia, my darling, I am *so* in love with you!"

And those words were what made my world sing. They put a lilt in my voice as I accepted, along with Damien, the Salters' invitation three weeks later to another celebration party, this time in honour of our engagement. That night, Damien's two-carat diamond ring sparkled on my finger—a finger that had never before carried a diamond. Desmond had told me he'd get me one someday and that day had never seemed to arrive. Damien, on the other hand, was insistent from the start, despite my objections, that we get one right away, a large one. "I'm not being a show-off, love..." He grinned. "Well, yes I am—because I want the whole world to know my heart belongs to the loveliest woman on earth. And I want to symbolize it by buying you a diamond the size of my love for you! Is that showing off?"

"In a way that makes me adore you, yes!"

Sarah and Simon—the nephew whose acquaintance Lorne Salter was finding true pleasure in re-making—were part of that celebration. Lorne and Lydia had also invited Mother, along with Joanna and her partner, Melanie. Carrie and Katie were enjoying a weekend in the care of Grandpa Connor. It caused a pain in my heart to have Connor absent, and yet Damien's estrangement from his father—and Connor's estrangement from me—made no other course possible.

We all toasted Damien's and my engagement and, once again, Joanna's and Melanie's upcoming parenthood, along with Melanie's acquisition of an office job just a short commute away. Consuela, assisted by a beaming Manuel, filled glasses with Asti Spumante but supplied peach punch instead for Joanna. I laid a hand over Consuela's when she reached for my glass to pour the Asti and said quietly, "Punch for me too, please." And when both Damien—whose arm rested possessively behind the back of my chair—and Lydia questioned my choice with their expressions, I replied simply, "I'm not sure yet. All I can tell you right now is that my taste buds rebel against alcohol."

Melanie, a ruddy-faced, carrot-haired Brit with kind eyes and a hearty laugh, let out a merry cackle. "Bet you've got one in the oven, luv! Bet you're going to be a daddy, Damien!"

Damien blushed, eyes blue-black in this light and filled with wonder. "That would overjoy me." Lorne, grinning widely as he passed tissues to Mother, brought glasses and chairs for Manuel and Consuela and invited them to sit down and join in our toast.

Only one more thing, I realized, would have completed my supreme contentment that evening, and that was Connor's presence amongst us and his blessing of our union. I'm ashamed to admit I'd put off calling him to that point because it was easier to communicate through Mother—who was now seeing him regularly. It was Mother who had arranged for him to take the girls during this weekend.

Watching Mother now, as she wiped away tears of happiness, I knew I was through hesitating. I would contact Connor tomorrow. I'd go over and see him and take steps to mend the rift between us. And—despite my promise to Damien—I intended to do all I could to mend the rift between *them* as well.

The right brother had been estranged from his father forever. It was finally time to topple that wall of estrangement—for the sake of the man I loved.

ﷲ

# Chapter 43

No long-standing wall comes down easily.

Dismantling the Berlin Wall, stone by stone, had to be an emotion-wrought undertaking. The strife and ugliness that wall represented made its destruction a symbolic farewell to a period of human history we wish we could forget. Yet people grabbed for remnants of it, mementos prized as treasures. Those who forget history, as the saying goes, are doomed to repeat it.

And besides residual pain, there is stubborn pride—the reluctance to lose face. Stubborn pride has spelled the downfall of nations, never mind human beings.

That pride is what had caused me to stay with Des and to be in denial for so long despite the warnings of others and my own persistent misgivings. It is also what caused my finger to tremble as I tapped in Connor's phone number several times during the following five weeks. And no doubt that pride is what caused Connor to be repeatedly 'unavailable'.

"A lot of us choke on humble pie, Mari," Mother told me, flicking a stray thread off my sleeve. "Connor loves looking after the girls on Saturday afternoons—and they love him. He reads to them, takes them for outings, and glories in showing them off as his granddaughters. That says it all. Keep calling. I guarantee he's summoning courage to pick up."

I had returned to work at the university. My students and my life there I valued as much as ever, and long-term, I knew I belonged there. But I would have to be taking more leave soon.

My pregnancy had been confirmed. To my delirious joy, I was carrying Damien's baby.

"Your handsome fella is strutting around like a peacock!" Sarah teased. "Anyone would think he was Adam and this was the first child on earth! Why in heaven's name haven't you two tied the knot yet?"

I gave a pensive smile. "I'm the one holding us up, Sarah. Damien would marry me tomorrow if it were up to him. Me, I was hoping against hope that I could convince Connor to attend, if not perform, the ceremony."

"That's tough when Connor isn't talking to you." Her tart voice mellowed. "But I'll join you, honey, in hoping."

Ultimately, I opted to give hope a nudge, or more like a shove. I decided it was finally time to get Connor where he lived—literally.

Mother always took the grandkids to see him and brought them back from his place. One Saturday afternoon I found the guts to change that. Damien was in the OR performing emergency surgery and Mother had a hair appointment. I bundled Carrie and Katie into my new Ford Fusion—a replacement for the Echo—and drove straight to his bungalow before I lost my nerve.

The smile died on his face when he opened the door and a Damien-like blush, to the roots of his hair, crept over his features. "Mari...!" he rasped. "I..uh..I've been meaning to call you."

"Then why haven't you?" I had already determined I was going to take the bull by the horns. Some things you can't force, and well I knew it. But this I wanted desperately—and in both their hearts, I was sure, Damien and Connor wanted it too.

"Grandpa!" By turns, the girls went into his arms and hugged him. He kissed them and ushered them downstairs to the basement where he had set up an old-fashioned electric train set for them to play with. They loved the novelty, preferring it to PlayStation any day. Later, he had promised to take them to a movie.

"Wait there," he told me. "I'll be right back."

"I intend to wait," I replied. "May I go into your kitchen and boil a kettle?"

"By all means."

Saturdays were his leisure days, the days when—provided he'd finished preparing his sermon for the Sunday and there were no pressing pastoral visits to make—he had time to chat. I steeped us both a mug of Earl Grey and awaited his reappearance.

By the time he emerged from the floor below, he was mentally braced. His voice had taken on firmness and resolution. He said, "Carrie and Katie are very dear to me. And their grandmother is becoming so as well. I can hardly ignore their mother, can I? I haven't meant to, Mari. I've just been...afraid to call you. Back in my schooldays, that kind of conduct was termed 'chicken'."

I nodded. "I understand. I *so* understand! The stubborn pride of my past immaturity had me knowing all the answers and refusing to listen to anybody. Damien is the one who changed that. Damien opened my heart to love, and to the desire to make things right with his dad. That's why I'm here, Connor, and that's why I intend to *stay* here until the two of us repair what should never have been broken in the first place."

He took a swallow of tea, his smile pathetically sad. "You, dear girl, are an eloquent orator. I should get you to help me compose my sermons!" Pained eyes warred with his quiet chuckle at the humour. "For a person who preaches love and acceptance, I've behaved inexcusably. Damien has every reason to hate me. You both do."

I dared tell myself that maybe this was going to be easier than I'd thought.

"Neither one of us hates you, Connor."

His shoulders sagged. "Damien always seemed so self-sufficient, so...unassailable. For years I held that against him, Mari. And, God help me, I *did* hold against him the fact that my wife died birthing him. That poor little boy...! Des put him through enough. He didn't need my putting him through any more."

Again I nodded. "You know now that *Damien* was the one who built the B-52 for your birthday and *Des* was the one who destroyed it, not the other way around? You know now that Des' psychotic game was to try and get Damien to fall in love with his women, so he could then destroy the women and break Damien in the process?"

His eyes blurred with tears. "I think part of me has always known it, Mari. I just chose to deal with it by not dealing with it." He sighed. "Look how Damien turned out! He won a scholarship and studied medicine and became a respected neurologist. And for all those achievements I've never once given him an ounce of praise or recognition."

Once more I nodded. "You so wanted to make the wrong brother right that you lost the right brother along the way."

Agony puckered his forehead. "In the end, I lost them both. I've made such a complete mess of things as a parent...! And I have the *nerve* to counsel others and to preach forgiveness...!"

It was then that I took his hand, pressed it gently, and breathed, "Don't you also preach that it's never too late?"

His tears coalesced, ran down his cheeks. I heard the quiver in his intake of breath. "But it *is* too late, Mari. Damien will never forgive me now. I stood by and allowed the woman he loves beyond life itself to be put in harm's way. Desmond nearly killed you, and I could have prevented it." With his free hand he took a handkerchief from his pocket and blew his nose. "I could have tried to get help for Desmond long ago instead of just going along with everything he told me when I knew, in my bones, that none of it was true."

"Connor...did Mother tell you I'm expecting Damien's baby? You're going to have another grandchild. You already have two granddaughters who love you very much. And who knows what the future holds? There may be more grandchildren." I increased my pressure on his hand. "I don't want any of them growing up without you in their lives. And I don't want you being a stranger from *our* lives, either."

He suppressed a sob. "My dear girl, you and Damien deserve each other. I should never have believed Teddy Kelly; the poor man has problems of his own. I as good as called you a whore, and here you are, telling me you want me in your life...!"

"It's forgotten, Connor. Truly, it is. Damien wants you in our lives as well, even though he's as stubborn as you are. I know he does! If the two of you were to really talk, he would forgive you in a heartbeat." I sucked in air, plunged on. "Connor, Damien and I want to be married as soon as possible. And I want *you* to marry us! Will you?"

He suppressed another sob. "I...would truly love that, dear girl, if it were also Damien's wish. But Mari, this isn't a fairy-tale. Damien and I have been estranged forever. You can't solve everything."

I smiled. "That's exactly what *he* says! It already proves you two are on the same wavelength. Besides—even fairy-tales are based on some truths." Impulse seized me; I went with it. "Come on over for dinner tonight! Drive the girls back to our place after your movie is done and be our guest for the evening. I'll cook. I don't know when Damien will be home, but I'll throw together something a bit special. Please, Connor!"

Doubt clouded his expression; he shook his head slowly. "I so appreciate the thought. But I hardly think it would be fair to Damien to spring my presence on him like that. And I think he might be very angry with you, Mari, for interfering. The last thing in the world I want—especially now—is to be the cause of any more trouble in my family." Almost reverently, he extracted from my grasp the hand I held and reached out with it to touch lightly the small mound of my abdomen. "I want this baby to love me the way the girls do, and I'll take that love on whatever terms it is offered. I'm thrilled that you and Damien are so happy together, and I think maybe it's best not to overstep boundaries and push myself in where I don't belong."

"Connor..." I placed my hand over his on my abdomen. "...shut up! Shut up and tell me you'll be there—for the girls' sake, and mine, and Damien's, and this baby's! If you care for me at all, in any way, stop throwing up roadblocks here and now and just tell me you'll be there!"

It was a pivotal moment. Possibly I had pushed too hard. Possibly he was right: Damien *might* be angry with me for interfering. Possibly, letting well enough alone would be the much safer route to follow. Suppose the two men talked and things ended up worse between them than ever? Neither one would thank me.

Not for a moment did I believe that would be the case. I went for broke, urged him yet one more time: "Just tell me you'll be there!"

Beneath mine—and still maintaining the new bond of touch he was forging with his unborn grandchild—his hand trembled. In a barely-audible murmur he breathed, "All right, my dear, dear girl. All right. You win. I'll be there."

# Epilogue:

## Of Magic Carpets and Disproving the Father Principle

*Truly happy endings where all is resolved are just about as elusive as is freedom from elephant thoughts while sitting on that rug that would otherwise fly you anywhere. Yet, even in a world of much sadness, those endings happen. The Father Principle, often so self-sabotaging, can be overridden. On the evening Connor Sparks is our dinner guest for the very first time, there is just such a wonderful occurrence. Magic takes place. Always I shall remember it that way.*

*Mother understands that my invitation does not include her. It's essential Connor and Damien not feel blackmailed, by having too many spectators on the scene, into behaving in any other way but a natural one.*

*I race to the grocery store to pick up ingredients for my planned meal: ham, scalloped potatoes, Caesar salad, and a key lime pie for dessert. I dress for dinner in a frilly blouse and a flouncy skirt. When the girls arrive back with their grandpa, they, too, want to dress up.*

*Handing Connor a glass of sherry, I install him on the buttery-soft stretched loveseat where Damien and I first made love.*

237

*While he sips, and I work in the kitchen, I listen to the sound of my daughters' laughter drifting to us from their bedroom as they rummage through their closet, trying on different outfits.*

*The careworn expression on Connor's face gradually softens. He accepts a top-up of sherry. When Damien crosses the threshold, he is chatting to me easily about the movie he and the girls have just seen, and his back is to the doorway. I see Damien freeze, see the jaw of the man I love harden with hostility.*

*"Damien...!" I rise hastily, go to give him a hug. "I'm the one who invited Connor. We're having a special meal. Go get changed into something more comfortable and come join us. Please!"*

*He remains frozen for several beats, then returns my hug and kisses me. Sea-blue eyes cloudy, he drones woodenly, "I lost the patient. It happens. Resigning oneself is never easy." His deep voice shakes as Connor rises also to stand beside us, still holding onto the sherry glass.*

*And then comes the miracle—the one that matches my wildest fantasies, the way loving Damien has matched them.*

*In the same deep shaky voice, Damien continues, "Mia, love, I think I could use a shot of what Dad is having."*

*"Of course!" I promptly go to pour another glass, hand it to him as I hold my breath.*

*Connor clears a husky throat. He says, "I feel for you about your patient. Loss is so hard and so cruel. Sometimes, though— as in my case—the loss has been well and truly earned. It's... it's tragic that a person can be too stiff-necked to admit he's been wrong. A person can waste years that way—and can even end up dying without ever having had the gumption to make things right."*

*Damien's brows draw together; he takes several swallows in succession before responding, his blue gaze glued to his father's. "Are you sick?"*

"No." Connor shakes his head. "No, I didn't mean to imply that. I am heartsick, though, about some of the things I've done—and not done." Again, he clears his throat. "This is good sherry. It loosens the tongue. And it's well past the time I had my tongue loosened, Damien... I wouldn't blame you if your answer was 'no'. But do you think you can bring yourself to forgive a pig-headed old fool?"

A slow smile settles itself over Damien's handsome features; he inhales deeply and is silent for several more beats. Then, in a half-whisper, he says, "There is a proviso, Dad. Certain conditions would have to apply. If you can bring yourself to forgive a pig-headed young fool, then maybe we have a deal."

There is a quiver to both men's voices. Connor's eyes brim, then overflow, and I sense, rather than see, Damien's tears. His head is down, that abundant, wheat-coloured hair hiding his face. I take their sherry glasses, so they can embrace. The hug, tentative and awkward, is an abortive effort; they draw apart quickly and opt for a handshake instead. No one understands the tentativeness and the awkwardness better than I. Their future will hold longer, more fervent hugs. Of that I'm certain.

Katie appears at that moment in a lovely pink cotton-print dress and matching shawl. Ever attentive, she picks up a box of tissues from the side table nearby and gives them one each. Her small forehead furrows in worry. "Grandpa, Uncle Damien, are you sad?" And, bending to kiss that furrowed forehead, Damien strokes her hair with a gentle smile and replies, "No, sweetheart. We couldn't be happier. Aren't adults crazy?"

The meal turns out well and receives many compliments. Connor and Damien load the dishwasher together while I slice up pie—which a sudden rebellion of my taste buds forbids me to eat. Very earnestly Carrie tells Connor, "The little brother or sister we're going to have sometimes makes Mom not hungry. Then we have to waste food by throwing it away. When Chimo comes over from the Salters' to visit, he eats the leftovers. If we had a puppy of our own, we wouldn't have to give the leftovers to Chimo or throw them away, right?"

We all dissolve in laughter. Damien says, "That's a very well-reasoned argument, muffin. I think we may be looking at a future member of the school debate team." His eyes twinkle. "If you guys can wait until after your new brother or sister is born, so we can make sure allergies aren't a problem, then maybe a puppy can join the family—always provided it's okay with your mom."

"After hearing a solidly-structured argument like that," I grin, "I wouldn't dare disagree!"

Connor says, "If and when you want help selecting that puppy, count me in!"

"Again, we have a deal." Damien lifts his wineglass. "We're quite the group for toasts around here, and I'd like to propose one right now. To this being a red-letter day of happiness for our family. And Dad...this is my opportunity to say words I should have said when I first came through the door this evening." His blue eyes hold the intensity I've always adored. "Welcome to our home. We want you to come back. Often."

We tap glasses, the girls and I hoisting our lemonade. Katie says, "Uncle Damien, you made Grandpa cry all over again! Is he still happy?"

"He's even happier than before," Connor tells her, surrendering to renewed laughter. "And his happiness would be complete, Damien, if he could see you and Mari married right away. I know you want that—and I want the honour of conducting the ceremony. Doing it ASAP would be just what the doctor ordered—wouldn't it, Doctor? What do you say?"

The familiar teasing eyebrow arches upward. And the man I love so profoundly replies, "My view parallels Mia's concerning the puppy. After hearing a solidly-structured argument like that, I wouldn't dare disagree."

'ASAP' is two short weeks later.

In the presence of those nearest and dearest, our wedding takes place in a tiny chapel built as an adjunct to Connor's

church. Carrie and Katie, as flower girls, both wear beautiful powder-blue dresses with elegant matching slippers. Mother, in a pale-green tailored suit that flatters her trim figure, proudly gives me away. "Y'all clean up real nice!" Sarah, my matron of honour, tells my breathtakingly-handsome groom in a mock Southern accent, widening her gaze to include bridesmaids Joanna, Melanie, and Lydia Salter. Lydia's husband Lorne is best man, his nephew Simon a groomsman, and his treasured employees and friends Manuel and Consuela witnesses and guests. It's the smallest and most intimate wedding I've ever attended. Each person there is very special to me. And I love it that way.

Damien utters his vows with heart-melting fervency, and I know my emotion is audible in my own. Eyes are liberally dabbed. Then it's off to a small but elegant reception held in a back room of Robert's Bistro. All during the usual speeches, I can't help noticing—with a tingle of wonder—how often Mother and Connor look into one another's eyes, and how Connor's arm drapes lightly over the back of Mother's chair.

* * *

Lorne Connor Simon Sparks makes his world debut but five months after Damien and I have spent a blissful two-week honeymoon in Kauai. He has Damien's sea-blue eyes and abundance of blond hair, and he emerges with a loud indignant wail that indicates a strong pair of lungs and general good health. Damien is ecstatic to take part in dressing him, changing him, and carrying him around to show off to others. If I'd had another daughter, I know the situation would have been identical.

Joanna gives birth to a beautiful little girl, Taylor Marie. She and Melanie are frequent guests at our home. We want the babies to grow up together. Already, Carrie and Katie love mothering them both and are very protective of them—as is dear Chimo, and even as is Freckles, our new spotted mixed-breed terrier, recently adopted from the pound. My life is very full at the moment, and—much as I love my career at the

## The End

_____

*Those are the words that don't just make my world turn. They make it turn cartwheels.*

"...more ways than I can say it—in love with you!"

"My gorgeous girl!" He murmurs it into the hollow of my throat. "I'm crazy, out-of-my-mind, over the moon, to the heights of Everest, to the depths of my soul—and in so many

*to be without it."*

*between his brows; I hear him groan, and I kiss the frown of pleasure and stroked; "Your lust thrills me. I never want*

*less lust-driven lover."*

*Lorne. But I do sometimes wish I were a far more patient and have you that I'm hardly in control. I would never un-wish wanted me to use protection. I'm...always in such a hurry to love, I've felt guilty for not considering that you might have restored my faith in fairy-tales. Since the first time we made forehead. "Darling Mia, you are my life! You have honestly blue gaze tenderly into mine, as his warm breath caresses my His eyes are closed, but he opens them to direct an azure-*

"...large-sized family these days but to me it sounds ideal!"

*my breast, "I think I'd like another of your children. Four is a finished making love and he has sighed his contentment against*

"Besides," I tease my husband one night just after we've

*quite yet.*

*university—I am in no hurry at all to end my leave of absence*

# Author's Note

I've been writing regularly since I was old enough to put pen to paper. So in June of 2010 when our daughter Colleen took her own life writing was my natural catharsis as well as a means to gain a greater understanding of mental illness. My journey of discovery is shared in my memoir, *When the Ship has no Stabilizers: our daughter's tempestuous voyage through borderline personality disorder* (Crossfield, 2014). I was touched and inspired by the supportive and encouraging response to my book. My husband Andy and I donated our proceeds from its sales to open a treatment centre for mentally-ill youth. We humbly received a 2017 Calgary Philanthropic Family of the Year award.

Writing Colleen's sad story left me no choice but to sometimes sound black and jaded. I now yearn for tales that leave the reader ultimately satisfied that a light exists at the end of what might sometimes be a very dark tunnel. I'm the last person anyone needs to tell that finding that light can be a major challenge.

Memoir is a genre where tragedy is often a necessary subject for in-depth exploration. What has always troubled me, however, is tragedy's extreme prevalence in fiction. As an English teacher of twenty-five years, I daily brought my students, already riddled with teenage angst, smack up against literature featuring even

*The Wrong Brother*

more angst-ridden characters. I wouldn't want my worst enemy, let alone a whole country, entrusted to the guidance of such a maladjusted, paranoid general as Othello or his petty, spiteful aide, Iago. Romeo and Juliet should have been marched down to the guidance counsellor's office long before their matters reached such a crisis! And Gatsby's more a pathetic figure than a 'great' one, making himself cannon fodder for the sake of such a shallow, self-absorbed fool as Daisy. I could go on...

Now that my literary efforts have moved into fiction I'm making it my mission to offer an enlightening alternative to the proliferation of dark and disillusioned works that sink readers irredeemably into the quicksand of emotional malaise. I'm rebelling against having the world's seamy underbelly reflected in and magnified by almost everything I read.

Romance is the most widely and continuously selling literary genre. There has always been a reliable segment of the reading public—not all of it feminine—that consumes a steady diet of feel-good fare. Accounts of passionate loves and lovers pull at human heartstrings, no matter the age of the reader. Descriptions of sex that is sweet and beautiful, rather than torrid and tawdry, evoke those wonderful well-being and immunity-strengthening hormones known as endorphins. And strongly ethical and sexy protagonists unencumbered by the '#metoo movement' evoke the same response. These are the types of heroes and heroines I want to portray!

*The Wrong Brother* is the opposite of a typical coming-of-age novel: its female narrator starts out cynical, rather than naïve. She's also not the stereotypical super-woman who goes traipsing all over the globe and encounters her white-knight saviour in some exotic and perilous setting. As a small-town scholar, she embraces academia's ivy walls and the quiet life they represent—even as she realizes that they leave some part of her unfulfilled. And her knight, while not riding a charger or wielding a lance, proves, in his own right, to fit the definition of hero very nicely.

*Fran L. Porter*

*The Wrong Brother* is purely escapist reading, not requiring analysis. It does use some recognizable literary techniques and has its lighter moments, despite being recounted by a smartass young girl who later becomes an abused wife. My goal was to receive good grades for both composition and character development, while risking the possible categorization of 'chick lit."

Primarily, this is a novel one can take to the beach and read solely on a plot-driven level. No assignment threatens to follow! I hope you, the reader, have exited with the same 'happy-ever-after' feeling you once derived from fairy tales. Producing that feeling was my number-one mandate – one I'd like to see more of in material prescribed on secondary-school reading lists!

To finding the light at the end of the tunnel,

Fran

# Acknowledgements

I wish to thank my publisher, Tina Crossfield, for her faith in me as a writer and for her professed adherence to high standards in publishing and to the production of quality materials. That is so important to me! It is such a pleasure to work with her!

As well, I owe profound thanks to artist Larry Stilwell, who designed the intriguing cover. Of Larry's artistic abilities I am in constant awe!

Thank you to Harald Kunze, for his attractive book design and keen eye for detail.

And finally, to my ever-supportive husband Andy, I thank you for that support and remain so grateful that you are a part of my life!

Blessings to you all,

Fran

ᘓ